To David

with best wishes

The Emperor's Servant

FIONA FORSYTH

Fiona Forsyth

16/7/2022

First published in 2020.

This edition published in 2022 by Sharpe Books.

To all the denizens of Milk Wood,
and especially BB, Blitz, Doyle, Edmund, Grease, Harri, Jaz,
KJ, Laraa, Nathaniel, Raina and Zoe

CONTENTS

Roman names

Roman men had two or three names at this time: everyone tended to use one of a very short list one of about ten first names. You will therefore find a lot of people with the first name Marcus or Lucius or Quintus whenever you read about ancient Rome. Girls were given a feminised version of their father's second name, and if there were more than one daughter in a family, the family would use nicknames to distinguish the daughters. In the Sestius family therefore, the two daughters were officially both called "Sestia", but I have decided that the elder daughter also took on her mother's name, "Albinia", and the younger was known by her nickname, "Tia".

There is often no logic as to which name we use for a Roman nowadays, and so I have followed this lack of logic (if that is possible), wherever I thought that it helped to clarify the narrative.

A list of the most important characters in the novel follows on the next page, and more information on ancient Rome, maps and topics such as names can be found on the author's website: **www.luciussestius.com**

Dramatis personae or the main characters

Sestius family

Lucius Sestius Quirinalis
Albinia his elder sister, the poet
Tia his younger sister
Publius his son
Sestia Caecilia (Celi) his daughter
Decius his all-round assistant
Sergius his estate manager
Titus the keeper of the vines
Marcella Titus' wife
Gallio tutor to the children
Helice nurse to the children
Melissa his Rome housekeeper

The First Family

Augustus known to us as the first Emperor of Rome
Livia Drusilla wife of Augustus
Tiberius Livia's son by her first husband
Julia daughter of Augustus
Marcellus nephew and son-in-law of Augustus
Maecenas friend and advisor of Augustus
Terentia wife of Maecenas
Agrippa friend and military right hand of Augustus

People from Cosa

Aponius an innkeeper
Larcius a doctor
and his son Larcius a ship's captain

At Rome

Piso Consul of Rome for the year 23 BCE
Popilia wife of Piso
Marcus Tullius Cicero friend of Lucius Sestius and son of a famous father
Horace one of Rome's greatest poets
Aulus Terentius Varro Murena brother of Terentia
Herophilus doctor and priest of Aesculapius
Marcus Primus governor of Macedonia
Marcus Licinius Crassus previous governor of Macedonia

Prologue – Rome, 23 BCE

He lies on the couch in the darkened room and is convinced that he is dying. His name is Augustus Caesar and he is the Princeps, leading citizen, but none of that can help him now. He lies in darkness and silence, in a room that is stifling in a warm May in Rome. He has always felt the cold, needing several tunics at a time in winters, but now his body is on fire.

They have summoned a famous doctor, their last hope, and he is hurrying from the Bay of Naples, but Augustus Caesar the Princeps does not believe that this miracle worker will arrive in time. The dying man has to prepare them all for his death. A twitch of his fingers summons an obedient acolyte, a whisper brings Livia, and he tells her what he is going to do. She isn't pleased but he doesn't care. Soon, in a quiet scurry and swish of draperies a group of men enter the room and stand awkwardly at the foot of his couch. Another flick of the fingers and Agrippa comes forward and kneels beside him. There are tears on Agrippa's cheeks, but Augustus does not think that many other men will weep for him.

Good, honest, hard-working Agrippa. His right-hand general, the most loyal follower you could desire, a man whose ambition is to support his best friend. Rome used to be full of men like Agrippa, now they are all self-serving and idle. But enough, thinks Augustus Caesar the Princeps, I must get this done. He can barely move or speak, but his mind is clear.

Slowly and hampered by another bout of shivering, he paws at the signet ring on his finger. Fortunately, it slips off easily – he has lost weight again during this illness. He is determined that nobody can mistake his actions; carefully and as dramatically as shaking hands allow, he holds out the ring to Agrippa. He can hear a suppressed gasp from someone and there is a distinctly unconvincing outbreak of coughing.

1

Agrippa looks aghast.

"Me?"

Augustus breathes out the slightest sound, but it is unmistakably, "You."

By the end of the day, all Rome knows. One man has transferred power from himself to his best friend: it is unprecedented, probably illegal, and any hope that Rome is still a Republic has died.

Chapter 1

Quintus Horatius Flaccus, Odes Book 1, poem 4

Spring frees up everything:

the dry ships are pulled down to the sea, the animals let out of their stalls.

The ploughman leaves the fireside and frost melts from the meadows.

The moon leans down to Venus as she leads the dance, the Graces keep the beat, and Vulcan checks up on his fiery factories.

Now is the time for a shining garland of green myrtle, of flowers set free from the earth, and a sacrifice of lamb or kid for Faunus in a shadowy glade.

Oh Sestius, you are so happy!

But death is pale and preys on the tavern crowd and the man defended by towered walls alike.

Life is short: no time for long-term hopes. Soon darkness and the weight of the dead, just like in the stories, will press upon you.

No chance to become king of the vineyard then, nor to marvel at young Lycidas, along with every youngster whose blood grows warm.

***

"Albinia sends greeting to her brother, Lucius Sestius Quirinalis, in Cosa. On a boiling hot day in July – we must be nearly into August by now. It is tempting to leave Rome and bring this letter myself!

Well, you have made it at last, my now-famous brother! I enclose a poem by Horace, to be included in the collection he is about to publish. Interestingly, he only wrote it last month, so

3

though he is putting it near the beginning of the collection, in honour of your long friendship, it is the last one to be composed. Although I suspect he has been thinking about it for years. I know you don't rate any poetry, but I think you will agree that this is clever. As you will see when the collection comes out, this one fits in beautifully in style and theme, but it is very definitely aimed at you, Lucius. I shall let Tia and Decius explain it all to you. And don't worry about the reference to "young Lycidas", Horace is just being Greek at you. He doesn't really think you fancy someone called Lycidas…

And now, onto other matters: Augustus is ill again, and rather seriously, though rumour says he has a wonderful new doctor who is getting results. We shall see. There was a very interesting scene when Augustus thought he might die…"

Lucius sticks his head out of the door and yells, "Tia! Letter!" into an empty corridor. He rereads the poem dedicated to him, this time frowning over any hidden meaning, and is relieved when his sister comes in.

"You could just walk next door, rather than shouting for me," she observes tartly. "I am not your slave, brother dear. Who is the letter from? Albinia?"

Lucius holds it out, saying, "Horace has written me an ode, apparently. Tia, do we have any myrtle in the garden?"

"Yes, of course," answers Tia, sitting down to read Albinia's news. She does not ask why myrtle, because she knows she will get the answer soon. And sure enough, there it is in the poem. Maybe Lucius wants them all to wear garlands at dinner that night. She will have to read the poem properly and think about it. The reference to pale death brings her father to mind immediately, and she steers away from that thought. It has only been a year.

"Augustus is ill – again?" she says, skimming forward before she can let herself speculate on a future without the Princeps. "Oh, he has been ill, and there is cautious optimism because of his doctor. But not before Augustus made his will and left his signet ring to Agrippa – Agrippa? Mr "I'm-just-a-loyal-soldier"? I bet there were people who found that hard to take."

"Agrippa is the only person who could carry on as Augustus has started," says Lucius sounding as if he is deciding what sauce to have with his eggs.

"Without the Princeps, we wouldn't have to carry on. We could go back to a proper Republic," says Tia carefully, casting the line into the stream as delicately as she can.

Lucius looks at her. "No, we can't," he says in the same calm tone. She makes no answer and reads the rest of the letter, finding the final paragraph worth reading aloud.

"Horace says to tell you that he is coming your way in about a week and asks for a bed for the night. He also says he might bring a friend. He was very mysterious while conveying all this so I shall expect a full account of whatever goes on when he visits. You should get this pretty promptly, so I hope I have given you enough notice."

Tia's eyes are thoughtful as she passes the letter back to him.

"Any idea what that is all about?"

"The mysterious visit from Horace and A.N. Other? No. This is Horace. Could be male, female, slave, free, animal, mineral, vegetable."

His sister laughs and gets up.

"I must check on the children. See you at dinner. Do you want myrtle?"

"Myrtle?" Lucius looks confused. "No, I don't think so – why?"

Tia shakes her head and goes.

Dinner is held as the afternoon is on the wane and is nothing special. Lucius' father always enjoyed the simple life at Cosa and the Civil War made this a necessity as the family's finances suffered. The Sestii have worked hard in the fifteen years or so since Lucius' pardon and return to Italy, and they have made up some ground, but Augustus' regime has kept them carefully simple. There is no ostentatious consumption here or at their Rome house, no remodelling and no interest in the latest developments in wall-painting. When old Publius Sestius died the year previously, he died quietly and with his family around him, as he wished. He had kept them going through a delicate period, and he was content to slip away from them all and join his beloved Cornelia.

And so, Lucius Sestius is the paterfamilias and master of a profitable and comfortable farm and a variety of industrial and commercial interests, which keep him in the senatorial class and make sure that his family are well-educated and don't starve. In fact, they will need the money for future generations: despite his own background in fighting to preserve the Republic, Lucius wants his son Publius junior – named after Lucius' own father of course – to enter the Senate. Augustus' regime promises the sort of stability which allows a family to plan ahead in terms of the next couple of generations, and while he is not enthusiastic about Augustus, Lucius finds that he automatically thinks of his children's future in terms of solid, respectable success. They don't bother with the traditional three-couch formation, and as Publius junior and his sister Celi are young enough to prefer chairs, the room usually looks a little cluttered. Everyone makes their own way to a couple of couches and a smattering of stools and chairs. A decent dining-set, suitable for when visitors arrive, is kept in the summer dining room under covers, ready to be whisked out when needed, but this room is everyday, decorated in a modest and old-fashioned style, the bands of colours running around the walls gentle and faded with time. The shades originally used were earth tones, no blaring red or stark black here, and the floor is plain, without marble or mosaic. Lucius looks around and automatically checks people off. Tia shares his own couch of course, and the children sit across the table from him, with their nurse Helice perched on a stool just behind them. Helice will spend the meal monitoring manners then eat in the kitchen with her friends. Gallio the tutor is absent: he often chooses to eat his dinner off a tray in the large library where he teaches the children. His daughter, Sestia Caecilia, known to her family as Celi, takes after her mother and will make a wonderful Roman matron one day. Young Publius Sestius is a curious mix, and for the life of him, Lucius cannot decide where his son gets his temperament. Publius is twelve, disapproves of poetry – except, as he says politely, his aunt Albinia's poetry – and wants to be a philosopher, although he has not been able to explain to Lucius how he intends to make any money at this. To Lucius' left, is Decius, a family freedman about ten years older than Lucius himself, who is Lucius'secretary, librarian, and all-round assistant: on the next couch is Sergius the steward of the villa. The family is usually joined by Titus, who is the vine specialist, but tonight Titus has decided on an early night. As spring marches into summer, this often happens, for Titus starts hovering around his beloved vines most of the day, willing on the grapes to mature to perfection and fussing over the number and size of leaves on each twig. The three managers dining around the table together should have proved troublesome but they have established a way of co-existing. When at the villa, Decius carefully tends to the businesses and dealings of Rome, Sergius sticks to anything to do with Cosa and Titus doesn't even notice that there is a demarcation of territory to be declared. It never occurs to Titus that he should worry about anything other than his vines and the wine made. Where the wine goes to, how it gets there and whether it makes a profit is none of his business.

Once satisfied that everyone who should be present is in fact present, Lucius nods to Sergius who by some invisible force of will ensures that the eggs and vegetables are brought in. Dinner begins. Publius and Celi, aware that Helice is hovering, eat nicely and wait to be asked before joining in the conversation. Like his father, Lucius believes in the family knowing what is going on and so once Tia, Sergius and Decius have discussed the day and told Lucius of the next steps in various domestic and farm issues, Publius and Celi are allowed to ask questions to ensure that they understand what is being discussed. Today, they talk about Horace's poem.

"I like it," says Tia, unexpectedly putting forward a definite opinion right at the start of the conversation. "I see our farm, as he describes the spring arriving, and our ships getting ready for the sailing season. I'm sure Horace was visiting when we sacrificed to Faunus in the spring a couple of years ago."

"And he describes our walls," says Publius. Lucius thinks of the walls which surround the main villa, not too high but punctuated with little towers along the way. That is how walls are in this area, a leftover from the Etruscans, the people who ruled before the Romans took over. The towers have been allowed to decay, but the one nearest the villa is used as a dovecote.

"So, if it is our spring and our farm and our walls – why does he get so gloomy at the end?" asks Celi. "Are you happy, like he says, Daddy?"

Lucius smiles at her. He is indeed happy.

"Horace is using a traditional idea you find in poetry," says Decius. "The poets have always warned us not to get ideas above our station."

Celi's wrinkled nose show what she thinks of that.

"Who is Lycidas?" she asks. "We don't have any workers on the farm called Lycidas, do we? And why should everyone's blood go warm?"

As the meal ends in a cacophony of throat-clearing, Celi is whisked off to her own room but Publius is allowed to stay. He serves wine with furious care and sits observing everything until his father gives him leave to retire. Lucius listens as Publius' quick light steps turn in the direction of the library and knows that later he will have to check that tutor and student have actually stopped discussing their studies. He hopes that Publius won't ask Gallio why Horace has beautiful youths called Lycidas in his poetry.

By the time they have finished a last cup of wine it is dark, and at some point Tia has slipped away to do whatever a single Roman lady of middle age does after dinner. Decius and Sergius say goodnight, and Lucius barely notices because the air is warm and still as only happens in the middle of summer. The skies are clear and he goes for a last stroll in the garden in front of the house, so that he can gaze at the blaze of stars overhead and wonder about the forthcoming visit of that poet and lover of life, spring and Lycidas, Quintus Horatius Flaccus.

Chapter 2

Guests often visit the Villa Sestiana – or "the farm" as the family call it – at Cosa, and the house staff keep several spare bedrooms ready, so the proposed visit of the esteemed poet Horace gives no cause for fuss or flurry. The poet's guest does not rouse much interest except in Tia who wonders why Horace has not written himself and why he has arranged this visit in such a clumsy manner. But everything is calm and prepared when several days after Albinia's letter, on a scorching first day of August, Horace arrives in unaccustomed style, accompanied by a litter, several tough-looking riders, and a small gaggle of attendants. Lucius puts on his best non-committal face as he follows Tia and Decius out into the main entrance yard. He goes straight to Horace and is enthusiastically grabbed and hugged and immediately knows something is wrong: under cover of the hug, his friend mutters "I'm sorry" directly into Lucius' ear. Horace gently turns him around and together they watch as an elegantly dressed man clambers a little stiffly out of the litter. The man stretches and calls to them, "Ye gods, that feels better!" He smiles at Lucius as though they are friends and advances towards him, arms outstretched.

"Lucius Sestius!" and Gaius Maecenas takes his hand enthusiastically. "So good of you to see me like this, Horace assured me that you would, and I promise that I shall be no trouble at all. In fact, I shan't even impose upon your hospitality, for I am borrowing your neighbour's villa up the road. Old Domitius Ahenobarbus, do you know him well?"

Maecenas has always struck Lucius as a surprisingly normal-looking man. In reality, Maecenas is not normal of course, he is the man who has crafted an acceptable face for Augustus' regime. If Augustus is at the top of the heap, he is there because

at dinner. He knows of course, what his words mean – and what they mean for Lucius.

Lucius sits and lets the words wash around in his mind, refusing to let them settle, because he knows immediately that they will bring confusion and he doesn't like anything upsetting the normality of his careful life. Over the last fifteen years, he has mended his feelings and got on, just as everyone said he should. He keeps anniversaries of bleak moments strictly in his head, and does not talk about anything to do with Julius Caesar or Brutus or how he had fought for the losing side all those years ago – except with Horace and Marcus Cicero who went through it with him. How dare the Princeps force him into the limelight like this now? And the consulship! The top role in Roman politics, the office which has been the aspiration of every upper-class Roman family for the last five hundred years?

He cannot trust himself to speak and he does not want to look at Maecenas. He gazes into his cup and swirls the liquid gently round and round. Maecenas will have to carry on. There will be explanations. In the meantime, Lucius sees what the prepared speech will not say. Augustus has been reminded of mortality and has been forced to engage in an examination of his achievements. He has decided upon a re-establishment of his power base. For some reason, the Princeps does not want to go on being Consul year after year, so he needs a convenient stand-in to see out the rest of this year for him. He has so much else to get on with, important things, and Rome's top office is a nuisance now, a waste of his time.

Naturally, Maecenas speaks eloquently and clearly, but he is also candid. Augustus wants to relinquish the relentless series of consulships without letting go of power. Lucius' job is to make sure that the Senate passes all requests with no objections.

"It might even be better if we can persuade someone to propose particular points," says Maecenas. "Maybe make them look like rewards?"

"A grateful state honours her favourite son?" asks Lucius.

Maecenas smiles and smoothes down the folds of his clean cream tunic. "I see that I don't need to say any more." Lucius disagrees. Augustus and Maecenas have thought this out carefully and cannot let any old has-been take up the challenge of the consulship. No, he is looking forward to hearing Maecenas explain why he, Lucius Sestius, has been chosen.

"You trust me to just go into the Senate and do all this?" says Lucius. There is a list of objections to himself behind that question, and he feels he should list them all out loud. "I chose to follow Brutus and Cassius, the men who assassinated Julius Caesar. I followed them when Augustus declared them public enemies. I fought against you and Agrippa and Augustus at the Battle of Philippi and fled into exile after. I only returned to Rome when you issued a general pardon to people like me. I keep busts of staunch Republicans in my study, as you can see."

He gestures towards the little stone heads on the bookcase, but his guest feels no need to look again. Maecenas is as smooth as a polished pebble and starts making the fidgety gestures of one preparing to move on. He brushes invisible flecks of stray wool from his tunic and shifts his weight in a cat stretch that starts at the shoulders and travels down his back.

"Gods, I need a bath and a decent massage," he sighs. "Yes, of course we know all that, and yes, we trust you. We have thought about all this, you know. Now I know that you will want to say yes straight away but we don't work like that. Of course, we do hope that you say yes officially, and to that end you are invited to dinner at Augustus' house as soon as you can get back to Rome. It is unfortunate that you have no wife as I'm sure Livia and my Terentia would have loved to meet her."

"Caecilia died several years ago," says Lucius.

"Yes, and I am sorry for your loss," Maecenas says. "A wife

can be a great blessing as indeed are children. You should consider marrying again. Children benefit from a mother being in their lives, and yours are young enough to appreciate having a maternal presence again. How are your children? You have a girl and a boy, yes?"

"Yes, ten and twelve," says Lucius feeling as though Maecenas is now showing off how well he has been briefed on the Sestius family.

"And do you bring them to Rome often?" says Maecenas, bright-eyed and already knowing the answer. "No? Well, you should bring them with you. Not to the dinner of course, but to be in Rome while their father is Consul will be exciting and good for them. Particularly your son."

"They have lived all their lives here in Cosa," says Lucius helplessly, wondering why he suddenly feels that he must be a failure as a parent.

"Ah yes. It's a decent-sized estate here, and if this is anything to go by, your wine will soon be making a name for itself," says Maecenas, and he peers into his wine-cup appreciatively.

"It's everyday stuff, really," says Lucius automatically.

"It's very good for everyday stuff. You should send a jar or two to Augustus – he has no palate, but he will appreciate the gesture."

High praise from the man who has carefully developed Augustus' taste in all things for the last twenty years.

Lucius has a more serious subject to tackle though.

"What would I have to do? And how do I actually become Consul?"

"Dear me," says Maecenas. "I didn't realise." His lightly ironic tone alerts Lucius

"I don't mean that I don't know what the Consul does or how he is elected, but – in the middle of the year? And I'm not a regular attender, so I don't know what is going on at the

15

present." For a wild moment he wonders if he should ask if he can bring forward a radical law but doesn't think Maecenas will find this funny.

"Don't let that bother you," says Maecenas. "It is all in hand. Let me see, today is the first day of the month, so on the first lucky day after the Ides, there will be a quick election, with whoever manages to turn up doing the voting. We shall announce it in the Forum just before the Ides, and Augustus will let people know that he supports your candidature. If anyone else turns up to run against you, it will be a joke. You will be elected and on the next official day, we shall swear you in and you can take your first Senate meeting. It will be a formality. Then we shall be into September and you will get going with some things that we are planning."

"Things?" Lucius can't help asking.

"We shall let you know," says Maecenas. "Don't worry."

Lucius has worked out that this timetable has made no allowance for his refusal of the proposition and he cannot see an obvious way of getting out of it. He looks at Horace who gazes back with nothing but a neutral smile on his face, eyes blank. His friend does not think he has a choice either. Maecenas coughs a little fake cough, and rises, arranging his tunic with a bit more fuss than is needed.

"Of course," says Lucius and he too rises. Sergius is summoned and asked to round up Maecenas' people, and Tia and the children come out into the atrium to be introduced. Maecenas is gracious and condescending all round, then steps out of the front door. His entourage appears and arranges itself. He floats into the litter without having to step anywhere normal or nasty, and the horsemen come clattering through from the stables, where they can barely have had time to water the horses. The litter is lifted and sets off, and the only sound is the slap of sandals in regular marching rhythm, until the horsemen start forward to fall in at the rear.

Sergius looking slightly stunned, shakes his head, and then turns to Lucius and asks if there will be anything else.

"More wine in my study please," says Lucius, feeling suddenly grey and boring. "Decius, would you join us as well? Quintus Horatius Flaccus and I have a lot to discuss." Horace grins, and stretches in the sun pouring into the courtyard, before following Lucius back into the villa. Tia exchanges a look with Decius, and shepherds the children back into the villa. She doesn't want to be part of this meeting, and besides, someone has to start organising the packing. She may not have been in the study with Maecenas and her brother, but Tia has a good idea of what is happening.

Decius finds Lucius and Horace sitting in silence in the study and decides on a neutral conversation-starter.

"I've been talking to Titus."

"And what does Titus have to report?"

"Excellent harvest expected, for a change."

Lucius laughs. "Really?"

"No, not really. When has Titus ever given us an optimistic prediction?"

"Never," says Lucius, thinking of Titus, of ancient Etruscan stock, short and scowling because the vines he tends so carefully never respond exactly as they should. Titus lives on the edge of famine, flood and disaster. He laments as he goes along his rows of vines, practically saying goodbye to each ripening bunch, convinced that he will never see the grapes arrive at that perfect moment when they can be picked. Every year, grapes nevertheless are harvested. Titus expresses relieved amazement and looks for rot, mould, insects and earthquakes to damn the year's wine to perdition. Once when he couldn't find a slave, Titus was convinced that the man had fallen into one of the wine vats and drowned. He had just been about to send

17

someone down into the enormous vat to search when the slave in question had been found asleep in the kitchens. Titus had shaken his head and wondered aloud if a human body added anything to the wine's – er – body. If only he had been joking. The slaves had been on their guard ever since.

"No, it is all as usual," says Decius. "The weather is wrong, and rain is predicted, and everything will be ruined."

"Has he talked about what to do with the surplus this year?" asks Lucius. Titus never has any ideas about marketing the wines, but Lucius makes a point of asking his advice. Every year, mainly thanks to Decius' work, the Sestius wines head further and further north. Last autumn, they even made it as far as Massilia in southern Gaul: when a Gallic wine merchant was touring the vineyards of northern Italy he made a deal with Lucius to take every spare amphora, even before the harvest was in. But he had liked their previous vintages, he said, so was willing to take the risk. Not surprising, thinks Lucius, when you consider what the Gauls usually consider a good drink. Beer. Good Jupiter above, beer…

Decius looks at him. "Maecenas?"

Lucius sighs. "An offer from the Princeps. He is stepping down from the consulship."

Decius' eyes widen immediately.

"You?"

"Me."

There is a silence. Then Decius says, "Congratulations. I think."

Horace groans. "Oh, you two! Pour the wine for the sake of all the gods. Lucius, I swear I didn't know anything about this until Maecenas informed me he would be accompanying me up to Cosa. I guessed something was up of course, so I told Albinia, when I sent her the poem. Now sit, Lucius, and let's discuss this."

"Discuss?" Lucius looks at him. "You heard Maecenas. What is there to discuss? I should be packing now. I'm being elected Consul in – what? – fifteen, sixteen days' time. Whether I like it or not. And I don't know if I want it, but I don't not want it. I mean, it is what it is all about. Becoming Consul. It still means something."

As he says it, he looks at Decius and knows that they both know that the truth of this is complicated. Under the Princeps, the consulship is a managerial post, someone who makes sure that Augustus' vision is brought about. And soothes the Senate and keeps Rome together and headed in the right direction. But he still wants to do it because he has been programmed since childhood. He wants to be able to say that he has been a Consul. He wants it written on his tomb.

And it may not be completely sensible to refuse.

"Yes," says Horace. "It does mean something because you are from a senatorial family. Your ancestors will be pleased. And your father would be thrilled. So now we must get you back to Rome and up to the Palatine for a dinner at Augustus'. I elect myself your unofficial campaign manager, seeing as it looks like a job with no actual work involved. Lucius, you must stop looking so idiotic. Sit down and drink."

Lucius sits and looks at the floor, and Decius moves to the door.

"Are you riding or sailing?" he asks. "The Swan is in harbour and I can send to get it ready," he says. "Lucius? Can you be ready to leave first thing tomorrow morning?"

"Yes, but let's ride," says Lucius, not having to think about the journey they have made many times. "Tell Sergius to pack light, will you? You'd better stay here, for the moment anyway, and Horace will come with me. I don't need anything special, I think. Oh, except a jar of our good stuff, Titus can pick something out. I'd better have a present for the Princeps."

Chapter 3

Several days later, it is horribly hot as Lucius strolls through an almost deserted Rome to the house of his elder sister, Albinia. He is in a plain tunic, old sandals and hat, and it strikes him that soon this will not be appropriate attire. Are Consuls allowed to dress down? He knows he will be given a group of bodyguards by the state, lictors, and they rarely allow their master to remain incognito. He wonders if he must take them everywhere and makes a note to ask. He won't be able to leave the city for the rest of the year either. No trips up to Cosa to help with the harvest or sample the new wines. A disconcerting thought stops him in the middle of the street leading from the foot of the Caelian Hill to the Forum: will he become a provincial governor? Most Consuls, once their year of office is up, have to go off and spend a couple of years managing a bit of the ever-increasing Empire. Slowly, he starts to walk again, thinking that if he keeps on making sudden stops like that it will annoy all those people in his entourage once he is Consul. Oh well, if he has to look after a province, then he does. It could be fun, and it isn't as if he will have to go fight a war or anything, the Senate and Augustus will give him a quiet little backwater. And musing in this manner, he strolls off the main street and into a series of left-right bends until he arrives at his sister's house.

Albinia lives in a rather nice and spacious house on the lower slopes of the Oppian Hill. It is a quiet area, known primarily for the workshops of the craftsmen who work animal horns into various things – combs, decorative cups, ornaments for your horse's reins. Not the most lucrative or famous of Rome's industries, the group of workshops do not produce a lot of noise, nor too many fires, though on the days when they are cleaning the horns there can be some evil smells. There is a very good wine-shop at the corner with a peaceable clientele, and Albinia's doorkeeper never has a problem with rowdy passers-by wondering who lives behind the lofty front door of the large house down the street. Albinia herself lives a quiet life and has done for twenty years since the death of her husband at the siege of Mutina. She has resisted all suggestions that she marry again – and has quietly and effectively invested her money from Apuleius and her money from her mother. As Lucius knows she has an intelligent freedman working for her as her financial manager (recommended by Decius so totally worthy of her trust) he rarely worries about his sister or what is to become of her. He is not one of those who thinks she should marry again. Albinia has no dependents and will leave behind nothing as important as her poetry; there is no pressing need for marriage, and her single state seems to suit her, so he does not see the point of his interfering. He is no hypocrite and does not have the nerve to ask her to remarry in line with modern thinking while he himself is so reluctant to try marriage again.

Albinia's staff are highly trained and have lived with their mistress for years – as, indeed, thinks Lucius, have his. He can never remember the name of her old door-slave, who nowadays barely manages a grunt in greeting before shuffling off to get the steward. Mentor, the steward, is a tall, elegant man, now freed, and the backbone of the household for at least ten years. He has the easy manner of one who knows his exact place in the world and doesn't mind. Lucius sometimes feels he could be friends with Mentor

After a civil and brief enquiry after the health and well-being of Lucius' own family as they cross the atrium and go down the back corridor, Mentor announces his presence at the doorway to Albinia's study. He then melts backward, and Lucius goes in to be hugged and sat down and fussed over. Albinia always enjoys this aspect of being his elder sister and Lucius as usual endures it. When the Cosa family come to visit Rome, Albinia comes to dinner every few days, and his children have a regular date with their aunt, usually a jaunt and occasionally a serious visit to a library or temple. Albinia does not impose her learning on her relatives, but Lucius knows that she would love his daughter to be just a little more intellectually inquisitive.

"You must have news," observes Albinia. "You never visit in the summer. I sometimes wonder what it is you do with your summer. Sit and read?"

"Nothing wrong with reading," says Lucius unwounded by his sister's jibes. "And I have an estate to run."

"Decius and Sergius have an estate to run," says his sister. "You could easily stay most of the year in Rome and attend Senate meetings, as is your duty. But you can't be bothered. So that mysterious visit from Horace – is this what this is all about? I imagine he didn't go just to read you some poems?"

"Well, let's say that I shall be making a bigger effort with Senate meetings soon," and Lucius laughs at her expression. "You are never going to believe it. Horace arrived with none other than Maecenas, and Maecenas had an offer from the Princeps himself – they have offered me the consulship!"

Albinia's eyes blink and a grin so wide breaks out across her face that Lucius has to join in and when Mentor arrives with cups and jugs the two of them are whooping with laughter. For the first time since Maecenas left the villa in Cosa, Lucius feels like an ordinary person again. Wine and fruit juice are mixed with water and served and brother and sister toast each other with mouths still quivering and eyes dancing. After a long drink, Albinia cocks one eyebrow at him and says, "What I should have said is, of course, that you will make a very good Consul."

22

She is serious. Lucius was going to make a rude comment but stops himself.

"You will take the job seriously even though..."

"Even though I don't think it is anything more than a token gesture anymore?"

"It is much more than that, Lucius, and you know it." Albinia stares into her cup of honeyed lemon with mint, and Lucius cannot remember the last time he saw her drink wine. Unlike him, tottering on the verge of happy cloudiness as a normal condition. As usual he pushes that needling little thought away.

Albinia decides to carry on. "Augustus clearly wants to make a statement by choosing you and that is fine. You are an acknowledged Republican, pardoned and welcomed back into the fold, and you make the new regime look good. That doesn't mean you can't get a few things past the Senate and into law pretty easily. Everyone is so relieved that Augustus has recovered that they won't be expecting anything much from you."

"Albinia, I am a night-watchman," says Lucius, slightly impatiently. "I'm to see the year through to its end then hand over."

"You might get a province," points out Albinia.

"Yes, I've thought of that," says Lucius. "It won't be anything much. A quiet piece of Gaul, Syria maybe."

"Marcus Cicero went to Syria, didn't he?" asks Albinia, knowing perfectly well that their friend Cicero had indeed gone to Syria. And had had a quiet and undemanding stint as governor while his legates ran the province for him. "Lucius, you need a break like this. It is a chance to get out of your routine. You could try getting some legislation through, you could do some good in the provinces, you could – I don't know – get living again!"

Lucius is surprised by this. Albinia is not one who lectures him, though he is aware that she worries about him, especially since Caecilia's death. And Albinia loathes Augustus and Livia and everything about them. He expresses his surprise.

"Well, yes, I don't get on with the whole thing, but I am not stupid either. I have to live in this world, and I do, quietly and successfully. And so do you, but maybe not as successfully, because you are a man and thus expected to achieve things." She is being ironic now, he knows. Albinia's poetry is good enough for public readings, yet she refuses to circulate them. A small circle of family and friends knows how good she is and this is as she chooses, just like the rest of her life; but Lucius knows that in a different political climate there is the possibility that Albinia could be Rome's first truly famous female poet. But now is not that climate.

"I haven't really expected to achieve things since Julius Caesar became Dictator," says Lucius, aiming for a light touch but realising that he is speaking the truth. "It isn't as though I really want power, Albinia, you know that. I have never wanted power."

"What did you want, twenty years ago, say?" asks his sister. "Did you ever know?"

Lucius thinks back and sighs. She is right. He had vague ideas about what was right and stumbled after those ideas until he fell over. Civil War and the emergence of Augustus have changed everyone's view of how power is distributed.

"I had this idea that I would be a pretty good speaker, have a career in the law, enter the Senate and climb the ranks, get to Praetor, and maybe Consul, but I wasn't sure about Consul really... I didn't want much, you know. I just wanted to be a small part of it all."

"Well, here is your first real chance," says Albinia briskly. "So, seize it."

"I'm not going to turn it down, am I?" Lucius grumbles in a

mock-suffering tone. "I don't really feel that I can do that without being ill."

"No, don't turn it down," agrees Albinia. "You wouldn't want to be rude." And the atmosphere lightens as they laugh again.

Lucius tells her about the dinner party at Augustus' house and asks if she would like to accompany him, but Albinia shakes her head firmly. "No, I am not the right person for that. Take someone else – like Horace."

"Not Horace," says Lucius. "He was embarrassed enough being used by Maecenas to smooth the path to Cosa. Poor old Horace!"

"Poor Horace nothing," says Albinia. "It is what happens when you accept a patron, and Horace does well enough out of Maecenas otherwise. He is getting Maecenas' backing for his collection of Odes after all."

"Yes, I meant to ask you about those," says Lucius. "Will you get me a copy when it's finally published? And tell me what to say about them? I couldn't make any sense out of the one you sent me."

Albinia looks at him. "I don't believe that for a moment, Lucius. You'd better have something ready is all I can say. People are going to notice that a poem to you is fourth in the entire collection, and they will want to talk to you about it."

"Who are the first three dedicated to?" asks Lucius.

"Maecenas, Augustus and Virgil," says Albinia with a dryness that could wither the first fresh daisy of spring.

Lucius' eyebrows climb his forehead as he takes in this exalted company.

"People are, I'm afraid, going to wonder why you are next," says Albinia. "Especially the people who haven't a clue who you are, who then ask around and find out that you are a dyed-in-the-wool old-time Republican who still worships Marcus Brutus and fought at Philippi."

"Horace fought at Philippi," points out Lucius. "He makes a joke of it."

"Which is why he is forgiven," says Albinia. "You have never joked about it, and you are going to have to now."

"Alby," says Lucius. "Why hasn't Horace dedicated an Ode to you?"

"What makes you think he hasn't?" asks his sister.

"Because you are angry that he hasn't," says Lucius and for once he is right. Albinia is so charmed by this perspicacity that she smiles and answers quite cheerfully.

"I am in the Odes but in disguise. Horace could not dedicate a poem to me, you know that, Lucius. I am too respectable a lady. See if you can spot me when you read them. If you read them." She hesitates. "Lucius, don't be too upset with Horace, will you? There will be some poems that you will find hard to stomach, but he must flatter certain people, you know. He is a freedman's son; he is reliant on his patrons. Maybe it would be better if you just left them. And it is a shame because there are some really lovely poems."

"If I read them, I promise I shall keep my opinions private," says Lucius. "Now – more pressing – who shall I take to this dinner?"

"Take nobody," says Albinia.

"I shall have to," says Lucius. "I can't think of anyone who is respectable enough that I like enough."

Albinia shudders at this sentence and he asks her how her own writing is going.

"All right," says his ever-cautious sister. "I should have something to read to you next time I come to dinner – that is, if you'd like me to."

"Providing it doesn't go on too long," says Lucius, with barbaric disregard for her feelings. Albinia laughs.

"Definitely time for you to go but I am coming for dinner

tomorrow for a full update on dining with the Princeps and family. I shall want to know who was there and what they wore and everything."

"Why?" asks Lucius.

"To annoy you," replies his sister.

"May I use your baths and get ready here?" asks Lucius.

"Of course," says Albinia. "Now push off and find Mentor and he will sort you out. I am going for a siesta. I probably shan't see you until tomorrow," and they hug farewell. Mentor mysteriously appears as Lucius leaves the study so that he can escort Lucius to the guest room he uses. Once the door is closed what does Mentor do? Lucius wonders. Maybe he vanishes into the breezes. Maybe he supervises the laundry. Lucius leaves all of that to the small staff permanently kept on in his own house in Rome and to Sergius and Tia in Cosa and he has no desire to find out anything about the mechanics of keeping a Roman clean, fed and fit for public duty. In the heat of the mid-afternoon, Lucius makes it as far as the couch and enjoys a nap during which his dreams are of such small significance that he cannot remember them when he awakes.

A slave escorts him to Albinia's tiny suite of baths, and Lucius appreciates the luxury of a completely silent wash and massage. No children splashing, no family wanting to talk, no one offering to pluck his armpits. Bliss. By the time he gets back to his guest room, his party clothes have arrived from home – a decorous pale yellow tunic, with a light cloak for the walk home. If he needs it. Someone clever has included some decent sandals and a nice perfumed oil, but Albinia's masseur has already made Lucius feel pretty so he leaves it. His hair is combed, he is shaved and dressed, and it is time to cross over the Forum and climb the Palatine Hill for dinner. The Augustus family, as is well-known, dine early and unfashionably, with no acrobats or fancy food – unless it is a special occasion. Albinia has lent him a boy to light the way back as well as the gardener to be Lucius' bodyguard, and they follow him as he makes his way across the city.

Chapter 4

The sun is low in the sky as Lucius walks along the road that takes him through the Forum. Despite the late hour, the Forum is busy. As always, there is building work going on, ubiquitous and even when you couldn't see it, you could hear it. Lucius sometimes wonders why the Princeps feels the need to change everything at once. Of course, building or refurbishing a building originally constructed by one's ancestors is quite normal, but Augustus just took over as usual. If it isn't his law-court, or forum or whatever then it is in the name of the Divine Julius (ha!) or one of Augustus' cronies. Poor old Agrippa is of course the one given all the boring practical projects – baths, aqueducts, sewers, anything involving pipes in fact. Augustus does most of the showy stuff himself, and lately his beloved nephew Marcellus has been allowed an arch or two. The whole of Rome must be clothed in marble, but nothing can quite hide the brick and concrete underneath. Augustus is fond of saying that Rome must be rebuilt in marble, but he actually fixes thin slabs over the cracks, literally and figuratively, and if the veneer wears through, what will happen?

Augustus is also making a big thing of refurbishing temples, though Lucius can remember being quite irritated when the Princeps decided to have a go at the little shrine to the goddess Minerva put up by Lucius' own grandfather and on their own street. The first the family knew was when a slave came back from market one morning and reported that a couple of workmen were busy hammering away at the shrine. When Decius and Lucius took a stroll to see what was happening, they discovered that a couple of sheets of marble had been pinned onto the brickwork. Lucius' father had still been alive then and had felt seriously annoyed at this usurpation of what he felt was a Sestius family privilege.

But the Forum is looking rather good to give Augustus credit. The Senate house is reassuringly plain and Republican, the temple to the Divine Julius is small though very fine, and the Speakers' Platform looks better for the new face-lift. The prows from the naval battle at Actium have been fixed up there of course, a small reminder that Augustus has got where he is by conducting a Civil War against his so-called friends. The loser at Actium was Mark Antony, and Lucius does not mourn the passing of such an odious man, but he is sorry that Cleopatra committed suicide: like any normal arrogant Roman, Lucius doesn't mind seeing an exotic femme fatale marching through Rome in chains. There is a statue of Cleopatra in the Temple of Venus, but Lucius knows that it looks nothing like the real woman. He once saw her on a shopping trip accompanied by a ridiculously large entourage and she really looked like any other woman, with, according to Albinia, truly expert make-up. Her nose was enormous. Cleopatra's that is, not Albinia's.

On he goes past the walls of the houses of rich men, until he reaches the house of Augustus. Off to one side, looking considerably more modest, is the house of Augustus. Here the scaffolding reappears, for Augustus is rebuilding his presence even in his own house. All trace of Octavian, the youth who took over control by wearing down his opponents one by one, must be covered up with the glamour of Augustus. A large but plain wooden door marks the house entrance and there is an exceedingly well-spoken slave on duty, wax tablet in hand to check that Lucius Sestius Quirinalis (of all people!) has been invited to dinner. A boy is whistled up to guide him to the small dining room where several people are already settling down onto the couches. Lucius looks around, expecting the famous

Augustan austerity to be evident but the dining room is classy and comfortable. Light cream walls are painted with a row of crimson pillars, and garlands of pinecones are depicted hanging between the pillars: the smooth floor is made up of thousands of tiny white tiles. The three couches are comfortably upholstered, and Augustus does not stint on cushions. Nobody will suffer from indigestion through having to lie on board-hard couches in this room.

Maecenas spots Lucius immediately and comes over with a big grin on his face.

"How nice! Lucius Sestius, may I introduce you? The Princeps and Livia Drusilla are on their way, of course. This is my wife, Terentia, and here we have the lovely Julia, daughter of Augustus, and her husband Marcellus, who is of course the Princeps' nephew. You haven't brought anyone? No matter, you will find that this sort of dinner is very informal. Augustus isn't fond of the banqueting scene."

"It is a complete waste of time and good food, the amount people drink," says a light and warm voice from the doorway. Lucius turns and sees the Princeps directly behind him. He suddenly realises that he has no idea of the etiquette, so smiles and hopes Maecenas will carry on with his introductions.

"Good evening, Caesar Augustus!" cries Maecenas. "This is Lucius Sestius Quirinalis and I for one am hoping that you won't be inflicting one of your grimmer meals on us or the wretched man won't know what to think."

"Maecenas, you know perfectly well I would never allow a guest to eat anything but the best," says the woman next to Augustus. "Lucius Sestius, take no notice of this irrepressible rogue. You are most welcome."

"Yes indeed," says Augustus with a wide smile. "And it is completely typical of you, Maecenas, to thrust the poor man into a group of strangers and confuse him. Behave yourself."

The young Julia and Marcellus are giggling, and Lucius suddenly realises that he is in the midst of a family not too unlike his own. Everyone – except him – is comfortable and relaxed, nobody has dressed up very much, though Maecenas' slightly too short tunic is an off-white linen this time. Augustus' own tunic is plain to the point of dull but made of very finely woven wool. The women are in light draperies which look comfortable without revealing anything, and Livia and Julia do not appear to be wearing any make-up even. Terentia stands out here: her cheeks are a little too pink and her eyebrows are a couple of thick black lines perfectly painted onto her pale forehead. Lucius feels that his own sartorial style puts him safely into the category of "unremarkable". He stops analysing, and says, "It is a pleasure to be here, Lady Livia. Where would you like me to sit?" And there is a cheerful scramble while Livia directs everyone – even those already settled – to places. It reminds him of dinners at home when he was younger.

As they settle onto the couches, a couple of slaves go round taking off sandals and putting on slippers, and a bowl of rose petal water is offered to Lucius to wash his hands. He is in the guest of honour's place, and the Princeps is to his right, on the host's couch with Livia. On Lucius' left is Maecenas, with Terentia beside him. Julia and Marcellus take the third couch. Lucius takes a quick and surreptitious look around the table and checks everyone, just as he does every evening when he is at Cosa. The Princeps is wearing well. His recent illness has made its mark, and he is on the thin side, but his hair, light brown and carefully cut in a shorter version of Alexander the Great's shaggy curls, is still thick and there is no sign of grey. Most Romans by this stage of the summer are showing the signs of the sun, with hair lightened in streaks and faces reddened or tanned. Nobody grows their beard in summer, or they risk a multicoloured face when it is shaved off. But Augustus is pale, a little tired-looking, a little gaunt in the cheeks. His manner is that of a perfectly healthy man, and his bony nose and sticking-out ears are as enthusiastically unGreek as ever. Livia is a different jar of pickled sauce. Lucius has seen her before at public occasions of course but hasn't been close and hasn't felt the need to gaze at her. Now he smiles at her and chats with her and after a while begins to watch her mouth. Livia's mouth does not move unless she is speaking, and she speaks relatively infrequently in this group of practised conversationalists. Her mouth is tucked away above her determined chin, small and curved and with the corners folded deep. Above this guarded line is a straight and perfectly proportioned nose and then two large and soft brown eyes, of such melting beauty, Lucius cannot understand why he has not fallen into them at first sight. Her hair is folded back into an unobtrusive bun at the nape of her neck, but the strands fall into waves as they curve around her head and her neat ears. Miniature gold chandeliers strung with beads hang from her earlobes and is her only jewellery. All in all, she presents as perfect – except for her mouth. Lucius finds that he cannot abide it. Too small, too pursed, and incapable of smiling convincingly, Livia's mouth broadcasts modesty, chastity and smugness. Lucius suddenly pities Augustus, and wonders if their lack of children together is down to that smirking, judgmental mouth.

The first course is eggs of course. Dips and seeds, sauce and little plates of chopped raw vegetables are placed on the table along with the bowls of different-sized eggs, and everyone helps themselves. It is all very normal. The talk is of the summer, how hot and uncomfortable it is, where common acquaintances are thinking of going for September if they can get away. Nobody at that table is going to go on holiday any time soon of course but talking about Baiae or the Alban Hills is harmless and pleasant. Lucius mentions his estate at Cosa, and they express interest in tasting his wine. He promises to send a jar the next day. In the confusion of today he has forgotten Maecenas' suggestion, even though Decius and Titus carefully decanted some of the prized ten-year-old vintage into a small amphora for him. Titus agonised about the wine's survival of a journey jogging on horseback down the Aurelian Road.

The table is cleared and a chicken stew and lots of fresh salad leaves and vegetables are brought in. There are sauces on the side though Augustus, Lucius notes, likes his food plain. Nobody is drinking much either. They don't need to, thinks Lucius, and wishes he had just a little more.

The conversation shifts to Augustus' illness, introduced by the Princeps himself, as if he wants Lucius to understand the situation fully.

"I was lucky to find this amazing Greek chap, Antonius Musa," says the Princeps, looking wise. Lucius has heard of this marvellous Greek doctor, of course. Antonius Musa is now all the rage amongst the upper classes in Rome. Rumour has it that he is going to publish a book to capitalise on the publicity of his recent success.

"Cold baths, that was the trick," says Augustus far too enthusiastically. Lucius can't help an inward shudder. The Princeps leans further forward, ready to continue his lecture, and across the table Lucius sees Julia nudge Marcellus. The two young people can't help grinning, but there is no malice there, just the affectionate teasing of the younger generation.

Augustus is clearly now a big follower of Musa's regime – brisk walks, plain food, water and cold baths. Lucius hopes to all the gods that he is not going to be questioned on his own healthy living. He listens and nods and eventually Julia bursts into giggles.

"Oh Papa, poor Lucius Sestius! He is terrified that you are going to insist on a run around the garden after dinner!"

Augustus is smiling but undeterred.

"I don't care how often you tease me about it, I think Musa saved my life. And I shall tell everyone so!"

"It was a very frightening time for us all," says Livia, with an air of bringing that particular conversation to an end. Lucius gets the feeling that she does that quite a lot. She turns to him and the change in subject comes.

"My dear Lucius Sestius, let us hear a little about you, for you know enough about us, I am sure. My husband tells me that you lost your wife in the autumn illness a few years ago. I am sorry to hear that. Do you have any children?"

Lucius is willing to indulge in her change of direction and they talk about families and choosing how to educate young children. Julia and Marcellus contribute anecdotes from their schooldays, and Maecenas and Terentia keep silent. Julia, it turns out, is nearly as well-educated as Lucius himself though she did not go onto his training in oratory and the law once she married. She confesses to enjoying poetry immensely and has heard of Albinia.

"I should like to meet her, Lucius Sestius, one day," she says with an earnest expression. "I love the idea that women can write just as well as men – on some subjects at least."

"And what subjects would a woman write about then, my dear?" asks Livia with just a hint of sarcasm. Terentia stirs at last.

"Love surely," she says lightly. "That is one thing where we are as expert as the men."

There is a definite hint of flirtation there, thinks Lucius, and he takes a quick glance at the Princeps. Augustus is frowning just a little, but Julia cuts in.

"Oh Terentia, we have so much more to say!"

"I'm not sure there is the market for poems dedicated to the art of weaving," muses Maecenas with just a hint of amusement in his eyes, and Julia, understanding him well, laughs.

"Oh, I could write a poem about weaving all right, but I'm not sure Papa would be pleased! I know that you feel that it is important and part of our traditions, Papa, but really it is so dull."

"You wove my tunic," objects Augustus.

"Our household weavers wove it under my supervision," sighs Julia. "And really, Papa, I don't mind that Livia or I see to everything you wear, in fact I always feel proud when you set off for some important meeting or other, and I can think to myself that I remember making that cloak or tunic or toga. But weaving is dull, and I am sure that when I meet Lucius Sestius' sister she will agree and then we shall decide what is the right subject for poetry. And women will show that they can write as well as any man!"

"Bravo!" cries Maecenas. "And I shall organise a recital for you to bring your epic work before the world! And I can get you a particularly good deal on publishing as well, you know."

"Only if Papa agrees to perform the recital," says Julia, and smiles beguilingly at her father. "You know you have a lovely speaking voice, Papa."

Julia is a child of happiness, and Lucius finds his heart melting as he sees her touch her father's arm gently. She is the perfect daughter. Her hair is tightly wrapped around her head and she has no hesitation in showing that she has inherited her father's ears. She also has his brows and grey eyes and on her they look beautiful, lending a serious cast to her face that suits it.

Livia leans forward and asks Terentia if she has any idea what the poet Horace is working on now that the Odes are finished, and Terentia looks at Maecenas with the question reflected in her expression. Maecenas makes a "wait and see" reply, and the conversation switches to which senators have good speaking voices and who delivers the best speeches nowadays. Lucius has little to contribute as he rarely listens when he is in the Senate but wishes he could talk about the politicians of his youth without making a faux pas. After all, Augustus had most of them killed. He risks a mention that long ago he heard Caesar speak and read his Commentaries on the various wars fought by the Dictator in Gaul and Egypt and Africa. Lucius thinks that having fought with Caesar in Africa and been wounded he has earned that at least.

"Oh yes, of course!" exclaims Augustus with unexpected enthusiasm. "You were there in the Thapsus campaign, weren't you? A nasty business it sounded but then war within a nation is never anything less. That is one thing I am proud of, that Romans are no longer fighting each other."

There it is. He has said it. Brought up the subject of the Civil War which was less than a decade away, and made it clear how he views the whole subject. And a sycophantic little murmur of agreement runs round the table. Lucius stares at the Princeps who looks up and stares back. There is a little silence, then Lucius nods his head and takes a long draught of the well-watered wine.

Everyone has finished the main course and the slaves clear and lay out dishes of nuts and fruit. Lucius has no appetite for anything other than leaving at the first polite opportunity and hopes that someone will make the appropriate noises soon. Surely the young newly-weds want to retire early? They are a likeable pair and Lucius thinks ruefully of his preconception that these next-generation Augustans were going to be arrogant and entitled youngsters, indulged and opinionated. Marcellus has excellent manners and his relationship with Julia is textbook Roman married. Although Lucius considers the two of them must have been hideously young when they got married, they work as a team already, presenting their conversation in tandem and every now and then turning to the other for assistance in making a point, finding the right word. There is clear affection, and every chance of a long and mutually rewarding marriage, he thinks, and is careful not to make that mistake of foolish old men, hoping that the young people will fall in love. Love is not high on the list of Augustus' plans for his family, but this arrangement is looking promising. Interesting, thinks Lucius, that Augustus has chosen his own nephew rather than one of Livia's sons to marry his beloved only child, but Julia and Marcellus seem so well-suited that he is pleased for them. He has no doubt that Livia's boys are just as worthy, but the opinion of the Forum is that they are going down the Agrippa path of military service and loyal friendship. Lucius hopes that the young Tiberius and his brother enjoy building sewers. The same Forum gossips thoroughly enjoyed Agrippa's recent venture down into the tunnels running under Rome and moving the city's rot unseen into the river and away. Apparently, Agrippa, the architect of naval battles such as Actium, sailed the length of the Cloaca Maxima – from sailing the Ionian Sea to paddling the Roman Wee, as one wit put it. Other jokes, even worse, followed. Lucius thought this was a little unfair as Agrippa had made sewers and aqueducts his business, giving the less glamorous side of Roman architecture its moment in the sun. Or not in the sun. Lucius shudders. Roman sewers are kept safely covered over and quite right too. He has been to too many places where "sewer" meant "open channel of filth sludging its way down the street".

As the end approaches the diners lean back, chat more informally. Maecenas disappears, presumably to the toilet, and Terentia wriggles herself a little closer to Lucius and smiles.

"So, are you looking forward to being Consul, Lucius Sestius? Nobody in your family has ever been Consul before have they?"

From another person – "Livia!" thinks Lucius – this could be made to sound like an insult, but not from Terentia who has the innocence of a completely inoffensive person.

"No," he replies. "My father was praetor though and was quite happy to make it that far. He was not an ambitious man and preferred his legal career and running the family estate to politics really. I am very like him but becoming Consul for the rest of the year – yes, it is an honour, and I will please my ancestors, I am sure. I just wish my father were still alive to see it."

Terentia's brown eyes grow sad, and she pats Lucius' hand, saying, "I'm sure that he is proud." And her fingers stroke the back of his hand lightly as she leans back and makes room for Maecenas once more. Lucius is confused and eats grapes steadily, feeling too embarrassed to look at Maecenas even though the latter is holding forth on the quality of wine in Italy nowadays. And doing so with all the charm and wit at his disposal. Julia is giggling, Marcellus watching and smiling broadly, and Augustus looks indulgent. Livia is clearly not paying any attention; indeed, she is probably planning the next weaving session. The look of determination and dry sanctity on her face does not promise any joy.

Julia and Marcellus are the first to excuse themselves, and Lucius smiles to himself. Once they have gone, he too makes his excuses, and a slave comes with his sandals and another slave with more water for washing. There is a flurry of domestic ritual, and Lucius finds himself nodding and smiling to Augustus and Livia, and leaving with Maecenas, Terentia strolling a little behind them with a maidservant. As they leave the complex of housing and temple, a stream of slaves joins them, Lucius' two and a cavalcade for Maecenas and Terentia. Over the Palatine they go and then along the road between Caelian and Esquiline until they part. Terentia, to Lucius' approval, has walked all the way. She smiles at him as he and Maecenas say goodbye and he feels both pleased and irritated. Musing on this he makes his way home.

Chapter 5

Now he has someone important to visit. Marcus Tullius Cicero the Younger is one of Lucius' oldest friends. They have known each other since childhood, at which point they didn't like each other, though they both idolised Marcus' father, the elder Cicero, who was a remarkable orator and the most self-centred man Lucius has ever known. Friendship with the younger Cicero came with the shared experience borne of seeing someone struggling and deciding to help him with the struggle. A long time ago Lucius, Marcus and Horace had stood alongside each other and the realities of a November battlefield, fighting against other Romans, had been distinctly grim. The Battle of Philippi was lost, and they had fled the battlefield like so many others. A few years later they had both been the recipients of Augustus' generous clemency. Such things bind people.

Fortunately, Marcus feels no need to exclaim that Lucius is back in Rome and ask how he is. Instead they get straight down to the wine, another hobby which they have in common.

"How long are you keeping it before drinking?"

"Most of it we drink within the year," says Marcus. "But this is from the year of Augustus' seventh consulship and doing nicely. My manager takes part of the harvest every year and experiments. It turns out that we have the world's oldest slave still working on the Capuan farm, claims he remembers all the great vintages from around the bay of Neapolis." He sighs. "He won't take his freedom, says he wants to die on the farm, treading the grapes. In the meantime, he and the manager have a wonderful time talking about pests, and soil, and heating and airing… I don't really want it to be so complicated."

Lucius says, "I let Titus take care of it all up in Cosa, and Decius comes and helps with the accounts and discusses the business. He loves it there. He's even bought a little bit of land nearby."

Marcus looks at him and says, "It is very peaceful walking around a vineyard. And the smell is fantastic. How is Decius? Is he ever going to get married?"

Lucius is used to this question. Marcus asks it every time. Marcus himself is not married, Lucius is a widower, Decius has never married. The three men have known each other for forty years and they all know that marriage is not for them. Marcus has chosen wine over a wife, Lucius has done his duty and is averse to sharing his life so intimately again, and neither of them know why Decius hasn't settled down.

"I think Decius may have someone in Cosa. He keeps making excuses to go up there when I want him in Rome or sorting out the tile factory. He does love Cosa, I know. Now he has land near the farm, he says he will build a house soon, so I imagine the plan is to marry his mystery woman and settle down. But I have to get through this consulship before life can go back to normal up in Cosa."

He realises that he has rambled on a bit, but Marcus doesn't mind. Marcus generally doesn't mind anything as long as there is a cup of wine within reach. Marcus leans forward to pour another cup and says casually, "Consulship?"

"Marcus – I need to tell you something."

His friend raises an enquiring eyebrow. Lucius ploughs on.

"I had a visit from Horace – and with him, Gaius Maecenas. He had a message from the Princeps. Would I like to take over the consulship for the rest of the year?"

Marcus looks blank for a moment then laughs from his belly in a single joyful and completely natural bark.

"You poor sod! And presumably you are going to accept this

offer? And now you are terrified?"

Lucius grins and relaxes. Marcus has hit just the right note.

"Wetting myself," he admits, and they raise their cups to each other.

He entertains Marcus with a description of the visit, which, looking back on it, now seems much funnier than it was at the time.

"How do you feel about Horace bringing Maecenas to you?" asks Marcus. Lucius sighs.

"I felt a little betrayed and mostly I understood that Maecenas was just using an asset. Horace is indebted to him for his support, and as I never read any of Horace's poetry I can't really complain, I suppose."

"What utterly twisted thinking," observes Marcus. "Thank all the gods I don't live in your head. And what did you think of Maecenas?"

"Oh, that is easy – he is charming and witty and clever and persuasive and beautifully-dressed. He stuck out like a – like a thing that sticks out – at the Cosa villa."

Marcus' lips twitch as they both enjoy the schoolboy humour. Lucius tries again.

"He was like a foreigner, maybe not even human. So clearly not part of the environment, it was quite strange." Lucius is struck by how much he himself feels a stranger to the world in which Maecenas moves. He does not doubt that being Consul will have no effect on that.

"You don't talk much about being Consul," he observes to Marcus. His friend frowns and shrugs.

"You wouldn't come round to dinner for a year, you were so keen to avoid me," he says, a little sharply. "Afterwards, I thought it better to just not mention it. I wasn't that enamoured of it that I wanted to talk really. It was fun being a governor though. Syria was an eye-opener."

43

Lucius manages to ignore this invitation to change the subject and decides to get the apology out of the way.

"I'm sorry, Marcus. That was ridiculously pig-headed of me. But I couldn't quite embrace the whole Cleopatra thing. The Battle of Actium was only just over and there was fighting going on in Egypt, but it still felt like civil war. I may have hated Mark Antony nearly as much as you hated him, but he and his followers were Romans. Or a lot of them were."

"Yes, they were," says Marcus quietly. "And it was indeed a civil war. A war between Augustus and Antony and we all neatly stepped behind whichever one we decided to support. Or rather, behind the one we despised less. You did that just as much as I did – you chose Augustus."

"He used you," says Lucius. "He made you Consul because he knew you would focus on getting Antony."

"Yes, I did," said Marcus. "I held Rome together behind Augustus because he was fighting Antony and I don't feel the need to make any apology for that. I got to pull down the statues of the man who ordered my father's death. It was worth it just for that. And the rest of it was just boring work. Actually, Maecenas was useful as well, a good man to work with. I can actually work if I have a good reason, you know."

He sounds defensive: the conversation has gone wrong and Lucius starts again.

"I did not mean that you shouldn't have been Consul. I understand that when Augustus asks it isn't really a choice. Not for Horace or you or me. What I want to know is – how do I get through this?"

"Sometimes," says Marcus, "you surprise me. People like you and me and Horace, we spend our lives apologising for following our principles and convictions. We all chose the wrong side at Philippi, we survived, we made our way back. At that point we made the decision to give up – and living in Rome under Augustus that means we don't lead opposition to him. We sit in the Senate when he wants, Horace writes poetry that doesn't criticise him, we make no waves. We have lost, Lucius Sestius, we lost nearly two decades ago, and we live with that. Being Consul will be easy, you'll have to read a lot of documents, chair a few Senate meetings and you'll probably have to go to dinner at Augustus' a couple of times. Depending on who his other guests are, you might enjoy the dinner. The food and wine are nothing to speak of, Livia is as scary as a pissed-off snake, and the younger generation are obnoxiously over-educated. If Maecenas is there, it will be fun, if it's Agrippa it will be painful."

"I've been to dinner already," Lucius tells him, "and everything you say is true. No, it was perfectly pleasant – but I had to deal with Terentia."

"Ah," says Marcus. "How did you get on there?" He is smiling.

"I was not comfortable. What on earth got her and Maecenas together?"

"Money and politics, of course," replies Marcus immediately. "Dear me, Lucius, you have been rusticating for far too long. And I can see you really are out of the loop." Marcus doesn't often get the chance to be superior and he enjoys his little victory. "Well, now you've already – er – encountered Terentia, you might just wonder why she and Maecenas are invited to our beloved leader's place so often…"

"You mean…?"

"I mean nothing," says Marcus, deepening his voice dramatically and for a moment sounding just like his father. "Now – the consulship. Did Maecenas tell you why you were chosen for the honour?"

"No, but I worked it out. My main attraction is that I am respectably Republican," says Lucius, only slightly bitterly. "I could see Maecenas noticing the images of Brutus and Cassius in my study, and I'd say he found it amusing. The Last of the Non-Conformers, that's me. How marvellous that even such as I can find a place in the Leading Citizen's Rome Reborn!"

"And the Leading Citizen's been ill."

"And he has been ill, and he is probably fed up of having to be Consul year after year, and he is never in Rome anyway."

"And you are the pair of safe hands he needs." Marcus is smiling again. "You have to laugh, Lucius, because it is very clever, choosing you. Nobody can say he is rewarding a crony, it looks noble to offer it to an recalcitrant old Republican like you, and you having those Brutus and Cassius busts in your study for anyone to see makes him look even more gracious. I bet Maecenas will be polishing that up into a little dinner party story, soon to be disseminated all over Rome. Take one piece of advice – keep on avoiding Terentia. And welcome to the Establishment!"

It is a sobering thought but not without its funny side. They toast each other again and the conversation moves on. Becoming Consul is only so interesting after all, and they have forty years of other things to discuss. Marcus pours more wine.

"Did you know that Horace is now publishing those Odes he has been writing for the last however many years?"

"So Albinia tells me. It's a big deal, then? I mean, obviously in the world of poetry it is, but for everyone else too?" asks Lucius, feeling again that he is out of touch.

Marcus laughs. "Everything Horace does nowadays is a big deal. He and Virgil can do no wrong. And as Virgil is never going to finish his mighty epic, then Horace gets all the limelight going."

Lucius is silent. His friends have changed almost in front of his eyes, and now he too has changed, finally joining the ranks of the respectable middle-aged members of the community.

Soon he will be spouting phrases like "For the greater good". Marcus leans across to top-up Lucius' wine and feels sorry for him. He, Marcus, made this transition much more easily, even willingly, but he knows that Lucius will not. And neither of them can do much about it.

Albinia comes round to dinner that evening, and finds her brother in a slightly bemused mood but ready to enjoy some good food and conversation with her. He brings her up to date on Cosa and the children and she brings around three thick scrolls in a fine red leather case – Horace's three books of Odes. Lucius gives the case of poetry to one of the slaves and asks him to make sure it has pride of place on the desk in the study. He really does intend to read some of the Odes. But not tonight.

Chapter 6

The next day, by arrangement – which Lucius discovers means trailing up the Palatine whenever a messenger summons you – Lucius goes for a meeting with the Princeps. Some nuts and bolts need to be discussed. Or rather, he needs to be inducted. He decides that a toga is needed and regrets it immediately. August in Rome is just too bloody hot. The streets and the Forum are quiet as he makes his way, and he has no trouble finding uncrowded shade for most of his journey. Crossing the Forum, Lucius reflected on how cluttered it was becoming, his mind running through a well-worn commentary. He is getting old, he thinks. He is getting tired of scaffolding and the noise of chisels on stone and the glint of all that marble, for Jupiter's sake! The path up the Palatine lifts him above the flurry and he strides on up to the top of the hill. Walking in Rome is the only sensible way to travel and Lucius walks up and down a hill or two every day. No matter how flabby the stomach gets, the legs are strong and defined. As he did for Augustus' dinner invitation, he goes into the square laid out in front of the temple of Apollo, and dawdles in the sun, to look up at the statue of Apollo which dominates the square – until one notices the temple, that is. And as Lucius stands there, the noise of the street recedes, and his bad mood drains away. The square is bordered on the two long sides by large pottery planters filled with flowers, and Lucius can see that they have been watered recently: the soil is dark, and the flowers have beads of water clinging to their leaves. Two slaves are busy tidying up rows of bright blossom. They work quickly, cutting at withered leaves and faded petals before the sun rises high enough to remove all shade. The Temple of Apollo rears up in front of him, its corners and facade still unworn and the paintwork immaculately fresh. The door stands slightly ajar, so Lucius climbs the stairs for a quick look into the interior. The god stands relaxed, leaning against a marble tree stump at the far end of a dim, cool room, looking down from his little plinth at an ancient slave who is dragging a brush around and stirring up puffs of dust. Standing slightly further back and a little more shadowy are the god's mother Leto and sister Diana. The trio are by three different sculptors but merge together into their family unit; there is no room for Jupiter. For the King of Gods and Men, Lucius supposes, this is just one of many little families he has sired and neglected. Lucius hears a constant muttering and realises that the old slave is talking to the god, every now and then glancing up at the statue and nodding in satisfaction. God and man seem perfectly happy with each other's company, and Lucius doesn't want to disturb, so he slips out once more. The door is inlaid with ivory panels depicting something or other mythological – people die in artistic confusion amid a welter of draperies. Lucius brushes his fingers across the smooth flank of an agitated ivory horse and turns to go back down the steps.

Crossing the square, and stopping in the shadow of yet another statue – Apollo again – he realises that he isn't quite sure where he is meant to go, and as he only knows two parts of the complex – temple and libraries – he heads for the libraries. The two rooms, one for Greek and one for Latin, flank a hall he has never entered, but he remembers that there is a door in the corner of the Latin library, so he turns into the little corridor that leads to the library and starts looking around for signs of a massive team of secretaries and slaves. After all, how can Augustus run everything, unless he has such a back-up team? Sure enough, in the corner of the hall is a desk, with a man sitting at it and writing, something which Lucius must have walked past before and never noticed. He will start there.

Augustus' set-up is efficient. The secretary summons a slave who leads him back to the square, dives into an unimpressive entrance, then turns into a corridor. Abruptly they peel off into a small room, then into a rather nicely-decorated large study, clearly designed for business. In the centre of this study is a podium, on the podium is a desk and at the desk sits the Princeps himself, Augustus. The empty expanse of floor between the door and the Princeps makes the isolated desk look a little ridiculous; surely Augustus had a more suitable room for meeting individuals? It seems to take an awfully long time for Lucius to be divested of his hot and heavy toga and then cross to the podium, and Augustus does not look up to see who has entered. The slave hops up to the desk, and whispers in Augustus' ear and the ruler of Rome nods, carries on writing for a little, then sits up.

When Augustus looks up, the cordial host from the night of the Palatine dinner is back in action, adorned with a generous smile, but there is work to be done and the Princeps does not waste much time on the niceties. Lucius is invited to sit at the other side of the desk, water and wine appear without asking, and the two men are clearly expected to serve themselves: there are a couple of slaves in the room but they have a desk at a respectable distance, far enough for privacy, near enough to be there if needed. They are not idle either, Lucius notices: even the one who brought the wine sits down and starts work on a heap of wax tablets piled up against the wall. He has no doubt that at this very minute Livia is personally supervising her household slaves in their various tasks. And may the gods help them.

Augustus has a list in front of him, Lucius notices, written on a small bit of papyrus which has been cut off a larger sheet. An economical man, Augustus has a small basket of similar scraps at his elbow, and the inkstand, by its smell, holds a cheap resinous ink. And with no time to waste, the Princeps starts briskly.

"Tomorrow, a notice will go up in the Forum announcing that I am stepping down as Consul. The election to replace me will take place six days after the Ides, which is an assembly day. I know people are away and there isn't time for many to come into Rome but that doesn't really matter. You can then take up your office in the last few days of the month, hold one meeting then in September it will be Piso's turn to chair meetings. Will that be all right? I don't anticipate any problem, though of course you will have to be seen out and about canvassing for the next few days, and your candidate's toga is going to be warm!"

His smile makes it clear that he sees trailing round yards of wool damp with sweat through the hottest days of the year as a triviality. Lucius realises that he must get a candidate's toga, specially whitened with chalk. He has never actually had to run for any office, so he has never had to undergo the formalities. Decius has another detail to sort out.

"Yes, that should be fine," says Lucius, trying to sound equally business-like. "At what point can I say that my candidacy is endorsed by you?"

"Oh, the very start," says Augustus. "I shall have tomorrow's notice end by announcing that I am supporting you. Maecenas doesn't think anyone else will go for it." He does not mention what Maecenas will do if anyone has the temerity to try.

"So, I would suggest that you go and get your entourage ready and make sure that you have a whitened toga and all that – are you happy about talking to people? Nobody will ask awkward questions you know. If anyone asks about me be completely honest and say I'm stepping down for the sake of my health. You don't know what my plans for the future are other than having a bit of a holiday."

"And if they bring up my past?" Lucius has to ask. "You know – Philippi and all that."

"Again, tell them the truth," says Augustus smoothly. "You were one of many at Philippi and all that is unimportant now we are all Romans, working together for the good of the state."

"Of course." Lucius feels vaguely saddened by this but doesn't try to analyse his feelings. Instead he asks about his responsibilities after the end of the year. "Will I be expected to take on a province?" He hopes that his tone conveys his hopes that he will be allowed to vanish once more immediately the year is over.

"I hope you won't be disappointed if I say no," the Princeps says, looking very closely at him. "We aren't in immediate need and if I am being completely honest I would prefer you to have had a lot more administrative experience. I hope I don't offend."

Through his relief, Lucius conveys that no offence is taken. He is even emboldened to make leaving noises. "Well, I must get going on my campaign speeches!"

This is a joke and the Princeps smiles and nods to show he understands.

"Oh, one more thing – my stepson, Tiberius. He has been my personal quaestor this year, a little young but after displaying wisdom beyond his years as military tribune, I decided he needed this chance. He has really been exceptional, and I hope you will continue to work with him. He isn't in Rome at the moment, he is on an extended inspection of the estate farms. We suspect that some unscrupulous landowners and their bailiffs have been using illegal workers – travellers captured from the roads, that sort of thing. The boy Tiberius is doggedly rooting out all that sort of corruption. He really is very good at getting to the bottom of things."

Lucius murmurs his delight at taking on a nineteen-year-old unknown as his personal assistant, and Augustus looks pleased.

He stands and holds out his hand. "By the way, our friend Horace should be somewhere around as you leave – try the libraries or the Temple. He is going to let me know what he thinks of the statues I've had put into the shrine. I'm rather pleased and so is Maecenas so I expect he will like them." Lucius shakes the Princeps' hand and the interview is over. He heads towards the door, but the Princeps calls after him, "Lucius Sestius!"

He turns.

The Princeps, still smiling, lifts one hand and says, "I'm looking forward to that jar of wine from your estate!"

And Lucius smiles back and leaves.

Lucius returns to the Temple of Apollo and once more enjoys that frisson along his skin as he slips from the square into the cool blurred interior. The slave has gone but, in his place, stands Horace gazing up at the statue of Leto. Lucius lets his eyes adjust to the gloom, and goes to stand beside Horace, wondering why it is the statue of the mother standing slightly back, who gets all the poet's attention.

"She's my favourite," says Horace, answering the unspoken question. His voice is relaxed, pitched low and quiet and still full of an energy which is not echoed in his appearance: Horace, happily middle-aged, looks as though he appreciates a good dinner. As Horace continues, Lucius enjoys the hint of a southern accent, adding warmth: "She is so proud of her children, so unaware of herself. She doesn't know that her love for them makes her quite the most beautiful of the three."

And Horace turns toward him and smiles. "Hello, Lucius Sestius," he says, his little dark eyes genuinely twinkling out from the nests formed by bushy eyebrows and generous crow's feet. "How is the Lady Albinia?"

"Well, thank you, and says that she is awaiting your acceptance of the invitation she sent you. She is dying to discuss

53

your Odes with you."

"Heaven help me," says Horace. "You know, it is fortunate for me and my fellows that she insists on such a low profile. We have enough competition amongst ourselves. And Rome is not yet ready to give a female poet a proper consideration, I think."

He sounds regretful. Lucius asks, "Would you be able to accept a female poet in Rome's literary circles?"

"I would adore to see such a poetess," cries Horace, and abruptly shushes himself as he glances apologetically at the god. "If the Muses were good enough for Apollo, I don't see why Rome persists in this ridiculous notion that women should not be creative in literature. I like poetry, I like women – a combination of the two would be very welcome, I can assure you!"

"Then I would like you to come to dinner soon with both of us," says Lucius.

Horace performs a pleased little bow, and the two of them gaze at the statues for a while in a completely comfortable silence. At last, Lucius stirs, knowing that he must get on, but before he can say goodbye, Horace has stopped him with a question.

"So how will you enjoy being Consul, do you think?" he asks, looking at Lucius far too shrewdly. Horace has the round slightly chubby face of the cheeky slave in a Menander comedy, and is just as cunning.

"Cicero says I shall find it – bearable," says Lucius, automatically adding, "That's Marcus Tullius Cicero the Younger," before remembering that he is talking to Horace. Horace laughs.

"Poor Marcus! Everyone always adds "the Younger". When will he escape being his father's son, I wonder?"

Lucius can hear the affection for Marcus Cicero in the words and approves. Marcus, despite being amicable and harmless, has few good friends and deserves more. He realises that he and Marcus and Horace should have some sort of get-together. It is a long time since they last held one of their "We didn't die at Philippi" celebrations. Maybe a dinner party is in order. Maybe he can persuade Albinia to come. She won't be his hostess of course, but he is sure they can dispense with that sort of formality. He promises himself the gathering as a treat for when he is Consul and fed up. He makes a note: he really must read Horace's Odes before he has the poet round for dinner.

"I have to go I suppose," he says and looks for one last time at the statues grouped in front of him. Horace goes back to his thoughts, and Lucius walks out of the cool and dark into the scorching day and cannot help wincing as the sun hits him. There will be precious little shade on his return journey. He goes home and prepares for government.

Chapter 7

The Sestius household is flustered. It is morning and Lucius is dressed in his whitened toga by Decius while nervously chewing on a bit of bread dipped in olive oil which he can barely swallow. As he walks about he is convinced that clouds of chalk dust rise around him, though he is assured by the entire household that this is not the case: he is almost convinced when Albinia arrives, takes one look at him and says, "Do you mind if I don't hug you? Only I don't want to get chalk on my dress." In the silence that follows this innocent remark, Lucius swears he can hear Decius' teeth grinding: Lucius knows that getting his best toga whitened took most of the afternoon the day before, and the slaves had served dinner with absurdly white hands and a muffled coughing.

In the atrium of the house on the Caelian Hill a small crowd of supporters is gathering, and the slaves hand out drinks and small honey cakes. Lucius will have a band of enthusiasts to support him as he walks down the hill and along to the Forum where Augustus' notice will already have been put up on the Speakers' Platform. The Forum will be busy as shops start to open and the word will get around quickly. With any luck a few curious people with nothing else to do will come and join the group and Lucius may well end up with a respectable procession behind him. Just as he is about to set out, he is pleased to see Marcus Cicero enter the house. With a huge grin, Marcus pushes his way through the crowd, and putting an arm round Lucius' shoulders, uses his other hand to clap him enthusiastically on the chest. The cloud of chalk dust this causes reduces Lucius to choking laughter and water is needed to calm down his coughing as well as dampen down the toga. He heads out of the door with Marcus at his side and is unsurprised to find Maecenas' litter waiting at the foot of the Caelian Hill. Maecenas emerges with less fuss than usual, though as they set off together for the Forum, a slave trots behind him holding a massive sunshade over his head. Lucius and Marcus exchange a brief grin and the three of them stride out cheerfully, Lucius waving and calling out "Good morning!" in the approved manner. Behind them is the little troop of Sestius freedmen, led by Decius, and then an assortment of friends, neighbours, favour-seekers, idlers, cadgers, small boys and a couple of stray dogs. The priest from the shrine of Minerva and the slave who assists him are there, as are the baker who supplies the Sestius household with their daily loaves, the builder who replastered some of their brickwork last summer, and the keeper of Lucius' favourite bar on the Caelian Hill. A few women join their menfolk, and the procession is neatly rounded off by Albinia's litter, carried by four matching and very good-looking German slaves (sold as a team at a knock-down price by one of Albinia's friends whose husband didn't care for them...). By the time they enter the Forum, Lucius feels quite cheerful. The day is sunny, he likes most of the people around him, and the walk has been entertaining. He enjoys observing the reactions of the people he passes: the busy just roll their eyes and carry on, the idle are visibly curious, while several stop and calculate whether or not it is worth their while to join in. He doesn't need to take anything seriously for the moment: he is about to become the first person in his family to become Consul. His father's spirit is approving, and Lucius wishes for one painful moment that old Publius Sestius were there to see this.

As his entourage enters the Forum, the buzz of people noticing pushes in a wave along the sides of the temples and law courts and breaks on the wall of the Speakers' Platform. Lucius knows that he is hardly the best-known Senator in Rome, but

Maecenas murmurs encouragement. "I've had men out here discussing you and your achievements in loud voices since dawn." Lucius thinks that they must have good imaginations. His achievements comprise of one stint as an unofficial quaestor minting money for Brutus and Cassius and failing to win the Battle of Philippi. But he need not worry. Maecenas' men have done a good job because lots of people appear to know him. He has his hand shaken a lot, and he gets questions shouted at him but nothing worse, no comments on his appearance or ancestry. A few people even wave wax tablets with petitions on them – how well-prepared were Maecenas' men exactly? He looks around, wondering how he is going to carry them all when Decius steps forward with a straw basket and rescues him. A basket? How did Decius know to bring a basket with him? Lucius opens his mouth to ask, but Decius winks and fades back.

On the Speakers' Platform is a respectable-looking figure in senatorial tunic and carefully-draped toga – this Lucius recognises as his fellow Consul (fellow Consul to be?), Calpurnius Piso. Piso waves at him with the large slow movements of an orator aiming at the back of the crowd, and gestures at him to come up and join him on the stage. There he takes Lucius' hand, lifts it into the air and makes a wide sweeping motion with the other arm, introducing him to the whole Forum. A cheer obediently arises and Lucius smiles and waves. Piso, still smiling, mutters, "And now thank all the gods we can go somewhere and take these ridiculous togas off. My house is just up the Argiletum if you'd care to join me? My wine-steward has got a nice Falernian chilling in the cellar, ready whenever we get there."

Lucius takes this as a good sign. Clearly, he and his fellow Consul are going to be able to work together. They stroll down the steps of the platform, and make a leisurely way through the crowd, shaking more hands, smiling, pretending to listen to people. As they reach the edge of the Forum, Lucius' entourage forms a human barrier between him and the rest of the throng, and he and Piso stroll off up the Argiletum towards the Fontinalis Gate. Piso's bodyguard of twelve lictors leads the way, holding the symbolic bundles of rods and axes, the fasces. As Lucius glances back he sees that Marcus and Maecenas are sending away the supporters – or rather they are standing and watching as Decius moves among crowd, talking and gesturing. Already the Forum is melting away into its everyday tasks of buying, selling and lounging.

As soon as they are out of hearing, Piso glances at Lucius with a grin and says, "Hail, fellow Consul."

"Are you an old Republican too then?" asks Lucius, irony making it clear that he knows Piso's past.

"It is interesting, isn't it?" Piso is smiling broadly still. "Do you know how I got this job?"

"Someone died, didn't they?" Lucius finds Piso's openness refreshing and wishes they had come across one another before.

"Yes, Murena popped his sandals in December last year, and Augustus needed someone in a hurry. He came round in person mind you and begged me to take on the consulship for the sake of the Republic. How ironic is that?"

"And did that argument sway you?" asks Lucius.

"No," says Piso shortly. "But I have two sons, neither of whom need to be burdened with my political past. So, I said yes. And I haven't regretted it. I have no principles left and have no intention of making any more stands for what I believe. I've quite enjoyed it, though the start was bit hairy. I hadn't taken any part in politics since I was pardoned after Philippi."

"Me neither," says Lucius.

Piso grins. "Well, try not to be a complete disaster," he says, striding up to a door and banging on it once. It opens immediately, and Lucius is struck by this efficiency. The two men go in and a housekeeper sweeps forward with a bevy of maids to help them with their togas. She bears off both garments with a promise to give them a brush and an airing. Lucius watches carefully and sees that the maid bearing his toga carries it at arm's length and keeps it well away from Piso's. Chalk, he hopes, rather than sweat. Piso stretches and yawns.

"Thank all the gods for that!" he says, and his voice seems lighter too, unburdened by being in public, being a Consul, being diplomatic. "Come on – there will be seats in the shade in the courtyard."

The lictors have disappeared and Piso leads him through the dark marble corridors to the little colonnaded garden at the back of the house, almost identical to Lucius' own garden on the Caelian. As promised, a group of wooden chairs and a small table have been put out in the shadow cast by the house's own walls. The sun is not yet too high. A jug of wine nestling in a bowl of cold water is being placed on the table by an elderly man in a good quality green tunic. He smiles and gestures to the chairs, and Lucius guesses that he is a freedman rather than a slave. He has the air. Piso sinks onto a chair and sighs.

"Thank you, Philo – Lucius Sestius, meet my indispensable right-hand man, Philo."

Philo smiles and nods at Lucius and asks if they would like him to serve the wine.

"No, you go and get on. We can serve ourselves," says Piso. The courtyard falls silent as Philo patters off and his steps fade away. Piso busies himself pouring and mixing and he and Lucius toast each other. There is barely a rustling of leaves as they take the first sip and savour it. It is a perfect moment, and Lucius holds it for as long as he can, knowing that once he starts to think or listen or speak, the world will return, and he will have to go on. He relaxes back into his chair and lets his gaze rest on the courtyard's garden, breathing in the warm, mint-scented air. When Piso speaks though, the moment fades gracefully and Lucius thanks it as it goes.

"Now, let's see, what do you need to know? You will find the job quite straightforward, just a load of admin and overseeing some weird ceremonies. We meet with Augustus and Agrippa and Maecenas three times a month on the Kalends, Nones and Ides. Fairly easy meetings, and sometimes we invite others if they have an expertise we need. In addition, Augustus' nephew Marcellus often attends, to get some experience according to the Princeps. Augustus has a squad of secretaries who do the day-to-day organisation, make sure that notices are sent out, that sort of thing. Our views on getting things done are welcome, our observations on how matters will be received by the general public are considered and our political heresies are expected to be conspicuously absent. My past life as a supporter of Brutus and Cassius is never mentioned, and every time someone says "the God Julius Caesar" I bite my tongue. I shall send you your lictors and the fasces – they have been at my house while we waited to see what would happen during Augustus' illness – to your house after the election. Then we shall meet with Augustus, decide an agenda for your introduction to the office and announce your inaugural meeting. There won't be any need for more than one Senate meeting while you are holding the fasces, and I shall make sure that I am sitting next to you in the meeting just in case. In September I take the fasces, chair the meetings and you are welcome to attend as many of them as you wish. Or none. After December we retire into obscurity once more and become a not-very-interesting footnote for the historians."

"Do you really find it that easy?" asks Lucius.

"Now I do," replies Piso. "I agonised over taking the job for two days and then my wife sat me down and pointed out the foolishness of refusal. She spoke a great deal of sense and then she and I went straight to Augustus and told him I would take the post. Livia was there and we made up a perfect quartet. Ever since then I've done as Popilia advised and looked on this as just a job. And I'm doing it for my sons and for Rome, not for Augustus. There is still enough room for patriotism of the old-fashioned kind. So, I just think of that. It works."

He looks at Lucius.

"Are you married?"

"Caecilia died in the autumn illness a few years ago," replies Lucius, the answer trotting out of his mouth with ease of repetition.

"I'm sorry to hear that," says Piso courteously. "You must miss her a great deal."

Lucius cannot find an answer to that. Eventually he says, "I almost wish I did. She was a very nice woman and we worked well together."

"You have children?" asks Piso.

"A boy and a girl. They are in the country for the summer. Actually, they live there most of the time."

"My boys and my wife are everything to me," says Piso, suddenly fierce. "Doing this has helped them. My older lad is already in his twenties, doing his military duty. He wants to climb high. The younger, not so much, likes his studies. But if I get to the end of this year without incident, I've guaranteed their future. Your children will find the same thing. Your daughter will make a better marriage, your son will have more options opening up for him. It will be worth it."

"Oh, I know," says Lucius. "And I have already enjoyed my first dinner at the Palatine house."

Piso laughs. "I hope you brought your own wine. Gods know where Augustus finds that terrible stuff he serves. Did you meet the family? Livia, Julia, etcetera?"

"Everyone bar Agrippa," says Lucius. "I don't know where he was."

"Agrippa is preparing to go and tour the eastern Empire," says Piso. "He will be setting off shortly. Augustus wants to show that Rome takes an interest, and he has not been too impressed with the quality of the governors sent out there recently. So, Agrippa will shake things up. He will be based on the island of Lesbos, and deal with matters arising as he sees fit. I quote directly from the minutes of the meeting I attended last week. So it must be true."

Lucius detected a note of cynicism. "And?" he asks innocently.

"And rumour has it that Agrippa has been a little annoyed at Augustus' obvious intentions regarding Marcellus. When Augustus thinks he is dying, Agrippa gets given the seal-ring so that he can take over. Otherwise, young Marcellus gets all the attention and he is barely what? Nineteen, twenty? So Agrippa suggests in a fit of pique that he should get out of Marcellus' way and do a three-year stint of touring provinces etcetera, and instead of saying "No, no, no, how can I manage without you?", Augustus exclaims that it is a great idea, will give Marcellus a chance to shine and how very noble of Agrippa to offer. Agrippa sat in silence practically all through the rest of the meeting, and if he wasn't exactly scowling, it was close."

"So he has basically condemned himself to a three-year exile?" says Lucius intrigued. "Gods above, I'd love three years on Lesbos at government expense."

"Really?" Piso's look is both sharp and amused. "When did you last leave the country?"

"To go with Brutus," admits Lucius with a grin. "I travelled the East with him and Cassius, then came to Greece, then fled to Sicily with Marcus – Marcus Cicero. Then everyone got pardoned and I've barely moved from Rome or Cosa since. I'm sure Marcus would have given me a post on his staff in Syria, but I didn't go near him while he was Consul. It was all too much still."

"Yes," murmurs Piso, his eyes fixed on a fading hibiscus flower in the centre of the courtyard. The garden is now visibly shrivelling as the sun moves nearer its zenith, but Piso and Lucius are still in shade. Lucius has noticed that Piso is good at looking calm and unconcerned. In the shade his eyes are difficult to read, except when he smiles. Piso smiles with full enjoyment and appreciation and that cannot be covered up. As Piso notices Lucius' scrutiny, the smile comes out once more and Lucius mirrors him without even thinking.

Piso says kindly, "Lucius Sestius, it will take time, but I think that you and I will become friends and learn to trust one another. And we shall make a success of this consulship. What is left of it anyway. Do you have any ideas for measures you would like to sponsor? I'm sure that with a bit of planning, we could get most things through very quickly. The tribunes are a tame lot, and quite capable of calling a swift assembly to push a law though."

"Land distribution?" asks Lucius wryly. Redistribution of land has been a contentious issue for over a hundred years. Nobody is going to touch that with an exceptionally long pole.

Piso groans and says, "I was wondering about something to reward the military. Something small but telling. Or building regulation. That always needs an eye keeping on it, despite Agrippa's admittedly excellent work in certain spheres. The problem of the urban poor is always with us." Piso quirks an eyebrow at him. "How about doing a boring little bit of good?"

"What an idea," muses Lucius. "Doing good. You are right of course. I don't have the money or inclination to build another theatre but between us we should be able to find something… and pass a Lex Calpurnia Sestia!"

"In honour of the recovery of our beloved Princeps of course." Piso can't help a little smirk as he says this.

"Naturally." And Lucius and Piso gently clink cups and settle back down to watching the sun climb over the rooftop and spread its heat over more and more of the little courtyard. When it reaches their table, they smile and say that it is time to be getting on.

"I can meet you in the Forum early tomorrow for some gentle canvassing," says Piso. "Better make a bit of an effort."

And Lucius leaves that moment of calm and steps out into the street to find Decius waiting. As they cross the Forum, a small group of supporters peel themselves away from various shaded locations and fall in behind him for the slog up to the house on the Caelian. Lucius takes pity though and dismisses everyone once they are away from the Forum. After all, he realises, he has left his candidate's toga at Piso's, so nobody will take any notice of him. Decius makes a note to get one of the slaves to run down later to collect it.

Chapter 8

Becoming Consul is straightforward. Six days after the Ides, just as Augustus and Maecenas said, the election is held. After a string of extremely boring mornings shaking hands in the Forum, Lucius feels relieved that it will soon be done and he can get rid of the infernal chalk-whitened toga, which leads to him having a constantly dry mouth and tickling nose. Decius has got used to standing near him with a drink and a handkerchief ready. Down on the Campus Martius, the new marble voting pens built by Agrippa a few years previously are opened and made ready to deal with the comparatively small number of voters who turn up. Lucius stands on the Candidates' Platform, accompanied by various grandees who make a show of coming to stand and wave at the crowd with him. Marcus is there throughout the hours of counting, and Piso, while Maecenas wanders around and makes frequent trips back to report that all is going well. The highlight of the day is when a small troop of lictors arrives, leading the Princeps himself to show his support. Augustus' appearance raises genuine cheers, and nobody seems to mind that he goes to vote straight away, leading his voting-group with him. Lucius has to admire the way Augustus handles being in public: the Princeps seems to give time to everyone while steadily making progress back towards the centre of the city. Lucius studies the technique carefully, and notices that two men are constantly at the Princeps' shoulder – one to whisper names and information as people come up to greet him, one to make polite excuses when the Princeps needs to move on. These two secretaries keep the Princeps moving while all he has to do is smile and chat and look apologetic. Once Augustus has vanished, a business-like air comes over the voting-ground and things speed up. A small army of slaves and freedmen and officials Lucius has never really noticed before divides up the crowd, funnelling groups forward to the bridges which every man has to cross before casting his vote, and neatly making sure that nobody can return to the pens where those who have not yet voted are held, like sheep at a market. Troops of men line up obediently, march across the narrow walkways and disappear, and there is a steady thump of feet over the wooden bridges. The voting pens have canvas awnings for shade, and enterprising salesmen have set out temporary stalls to sell food and drink, but there is not enough entertainment to tempt even this small crowd to hang around, and when the result is announced it is more with relief than genuine emotion that everyone cheers. Another step along the road, thinks Lucius as he shakes hands all round. The toga comes off immediately. His sweat-soaked tunic begins to steam gently as he walks slowly across the Campus Martius, thinking of nothing more than a bath, and his dinner. His entourage fades away tactfully, Decius takes his toga and walks on ahead, and Lucius makes a small detour to the baths at the foot of the Caelian Hill. It is only when he is sitting on his own at last in the hot room that he suddenly starts to cry and for a few minutes just cannot stop. He doesn't make any noise but now that everything that has been going on about him has subsided, all the surplus emotions flow out. He thinks of Philippi, a horrible battle of mud and rain that stretched over weeks and ended in the suicides of Brutus and Cassius. He remembers the months of flight and exile and living with no clear future. And here he is, sitting in a steamy room in complete solitude, safe and old and Consul of Rome. He shudders to a stop, and after a few minutes goes for a massage. He then takes a long time to walk home, misses dinner and sleeps until dawn.

Over the next few days, he reads Senate minutes, reports

from overseas and Treasury accounts. It is almost completely uninteresting. Augustus keeps a tight hold of any path to power and nobody shows any signs of challenging that. He meets the chief of his group of lictors and is told how his state bodyguards expect him to behave. He holds several meetings with his fellow Consul and Piso is extremely helpful in answering questions and giving guidance. Lucius finds that working with Piso is, as expected, a benefit, as is the flattering attention he receives everywhere. Several people invite him to dinner and others not yet in Rome write charming letters. He pleads the pressure of work to get out of any invitation not from Piso, and Augustus leaves him alone to get on top of everything.

Then comes the day when he will attend and preside over his first Senate meeting of the year. Lucius puts on his best toga first thing in the morning and is welcomed into his own atrium by his neighbours and clients, who are all impressed by the gang of lictors waiting for him outside. These men will go everywhere with him when he is on official business. They carry the fasces, bundles of rods and axes, which symbolise his authority, though Lucius feels that beating or beheading anyone is unlikely to happen on his watch.

Everyone troops up to the Temple of Jupiter Best and Greatest, lictors marching smartly in front and clearing the street in a needlessly officious manner, and his band of supporters trudging behind him with huge grins on their faces at the thought that their patron, after years of being frankly unimpressive, has made it. A few senators, including Marcus Cicero and Calpurnius Piso, have graced the temple with their presence, and two aged worthies step forward, one acting as priest, another looking out for auspicious flights of birds. A weary-looking ox trudges up to the altar, stands patiently to get stunned and sighs out its last breath with a hot gush of blood as its throat is cut in Lucius' honour.

After this the heat begins to make itself felt and everyone strolls down the hill. The Senatorial contingent makes its way into the dark of the Senate House, where sweaty backsides enjoy the bliss of the cool marble. Lucius gets to sit on a spindly Consul's chair, and the clerk hands him a small tablet with an incredibly brief agenda. Prayers are said, and the bird-watching senator stands to describe the extremely pleasing sighting of several birds of prey over the Capitol Hill as the sacrifice was taking place. He offers Lucius his congratulations and Lucius smiles wondering if anybody there does not know that the birds had been set loose at the foot of the hill by a temple slave. Several senators of high rank rise to welcome Lucius as Consul, and between them cover his service to the state ("diligent quaestorship") his prowess in battle ("veteran of many campaigns") and reputation ("unostentatious loyalty and diligence"). Lucius is impressed. He thanks the Fathers for their kind words, and, reading from the tablet passed to him, he announces that in a few days' time, on the Kalends of September, the senate will be recalled to discuss the plans for honouring Augustus which are summarised on the wax tablets each senator will find waiting for him at home. Senators still absent for the summer can of course make their way back to the city if they wish. Even as he speaks, Lucius feels as though he is actually one of the audience listening to him, he is so impressed by this smooth organisation. He does not indulge in wondering what is waiting for him at home, for Augustus has dropped some hints, and anyway, Decius will have already read it and drafted some suitable views. Not that Lucius needs views. Piso will preside over the minimal debate required to approve the measures – whatever they are – and Lucius will not be required again until October, though he might make a point of popping in to the meetings of the Senate just because he feels that he ought to now he is Consul. He expects that he will be told if he misses too many. He looks around the Senate House to check in case someone wants to keep them all in here while the morning heats up, but nobody is keen to introduce any business, and there is no news from abroad. Lucius ends the meeting with an invocation to Jupiter, and everyone prepares to dash across the now-sweltering Forum to find shade and get out of their togas. His first day as Consul has gone boringly well, as things tend to under Augustus of course. You have to admire the way that the Princeps does his groundwork.

Outside the Senate House, one of his slaves meets him with a flask of water and a hat, both of which Lucius takes gratefully. The lictors fall in and they all march home. The summer is nearly over and by the time the Senate meets again it will be a much more crowded gathering, and Calpurnius Piso will be in charge.

He finds Decius waiting in the study when he arrives home. Decius has cleared the two desks and on each of them there is a stack of wax tablets. Augustus' messengers have done their rounds and like every other Senator, Lucius has his orders. On those tablets, he supposes, is the price of his consulship. A slave comes in with jugs and cups and as Lucius sits down heavily, gazing at the wax tablets, pours an almost neat cup of wine and places it in front of his master. With a pang, Lucius notices that the red leather carrier containing Horace's precious Odes has been moved to the bookshelf, and he hasn't read a single poem yet.

"Would you like a run-through?" asks Decius calmly, as he mixes himself a cup of wine and water, much weaker than Lucius'.

Lucius sighs. "Yes. And thank you for already having read all this and decided what we are to do." Decius just smiles. He settles himself down behind his own desk, facing Lucius and picks up the top tablet from his pile.

"Augustus wants to shore up his own position in view of him not being Consul any more," he begins, and the afternoon is spent in carefully analysing the terms of Augustus' return to "ordinary" life.

It is all to do with power and protection. Augustus already has the most important power, the power of a name and a background. Heir to a deified Julius Caesar, he is now the one and only Augustus. Rumour has it that the Princeps originally wanted to change his name to Romulus and as always the persuasive hand of Maecenas had gently steered him away ("Romulus was a barbarian who murdered his own brother to take the rule! I don't think so") towards a less royal and more respectable title. ("Hints of reverence without actually saying so – very suitable") And now the power is developing once more. You have to admire Augustus; he doesn't stand still or allow things to stagnate. He also has the advantage of twenty years of success in war, titles and honours laden upon him, rows of consulships. Lucius could remember his first sight of Augustus as a short and unprepossessing eighteen-year-old called Octavius, returning to Rome as the unlikely heir of the assassinated Julius Caesar. Like many, Lucius had taken no notice of the shrimp, and why should he? He was completely taken up with preparations to leave Italy, following his new commander Cassius. But in Octavius a new Julius Caesar had been created, and his links to the old one had been constantly and remorselessly underlined at every opportunity. Strange to think that at the time they had all thought Mark Antony was going to be the problem.

Decius finishes reading and Lucius says nothing. He starts to read through the documents himself, homing in on the bits highlighted by Decius. Maecenas is clever: the terms of the new arrangement are startlingly clear in their purpose and their individual proposals are blurred at the edges, just enough to give

Augustus leeway. Blurred edges are also smooth, like Maecenas himself of course, and once more Lucius has to admire the organisation behind Augustus. He wonders if Livia has a role in this and decides he would not be surprised.

Augustus is replacing the power he would have as Consul. He will still be able to interfere in matters to do with the provinces, he will directly manage the most important provinces himself and he will be able to initiate legislation. Combine this with the immense authority he has already just by being himself, and nothing will happen that he does not approve first. Lucius wonders if anyone in the Senate will dare to protest. Four months, he tells himself. I shall only be Consul for four months.

Chapter 9

That night Piso and his wife Popilia come to dinner and Lucius has managed to persuade Albinia to come and meet them. He thinks this will do her good and he is still hoping that she will rise to the challenge of helping him to host his consular dinner parties. He has a feeling that he will be expected to entertain over the next few months, and he can hardly refuse if Augustus wants to come to dinner. In fact, he supposes, it is his turn to ask the Princeps. And if he asks the Princeps – and Livia, gods above! – he should ask Maecenas and the delectable if worrying Terentia. At least if Albinia gets on with his fellow Consul, then that will be one agreeable couple for her to talk with. And to make the traditional ninth guest he could ask Horace, and then he could seat Horace and Albinia next to each other and they could talk about poetry. Lucius smiles, pleased at his unexpected skill at domestic planning. But one step at a time, and to his pleasure and relief, Albinia clearly likes Piso and Popilia.

Popilia is a comfortable and sweet woman, smiling from the moment she enters the atrium, and effortlessly pleasant. Her social skills seem aimed at making everyone around her relax, and she is formidably intelligent and well-read. She and Albinia are immediately immersed in a conversation about the new library being built and what should be stocked in such a library, and what texts are essential for any Roman's personal collection. They agree that Virgil has progressed marvellously since writing his Eclogues, and lament the death of Catullus, who has been dead at least twenty if not thirty years, thinks Lucius. Popilia is keen on the recently deceased Cornelius Gallus and Albinia thinks Gallus' poetry has been improved

73

considerably by the poet's death. They barely notice the arrival of the eggs which mark the beginning of dinner and are well into the main course – Melissa's famous seafood stew surrounded by a constellation of dishes of vegetables – before either of them addresses their menfolk. Lucius and Piso are thankful for this piece of luck and chat comfortably about the oddities of Senate tradition, and indeed the oddities of some Senators. It is not long before they are discussing that favourite topic of dinner parties – why has Maecenas never been a Senator?

"He isn't really in the heart of things any more, you know," observes Piso.

"Really?" Lucius is puzzled. He had assumed that Maecenas was masterminding Augustus' return to public life after the crisis of his near-death. He had distinctly received the impression that he, Lucius, was Maecenas' own choice for the consulship going spare, and should be suitably grateful.

"Well, I think it is Terentia," says Piso. Lucius is more confused and must look it because Piso suddenly laughs and says, "You don't know! Of course!"

"Know what?" asks Lucius and remembering those odd remarks by Marcus Cicero, it all suddenly becomes clear. "Oh," he says. "She and Augustus?"

"For about a year off and on I'd say." Piso is enjoying this little piece of gossip. "Popilia! What is the verdict of the ladies of Rome on the Augustus/Terentia affair? When did it start?"

Popilia looks startled and takes a moment to descend from the lofty regions of philosophy and poetry. "Terentia? Oh years, I would think." Lucius is a tiny bit amused at the surprise on Piso's face. "Yes, I think it started before he went off to Spain. And as soon as he got back, they picked up where they left off. Quite a long time for Augustus, I don't know about her. I wouldn't give it much longer though. I've heard that Terentia gives every sign of being on the lookout for pastures new."

Lucius suddenly feels completely out of his depth. This is a new world to him, and he realises ruefully that he really has lived very quietly for many years. A memory returns and he exclaims in horror.

"Oh gods! That dinner I went to on the Palatine... She was..." He can't finish and everyone laughs.

"Don't worry," says Popilia kindly. "I'm sure you are quite capable of resisting Terentia. Poor Terentia. She doesn't have much else in her life, and considering her family and her marriage, she had every reason to think that her life was going to be more – fulfilled maybe? – by now. But I don't think Maecenas has treated her very well. Oh, I'm sure he is perfectly pleasant, charming even, but he isn't really husband material, is he?"

Albinia arches one eyebrow and says, "Many women would be grateful for a husband who leaves them alone."

Popilia shakes her head. "That is just something to say when a man is – well, you know... But this is something altogether different. A woman like Terentia with few of her own resources, really needs a family and a devoted husband to thrive. Instead she got Maecenas who goes through life pretending she isn't there. No wonder she fell for Augustus, she was bored and frustrated, and here was the most powerful man in Rome saying nice things to her."

Piso is a little more cynical. "If you ask me her brother had a lot to do with it as well. He isn't above pushing his sister at Augustus and hoping that he benefits by the association. He thinks that the state owes him because he lost out when his cousin, the Murena who was to be Consul this year, fell ill and died. I replaced the dead Murena, and I found out more than I wanted to about that family. Terentia really has been very unlucky in her relatives."

"What did you find out?" asks Albinia, bright-eyed with interest.

"Well, the Murena I replaced was a grumbler," says Piso. "Very highly born, but ineffective and always moaning about unlucky he was. Stupid to let everyone know, but he didn't get anywhere."

"He wasn't so unlucky that he didn't make it to Consul," Lucius points out. Piso looks at him, and they both grin.

"He was duly elected by an assembly of the people of Rome," says Albinia, severely. "And having the noble name Licinius Murena did no harm at all."

"It was his turn," says Piso.

"Here's to everyone having a turn!" cries Lucius raising his cup and they toast him and laugh.

"And the rest of the family?" asks Lucius. "Anyone to worry about?"

"Terentia's brother is a useless, pleasant character," says Piso and Albinia can't help letting out a yelp of laughter at this brutal evaluation. "But he is ambitious, and you watch, if his sister falls from the Princeps' favour, young Aulus Terentius won't be happy. He will become like his unfortunate cousin, one of the permanently dissatisfied."

Lucius shrugs. "The generation below us are going to have to put up with being dissatisfied."

Piso looks at him. "And one of the things your friend Maecenas has got particularly good at is spotting those people. So, while he is not as important as he used to be, he could rise again if he spots another plot in the offing."

Lucius feels very unhappy at the thought that Maecenas is his friend, but Piso was being ironic, and there is no need to challenge this.

"Next time we do this," says Albinia, "would you invite Horace?"

Lucius agrees happily. He can see Horace fitting into this circle very neatly. Piso and Popilia have over the course of an evening become family friends, and this is an unexpected benefit of the consulship. Lucius Sestius the dozing back-bencher who attended Senate meetings once a month if he happened to be in Rome, would never have even spoken to Consul Calpurnius Piso. He looks at Albinia and sees her pleasure in this genial company and for the first time feels a real enjoyment in his sudden promotion. Relaxed dinners with interesting people and coaxing Albinia into public just a little more... And he must get Marcus Cicero around as well...

As the evening ends, Popilia and Albinia have already decided the best date for the next dinner, at Albinia's – Albinia's! Lucius cannot remember when she last entertained – and with Horace as guest of honour. It will be on the Kalends of September, after the first senate meeting of September. Lucius and Piso exchange glances, knowing that they will need something to look forward to after that particular meeting. Hands are shaken, thanks exchanged and Piso and Popilia are off down the street in a small but well-lit cavalcade, surrounded by lictors. Nobody will bother them as they make their way home in the dark. And, thinks Lucius, we avoided talking about the settlement we have to get through the Senate for Augustus. Quite right too. Tomorrow is soon enough for that.

Chapter 10

Augustus' proposals regarding his position in government generate much quiet debate amongst senatorial ranks, and over the next few days Lucius and Piso meet every day to decide their approach. Decius is allowed to be present to keep notes and at each meeting a few senators come round and add their ideas. Nobody of course talks openly about opposing the measures but there is an undercurrent of anxiety. What Augustus is proposing is not a dictatorship, not a monarchy, but it still gives one man a lot of power, some of which is not clearly defined. In the end, everyone knows that they will agree: Lucius and Piso soothe and encourage, and gradually the anxiety is stilled. Some are resigned to this settlement: most are persuaded that they don't care that much.

On the Kalends of September, Piso opens the Senatorial meeting with a short and clear speech.

"Fathers of the Senate, Roman values have always made certain things clear: we must honour the gods of our forefathers; we must preserve our great city and its empire; we must make sure that we bequeath a stable and prosperous government to our sons. The measures put before us today will ensure all this. Augustus has saved Rome and works tirelessly on its behalf still, and we must ensure that this service is both rewarded and enabled. Let us join with Augustus in putting Rome first and ourselves second. I put before you the new Julian Law and urge that you recommend it to the people of Rome."

This speech took Lucius and Piso an hour to put together and every word has been weighed, found to be mostly true and welded into its place. It gets applause from the Senate and the Julian Law is approved to be taken before the people. The whole thing takes five minutes, then the Senate move on to listen to a particularly boring letter from the governor of Egypt predicting a good harvest. Egypt always has a good harvest. Ironically, Egypt is under the direct control of the Princeps, so the prefect is writing to the Senate out of courtesy, and it cannot escape anyone that Augustus has in his new settlement taken similar control of a much larger section of the Empire.

An elderly Senator gets up to point out that the harvest in Italy is not looking quite so good, and wonders if there will be a lot of rain this month. Another Senator says that the signs from the gods so far indicate nothing special about the weather. The Consuls are asked to keep a careful eye on the situation. Piso, in a voice which only just restrains itself, promises that the Consuls will watch the weather. The Senate make getting-ready-to-leave shuffling sounds and Piso reads out the prayer to Jupiter. The meeting is over. Augustus is openly confirmed as the most powerful man in Rome, and nobody can quite tell the limits of his power. Maecenas will be pleased.

Lucius and Piso wait until everyone has filed out, looking carefully for any signs of dissent, but see boredom and a few disgruntled faces, nothing more.

"Should we go and report to Augustus or will that be too obvious?" asks Lucius. Piso grins.

"No need," he says. "If you come back to mine for a drink, there will be someone waiting for us. If there isn't, you can have your pick of my bronze collection."

"I didn't know you collected bronzes," says Lucius.

"I don't," says Piso. "But it doesn't matter because this is a bet I won't lose. I just wonder who they will send. Maecenas probably."

He is wrong about that at least. They send a young man, Tiberius Drusus, elder son of Livia, and he is also looking for a job.

After all these years in a political wilderness, Lucius finds it quite amusing that he is meeting and liking so many important people. And Tiberius is important. He is still a young man, about nineteen, but he has served in Augustus' army in Spain already and is now a quaestor. In fact, as he swiftly makes clear, he is Lucius' quaestor.

"My stepfather Augustus asked that I serve this year as quaestor to him as Consul," explains Tiberius Drusus earnestly, "and with your permission, sir, I'd like to carry on as your quaestor."

"You are fortunate," says Piso to Lucius. "I've forgotten the name of my consular quaestor."

"Not everyone finds service to the state to their taste," says Tiberius with a dryness well ahead of his years. However, he is Livia's son. That would dry out anyone.

"Well, come into the study with us and have a drink," invites Piso. "And we can bring you up to date on the Senate meeting, because I don't believe you were there?"

"No. I didn't want my relationship to Augustus to be recalled and have everyone think I was representing him in any way," says Tiberius, very properly. "Also, I only came back home yesterday, and I slept in a bit," he adds. Lucius grins and slaps Tiberius on the back. This is uncharacteristic, but he is warming to Tiberius.

"You get all the sleep you can while you can," he says. "And I shall try to keep you in Rome, so you don't miss out on the joys of city life any longer. You can tell me all about your roving mission later because I think you need to hear about the Senate meeting first. We would be obliged if you conveyed it all to your stepfather as well."

"Oh yes," says Tiberius. "I expect you realise that he asked me to ask for your thoughts while I was here."

Lucius is glad to see that his new quaestor understands his role perfectly.

That night Albinia holds her dinner party for the Consul Piso and his wife Popilia, the Consul (and her brother) Lucius Sestius, the poet Horace and family friend Marcus Tullius Cicero the Younger. The numbers are all wrong and there are only two women and for one moment Albinia wonders if she is being too eccentric. Her brother who has arrived earlier and brought Marcus Cicero to calm her nerves and drink her wine reassures her.

"You could set a new trend for inviting people you like," he points out.

"I've invited four men who all fought on the wrong side at Philippi," Albinia muses. "That isn't going to go unnoticed."

Lucius thinks about that but cannot see any reason to be too concerned.

"We have all ingratiated ourselves after all, and are now part of the Establishment," he says reasonably.

"Especially me and Horace," says Marcus unexpectedly.

Albinia sighs. "You are right. I'm just worrying because I don't entertain really, I go to other people's parties and even then, it is just a few people."

Lucius looks at her, but she seems to be commenting on a fact not lamenting her loneliness.

"Mentor will make sure everything runs perfectly and when you look at the thing it really is just a meal with friends. Friends who aren't going to comment on the food you serve or gossip about your clothes or whatever else it is you are bothered about."

Albinia seems genuinely amused. "It is a long time since I worried about what people thought about my clothes! Really, Lucius!"

Marcus catches up on the conversation and assures her that she looks very nice. Albinia pats his hand and continues, "No, this is just worrying about the unknown. When I think about it

81

logically, this is going to be a perfectly nice evening. And it is quite something getting Horace at all as he is rather in demand now that everyone has read his Odes. Everyone except you, Lucius, of course."

"Everyone except me," agrees Lucius, too comfortable to worry about that yet again. "I still don't really get why he has written one to me, and as to what it means... Well, it is nice that someone has actually written a poem to me, so I shan't bother too much about meaning and whatnot."

"Meaning and whatnot..." murmurs Albinia. "You are such a barbarian, Lucius."

"He hasn't dedicated anything to me," says Marcus, sounding a little grumpy. "And I met him in Athens, way before you did, Lucius."

And the first guests, Piso and Popilia, can be heard, being ushered into the atrium, having their cloaks taken, and sorting out where their lictors can sit and wait. Lictors are rather cumbersome, Lucius has discovered. Wherever he goes now, there must be accommodation of sorts for an extra twelve men. His own lictors have been sent off to the inn down the road and will take turns to guard the front door of Albinia's house. No doubt Piso's will do something similar. The innkeeper will be pleased: lictors are thirsty beings.

The noise dies down, and the guests are ushered in by Mentor: Piso is wearing a plain tunic and says how good it is to feel so welcome and comfortable. This is just the right thing to say and Albinia beams. Popilia retorts that she has enjoyed the opportunity to dress up a bit what with Piso never going anywhere nowadays, and Albinia nudges Lucius into paying a hurried compliment which fools nobody and makes Marcus grin into his wine-cup. Popilia however just laughs and thanks Lucius and asks when Horace is going to arrive.

"The Odes are so clever and graceful, I want to thank him for lightening the atmosphere," she says approvingly.

"He will be pleased to hear that," says Albinia. "The poor man has not had the rapturous reception he had hoped."

Popilia looks surprised. "I don't see how anyone could read them and not find something to enjoy," she says thoughtfully. "Do people actively dislike them or do you think they aren't moved by them?"

"I think," says Albinia, "that people find them too Greek and clever. Of course, anyone who thinks that is wrong."

"Do his Republican roots count against him?" wonders Popilia and answers herself, "No, of course not, he and Maecenas are friends, and everyone knows that. He is a poet of the Palatine."

Albinia pulls a face at that. "Yes, but he manages to be his own poet too."

And with that, Horace enters, and everyone is slightly embarrassed because he might just have heard Popilia's assessment of him as a poet of the Palatine. He has but manages to make a joke of it with his first words:

"Hail, fellow Palatinians!" he cries and after just a moment, Piso snorts with laughter. The Palatine drinking club is born.

"And the only qualification you need is that you or a family member chose the wrong side at the Battle of Philippi," Marcus Cicero says dryly. Horace raises his first cup of wine in a toast and everyone joins in, as Albinia signals Mentor. She wants Lucius and Marcus to get some food inside them before they drink much more. And to keep her guests distracted she says,

"Horace, I know we should not even ask until dinner is over but this is the right moment for you to give us a recital of one of your Odes – you know the one I think?"

Horace knows the one she means: it is perfect for this moment. He does not stand or clear his throat or make a fuss: lying on the couch next to Albinia, as a slave removes his sandals and puts on his slippers, Horace recites:

Philippi

Friend, once we were taken to the edge
by Brutus, noblest Roman of them all.
Now someone – who? – has spirited you
back to Rome.

In dangerous times, we – fine Romans! –
put off the reckoning and
were garlanded with the East, drunk
on date-wine.

You, my comrade of choice, and I
got through the battle and flight.
Nobility was crushed and kissed the mud.
Shield thrown down,

I ran, till Mercury whisked me away.
You made it to the sea and found
a battle still had to be fought, with
waves of fire.

And now we owe the gods a feast, so
put down the weight of war.
Under my laurels drink Italian red.
My old friend.

And Mentor times things perfectly: into the silence following this, comes the bustle of serving, a rattle of crockery, the minutiae of "Now where shall we put this?"

Across the tables, Lucius lifts his wine-cup to Horace, and lets go of the picture of the disaster that was Philippi. He makes a note to himself: he owes it to Horace to read those Odes.

Chapter 11

In the middle of the busiest time of his recent life, Lucius welcomes his children who have been clamouring to come to Rome to see their father the Consul in action. One afternoon, the atrium suddenly explodes with noise and movement as young Publius Sestius, Sestia Caecilia, their tutor, their nurse and their aunt Tia all try and get their luggage sorted and into the correct room while loudly telling all the household what a fantastic time they have had on the journey. Lucius watches from a corner until his son notices and comes across for a hug. Publius never seems to mind that Lucius is a little restrained. Celi has definitely grown in the few weeks since he left and he finds himself remembering her as the tiny child wobbling her way from Caecilia's arms to his, and determinedly saying "Celi go Papa." This has turned into a family joke, and as he hugs her now, she looks up at him and says with a mischievous grin, "Celi go Papa". His sister Tia waits dutifully for her turn and says quietly, as she kisses his cheek, "It's good to see you, Consul." She nearly manages to get through this greeting before she giggles at him.

Gradually, slaves remove bags and bundles, the porters who helped carry luggage from the city gate are tipped and sent on their way, and the children are whisked off to their rooms for a wash and change of clothes. Tia retires to the room she has occupied since she was born, and the kitchen staff are bustled away by Melissa to oversee a special homecoming dinner. Lucius looks around his empty atrium and listens to the sounds of his household, then walks to his study, and carries on reading documents until he can talk properly to his family over dinner.

Albinia arrives to meet her favourite niece and nephew –

"Your only niece and nephew!" scolds Celi as usual – and the meal is taken up with the children's excited descriptions of the time when everyone was convinced that there was a wild boar ravaging all over Cosa. But apparently, in the end, there wasn't, though Publius makes it clear that he was disappointed with his aunt for not allowing him to go off into the woods behind the farm by himself, with only his new hunting spear and a six-month-old puppy for company.

"Shocking," says Lucius drily, and winks at Tia. She pulls a face back, and remarks that next summer she will feed Publius to the boar herself.

"I think Gallio and Helice will find it good to be back in Rome," she says, referring to the children's tutor and nurse. "And Helice has suggested that we start looking for a maid for Celi, someone nearer her own age, who can grow up with her."

Albinia nods. "A good idea," she observes. "Would you like me to ask around, Lucius?"

"If the harvest is as bad as Titus says it is going to be, we shan't be able to afford a maid," says Lucius gravely, and for a moment Celi's excited face wavers.

"Your father is teasing," says her aunt Albinia. "Don't worry, Celi, you and I will sort it out. And we shall also make sure that he pays for it!"

Tia has reinforced the children's manners over the summer despite the long hot days of license, and so Publius and Celi excuse themselves at exactly the right time and give every indication of dutifully sleeping until early morning. In fact, Celi is clearly going to fall asleep as soon as she gets to her room. Publius declares his intent to read some Plato and the adults nod and keep straight faces until he is out of the dining room. Lucius and his sisters are now, as they have often been in the past, a unit, and Decius quietly makes to leave – ever the soul of tact. But Tia catches hold of his hand as he passes her couch and says very firmly, "Stay." And Albinia lifts her cup to him and says, "You didn't think for a moment that we would want you to leave, did you, Decius? Sit down and don't be silly." And Decius sits on the end of Lucius' couch, colouring just a little. Lucius is amused because usually nothing ever gets to Decius. Albinia and Tia exchange a look that really is a smirk, and Lucius refills Decius' wine-cup.

"So," he says. "How was the rest of the summer really?"

"It was fine," says Tia. "Really. The children had a great time and I loved seeing them having a great time. As you saw just now though, Publius still wants to be a philosopher I'm afraid."

"Better than being Consul," says Albinia. "Eh, Lucius?"

Lucius pauses. "I don't mind him being a philosopher. But being Consul is – well, not as bad as you might think… what's so funny?" His sisters have burst out laughing.

Tia says, "We are so proud of you, you know. You've really hated every moment of this and yet you are still doing it, and we love you for it."

"Actually," admits her brother, "I haven't hated every minute. And Piso and I are going to push through a law to do something useful, dealing with large-scale disease in the city." There is a brief silence as they all think of their stepmother Cornelia and Lucius' wife Caecilia, who both died in an outbreak of the disease which breaks out in Rome nearly every autumn. "I suppose I have to thank Maecenas – and Horace maybe, for making Maecenas remember me."

"And have you read any of the Odes by Horace yet?" asks Albinia.

"Of course not. Well, just that poem you sent to me at Cosa. It's all right. I like the fact that it is about Cosa, and I like that Horace has put those little glimpses of the farm in it. The stuff about death is ridiculous but I suppose it is traditional. And I really did like the one he recited at that dinner you gave, when

87

Piso and Popilia and Marcus came."

Albinia notices that he has already forgotten the copy of the Odes she bought for him and chimes in determinedly, "Well I've brought another of his Odes with me and I shall read it to you and then you can at least pretend you care about his life's work."

Tia is pleased. "A bit of culture after months in the sticks will be nice – go on, Alby." And she curls up on her couch.

Albinia smiles and sits up. "This one is from the end of the collection he has just published." She waits a moment and then recites:

I used do all right with Love,
And won my spurs in her melee.
But now, thank all the gods above,
I'm done and all my weapons lay

In Venus' shrine. Hang on the wall
My lyre and shield, and, goddess, take
The torches, crowbars, bows and all,
I only used them for your sake.

O Venus, summer's queen, sea-born,
From Cyprus, look upon your bard!
For Chloe now I shall not mourn,
The whip, once lifted, comes down hard."
***

"Neat," says Tia. "Almost funny. The poet compelled to retire through being finally conquered. And just a little naughty in the reference to whips… dear me! I hope that doesn't annoy Livia…"

"It's probably about Livia," says Lucius. "I can see her with a whip."

A snigger runs round the table and they settle down again.

Decius looks thoughtful.

"He hasn't really given up on love though, has he? You would not dedicate your last love poem to Venus if you really meant to give up. I think the poet is quite keen on love still."

"Horace is never completely serious when he writes about love," says Albinia. "Crowbars, indeed! He is intricate, cool, and so, so clever – but he doesn't reveal anything. Some people are actually convinced that he can't like women, which is not true. But when he writes about other things – well, listen to this one:

Offerings to a spring of water
Tomorrow those cool waters will get
flowers, wine and a baby goat
so young that the horns have not yet grown,
his future of battle and love now lost.

His life is given to stain your waters.
Hot blood tangling the icy stream
will ensure you water my flocks
in the blazing days of summer.

To make you like the great rivers,
I shall sing of the oak tree
clinging to the rock as
your waters leap down laughing."
***

They think about that one.

"So, Horace's real love is his estate?" asks Lucius. "The old traditions, the service to the gods of his farm and the countryside?"

"So it would seem," says Albinia. "He certainly writes much better poetry – just as clever but it gets to you. I like that one very much. Others less so, but I suppose he must bow to the will of Augustus and Maecenas and write the poems they want. He certainly isn't as good at patriotic poetry, but he must pay his way somehow. We all have to do that, don't we?"

"I really need to read them," says Lucius with a sigh. "Three scrolls, collecting dust in my study, that must be nearly a hundred of them, right?"

Albinia thinks of the money she spent on buying Lucius the collection and echoes his sigh. "Yes, dear brother, he published nearly a hundred poems just a few weeks ago. I was fortunate enough not only to get a copy – and read it! – but to be present at several occasions on which the poet recited his work. I was impressed by many of the poems and told you about them on several occasions. I must also tell you that even if the collection wasn't as well-received as Horace hoped, it was noted by many that the poem addressed to you came right at the start of the collection, up there with all the important people! And I still find it strange that nobody has asked you about this. However," she turns to Tia, "I have to say, being Consul has really done wonders for our brother. He has a serious purpose. It is strange, I was really worried about how working for Augustus would affect him, but he seems to be handling it really well so far."

"I'm blushing because I can actually hear you, being here and all that," says Lucius mildly, used to his sisters talking through him and about him.

Decius stirs and tactfully brings the conversation back to Horace. "I still think the first poem you read, about hanging up his weapons, is deeper than you think," he says. "It is playing the game, but it is also about someone who has been hurt and that is serious. Maybe Horace finds peace and quiet in farming and maybe the traditions and the rhythms of country life move him, but he is still a slave to love and he knows it. The countryside may not be his freedom, because he does not really want to be freed."

"And your freedom, Decius?" asks Tia quietly.

"Oh, I have all the freedom I need, and have had since I came here to work for your father," he says lightly, but he does not look up.

"I'm sorry," says Tia, and Lucius finds this catches his attention because he does not see why she is apologising. A thought so disturbing runs like lightning across his brain and is dismissed immediately. He looks at Albinia whose face is wearing a smile, but it is the secret smile of a stone lady on an old Etruscan tomb, like the ones on the roads leading out of Cosa.

"What about reading us one of yours?" he asks.

"Dear gods," remarks his sister, "by that do you mean one of my carefully crafted little jewels of verbal purity? Because, yes, I do happen to have a new poem ready."

"Recite away," invites her barbarian brother.

"<u>Writing</u>," she begins.

"When you write upon papyrus
first you need to smooth the surface.
Get your pumice stone, and draw it
against the grain of the fibres.
And then –
slow
down…
long sweeps over the
                    criss-cross
        of lines
feel a gentle snag,
then glide on…
blow gently, to remove the grey dust.
Then wipe with cloth – linen, not wool.
Stroke the surface with featherlight fingertips,
checking for rough edges. But remember

91

don't polish the surface too much!
It wears through: hold it up to the light
And see the fossil patterns of leaves
in the weave of layer upon layer.
Think carefully.
Once you scratch that first word
the clean cream sheet is no more.
Make sure that what you write
is worth the papyrus' loss."
***

There is a silence, broken by Decius sighing and getting to his feet.

"Lady Albinia, I think you have just brought this dinner to the best possible end. Certainly, I couldn't follow that, so I am going to excuse myself. And thank you."

Why is Decius always so right?

Chapter 12

Young Tiberius Drusus turns out to be a gift from the gods. Lucius finds Tiberius waiting in his atrium every morning, briefed and eager to serve. He is knowledgeable and puts Lucius to shame frequently.

"My mother and stepfather have kept me informed on current affairs ever since my younger brother Drusus and I moved to live with them," says Tiberius when Lucius congratulates him. Lucius imagines family conversations round the dinner table as briefings and pities the young man in front of him. Tiberius has been born into an ideal aristocratic family, mother a Livia Drusilla, father a Claudian no less, Tiberius Claudius Nero. With connections like that young Tiberius is set fair for the smoothest ascent of the political ladder imaginable. But many years ago, his father chose the wrong side in dramatic fashion, and his mother caught the eye of Augustus. Tiberius was not yet two years old when he and his parents managed to escape the terrible siege of Perusia and by the time his younger brother Drusus was born, Livia had already married Augustus. It had been a scandal at the time though Livia and Augustus now live lives of ostentatious respectability, and Lucius looks at the intense young man in front of him and wonders how it has affected him. Tiberius seems altogether too serious for his age, though he has a sense of humour. Maybe it is the frown into which his face naturally settles when he is concentrating, but there is something which makes you just a little bit cautious around Tiberius.

Tiberius has had a busy year as Augustus' quaestor. He has reorganised the checks on the public grain ships coming over from Egypt and Africa, and has carried out a series of spot inspections on the great slave barracks in the south of the country. Slaves claiming to be Roman citizens have had their cases investigated and a shocking number of people returned to their former lives of freedom, while Tiberius has passed on details for prosecution by one of the year's praetors. And it is only September. Lucius wonders if Tiberius prefers to be away from Rome. He has certainly made the most out of his independence.

Lucius has considered asking Tiberius to be his Senatorial spy to gather information on how the new settlement of Augustus' power has gone down in the upper classes, but he quickly realises that this is unfair on the boy and unlikely to work, given that he is so close to Augustus. Nobody is going to talk in front of Tiberius. Instead, he puts Tiberius to the task of gathering facts and figures to back up Lucius' own bid for immortality – a new law planned by himself and Piso.

The grandly titled Lex Sestia Calpurnia will address an uncontentious but important issue – the reaction of the authorities to outbreaks of disease in the city. Over recent years, there has been a wave of serious illness nearly every autumn and winter, with the very old being affected in particular though not exclusively. Lucius thinks of Caecilia, dying barely two days after saying how tired she felt one evening. For some reason, nobody else in the house caught this particular wave of the disease, not even Melissa the cook who nursed her mistress. But the effect of the onslaughts in the poorer areas needs to be addressed and the law will put into place emergency measures designed to halt the spread of disease once it has taken hold.

When Lucius explains the idea behind this proposal to Tiberius, the young man thinks for a few seconds then says, "Why don't you also talk with the priests on Tiber Island?" and Lucius is impressed once more. He and Piso have already decided to do this but it shows that Tiberius' practical turn of mind will back up their efforts.

It is on a windy day in September with clouds streaking the sky that the two Consuls and their quaestor set off for a meeting with the Greek who is both chief priest and doctor of the Temple of Aesculapius on Tiber Island. After meeting at Piso's house, the three do not have far to go – around the base of the Palatine then through the Forum Boarium. Normally this would be a mistake, what with all the market stalls and noise and dirt, but when you have a gang of lictors preceding you, space appears, and your progress is smooth. Over the Fabrician Bridge and the little Tiber Island suddenly opens up, quiet and peaceful and far away from crowds and bustle.

The island sails along the river, it seems, with its two bridges looking like a sweep of oars caught mid-flight. This image is reinforced by the fake boat prow built out at the downstream end of the island, but this is a boat that goes nowhere, forever cutting up the river into two streams just as the Tiber curves around the heart of the city. Dominating the whole island is a temple to the god of healing, Aesculapius, brought from Greece hundreds of years ago when Rome was in the grip of another pestilence. The god had stopped the pestilence and stayed. Most of the southern part of the island is given over to a hospital, comprised of a large courtyard surrounded by a deep covered colonnade and bordered by myriad rooms in which the doctors and their assistants see a stream of patients. The hospital is well-staffed: every doctor who qualifies in Alexandria, it seems, comes over to do a stint in Rome on Tiber Island. It is quite something to be proud of, that Rome has more interesting illnesses than the mighty Alexandria. The doctors have a huge number of slave-assistants as well, because once a master has taken a sick slave to Tiber Island, the slave belongs to the god. Fresh air and good food do a lot to cure a damaged slave. The hospital and temple are run by its Chief Priest, a Greek named

Herophilus, a tall and bony man with a nose so curved and thin he reminds Lucius of a parrot. His tunic is long and immaculately clean, and he doesn't look as if he ever touches a patient. Why would he with so many slaves around?

The Consuls sit (and Tiberius stands) in a rather nice office where the Chief Priest receives the more important visitors to his hospital. When Lucius and Piso explain their plan, he gets quite animated, and starts hunting through the books on his shelves.

"This pestilence never quite vanishes from Rome, but seems to have years when it is worse and we don't know why," he says apparently to the books, for he is turned away from them, and his voice sends puffs of dust up from the scrolls in front of him. When he turns back to them, trickles of dust are sliding down his lovely clean tunic, and he deposits the scrolls in a cloudy mess and pats at himself with no real determination.

"I don't let the slaves dust the scrolls," he explains. "I need everything to be left just as it is. But I never have time to dust anything myself of course. Now, before I get to work on these," he gestures at the scrolls, "I'll tell you what I know off the top of my head. Give me a few days to do some reading and I shall let you have a paper with my findings."

Young Tiberius nods approvingly at this efficient approach.

Herophilus sits down and takes a few moments to frown at his desk while he gathers his thoughts.

"The pestilence is a product of breathing bad air," he pronounces. "And as the illness seems to be particularly virulent in Rome, we must conclude that the bad air is a product of so many people living together. When people fall ill, they breathe out more corruption and the air in general becomes worse, so more people fall ill. In my opinion, therefore, the sick should be isolated immediately. In addition, the public latrines, producers of much foulness in the air, should be cleaned regularly, and properly maintained. It is also noticeable that Marcus Agrippa's work on the water supply and bathhouses has not resulted in a reduction in the pestilence, so I feel that the pestilence is not affected by the availability of clean water. It is also noticeable that the pestilence does not reach the tops of the seven hills but concentrates in the valleys. Consuls, in my opinion, if you could move the people of the Subura out of Rome every summer and clean the city thoroughly while they were away, you would do much to reduce the disease. But I realise that this is not practical."

"What do you do if your patients here fall ill with the pestilence?" asks Tiberius.

Herophilus looks surprised. "We isolate them, as I recommended to you. We leave food and water at the door, and the ill wait on themselves to the best of their ability. With so many people in the hospital already weakened through injury or the like, we really cannot afford to let the disease spread here. If one of the sick dies, he is wrapped up by the other patients and left at the door and a special group of slaves purify the body and take it to the grave pit that we maintain well outside the city on the western side of the Tiber. We make offerings to Aesculapius and burn cleansing herbs. None of the slaves who deal with dead bodies ever catch the pestilence. We think that the god gives them special protection. Interestingly, to my knowledge few doctors have fallen ill either. Again, I think this is due to the god, but I have no doubt that our policy of never approaching a pestilence victim is also helpful."

Yes, thinks Lucius, the gods know we wouldn't want our doctors to actually approach us when we were ill...

This visit gives Lucius and Piso a good idea of where to start with the Lex Sestia Calpurnia, and while it doesn't exactly mean that they tour the public latrines – they are not Marcus Agrippa after all – Lucius finds himself scrutinising all facilities he happens to use with a more discerning eye. And over the course of a few days, the two Consuls and their quaestor draw up a set of simple measures to help tackle city-wide epidemics. The proposed law merely lists arrangements that will set up temporary hospitals, dispose of bodies, distribute food and limit movement. It is so simple; Lucius cannot fathom why it has not been addressed before.

Piso says, "People have fallen into a lethargy. Augustus does everything in times of emergency – and at most other times too, actually. So, they think that they don't need to do anything themselves."

"Augustus must get frustrated," observes Lucius.

Tiberius grins, quite an unusual sight. "Oh, he does."

Lucius has an idea and adds a final clause to the proposed law.

"All doctors residing within the official boundary of the city shall be exempt from tax, in honour of the recovery from illness of Gaius Julius Caesar Augustus."

He reckons that the law is now guaranteed to be passed.

Chapter 13

It is several days before the end of September and Lucius is not particularly looking forward to the dinner that night. He has finally got around to returning the invitation to Augustus and Livia and Maecenas and Terentia. He has also invited some friends but has no expectations that this will be anything other than a duty. It is with some confusion that he welcomes his first guests, Terentia and a man who is familiar to him without his knowing his name. Clearly, he should.

"Dear Lucius Sestius! Maecenas sends his apologies, but he really isn't feeling well today," says Terentia with a tone of such dismissal that her husband's illness has clearly given her no distress whatsoever. "But fortunately, my brother came calling and agreed to make up the numbers – I am guessing that you have worked hard to put together the perfect nine guests!"

Lucius is filled with dread at the thought that Maecenas will not be there but turns to his new guest and politely welcomes him into the dining room.

"Oh, we are first!" cries Terentia. "Oh good, then I may just slip next to you Lucius, if you don't mind?"

Lucius can think of nothing that will answer this politely and truthfully so mumbles something about being delighted while Terentia's brother, still unnamed, rolls his eyes at him and looks resigned.

"I can see that I must introduce myself – again," he remarks. "Terentia, do you really have no manners or is it just that you have no sense?"

Terentia laughs at this insult and carries on settling herself and her many draperies on the couch. Decius has sent in one of the maids to fuss over Terentia, with slippers to exchange for sandals, and the two women twitch the folds of Terentia's dress until they are just right.

Terentia's brother sighs and says, "My apologies for my sister, dearly as I love her! Let me introduce myself – Aulus Terentius Varro Murena. Thank you for your kind welcome, Consul." He emphasises the last word and gazes sternly at Terentia, then his face breaks out into a charming smile, and he suddenly looks very like his sister, with his dark hair curling slightly too long at the base of his neck and his round face slightly chubby in the cheeks and chin. He also has Terentia's delicate little nose, which he wrinkles at his sister, so he looks for a moment like the picture of a naughty younger brother. Terentia is settled to her liking, and the wine is served.

"You don't know me because I've not been in Rome a great deal recently," Aulus Terentius says to Lucius. "I can tell you it is good to be back, I've had enough of dealing with Gauls and Germans and things."

"Oh my," slips in Terentia, with a smirk.

Aulus Terentius groans. "And I'm getting used to all our silly family jokes again," he says and smiles at his sister.

"Gauls and Germans?" asks Lucius, a vague remark of Piso's coming back to him. "Are you the mighty conqueror of the Salassi tribe?"

"Oh yes," says Aulus Terentius. "That's me. Though "conqueror" is being very polite. Three endless years of riding through forests and bogs in the freezing cold winters and stinking, hot, fly-ridden summers chasing hairy men with tattoos. Total joy. Why on earth we want to conquer people like that I shall never know."

Lucius is saved from trying to reply to this by the entrance of Albinia and Horace, who have met outside the front door, and have managed to have a deep and meaningful conversation about some obscure Greek lyric metre between the atrium and the dining room. They look extremely pleased with themselves. There is no doubt that they will sit next to each other and Lucius mentally fills up the couches. Aulus Terentius on the other side of Terentia, Augustus and Livia on the couch for the guest of honour, put Popilia next to Horace and Albinia, and Piso can entertain Livia. He sighs in relief. That should work. Piso and Popilia are next and they all perch on the edge of their couches with cups of wine and wait for their guests of honour. Terentia perfects her elegant lounging.

At precisely the right time – just a tiny bit late – Augustus and Livia arrive, and amid laughing apologies, are settled onto their couch. Livia shows every sign of delight to be next to Piso, and indeed the two of them seem to get along rather well. The cynicism which Lucius has noticed in some of Piso's comments about their fellow senators matches Livia's dryness rather well, and she laughs much more than at their only previous meeting. Lucius relaxes, perhaps a little too much, and Terentia does not even wait before the end of the first course before she is snuggling into him closely. He looks at Albinia, trying to signal to her while covering his panic, but she toasts him and turns back to Horace. He snatches a look at Augustus, but the Princeps is enjoying a heated discussion with Aulus Terentius, and neither is paying any attention to his problem. Only Livia notices his discomfort and to Lucius' amazement she gives him a wink. As the first course is cleared, she gives a genteel cough and announces her intention of going to repair her face. She looks steadily at Terentia as she says this. Albinia, as Lucius' hostess, gets up too and with a shrug Terentia joins them. Popilia smiles at Piso, and trots off on their wake, knowing what is expected of her. Lucius adjusts his tunic and wonders how on earth he is going to deal with this.

Suddenly Aulus Terentius says, "You are an excellent host, Lucius Sestius. Thank you for making an uninvited guest so welcome," and he lifts his cup to Lucius. There is a muttering of agreement and raised wine and the Princeps graciously steps in with a question about how Lucius is managing the increased demands on his time. Lucius realises that he can relax, and when the ladies return he even smiles at Terentia. He has no intention of allowing anything to develop though. It is far too public a flirtation for his taste.

By the end of dinner, despite some nudges from Aulus, Terentia has made it clear that she will stay if given the slightest encouragement. Lucius can't quite believe that he has interpreted everything correctly though – is she really hoping to stay the night? Is that acceptable nowadays? And Augustus? How does he feel? Lucius really cannot begin to work out what is going on there and he hopes Albinia has a better idea and can explain later.

One little incident sticks in Lucius' mind and lightens his nervousness at Terentia's invitation. Terentia has turned her attention to her brother and is teasing him, pretending to introduce him to Horace.

"Horace, meet my brother, Aulus Terentius Varro Murena, though what he needs with all those names, I don't know." She sips from her cup but from the tone of her voice, Lucius can imagine that she is also waggling her eyebrows at her brother. He recognises the tone from Albinia. This is clearly a long-running joke, and in line with the slightly acidic nature of the brother/sister relationship he has observed so far.

"My sister – Terentia –" says Aulus pausing to emphasise the single name, "is just jealous."

"Ah," says Horace brightly, "name envy."

Augustus barks a sudden laugh and toasts the poet with an appreciative nod.

"So much better than other types of envy," says Livia sweetly, and is rewarded with a round of laughter. Livia does not say much but everything she does say gets a response. The conversation moves on and Lucius thanks the gods for his own relatively simple name, enough to make him a Roman citizen. That is all he wants. Aulus Terentius Varro Murena must have gained all his names through a father or grandfather being adopted and is signalling his links to two major families in a very unsubtle way. Lucius hopes Aulus' talents will match his name and his connection to Augustus, because it is clear that he has no intention of going down in history as merely the brother of the woman who married a friend of Augustus. Still Aulus seems nice enough, has his sister's looks and charm, and Augustus will surely reward him one day, for his sister's contributions to the Princeps' happiness, if nothing else.

As the evening ends, Albinia takes pity and sticks close to her brother, loudly asking if her room in the house can be made up so that she can stay the night. She stands and waves off all the guests alongside Lucius, and as the last guests, Aulus and Terentia leave, she firmly closes the door herself, and turns to grin widely at her brother. "Safe at last!" she declaims dramatically, and the two of them break out into whoops of laughter as they stagger around the atrium. They collapse together on the wooden bench where Lucius' clients wait for him every morning, and the slaves glance indulgently at them as they bustle in and out of the dining room, clearing up. Of course, the slaves know exactly what has been going on.

"Dear Juno and all the gods, I distinctly saw Terentia pouting as Aulus dragged her off!" says Albinia, shaking with laughter. "My poor brother, what did you do to deserve that?"

Lucius sobers up a little. "I wish you could explain it all to me," he asks Albinia sadly "I felt all evening that I was two steps behind everyone else."

"It is easy, my dear Lucius," says his elder sister in a slightly condescending manner. "Terentia is bored and childless and frustrated. Augustus is tiring of her. She isn't really fond of Augustus, but she is used to the attention, and so can't help flirting in front of him in the hope of making him take notice of her. If that doesn't succeed, maybe at least you will be nice to her, she thinks, and she will enjoy that. She is also on the look-out for her next husband, and if you turn out right, and if she can persuade Maecenas to divorce her, she will actually make you a very good wife. I find myself liking her: she is pretty and clever, and I think that if she is happy she won't cling and be boring. But her brother will never let her leave Maecenas. Ambitious Aulus!"

"Poor Terentia," says Lucius, a little more sympathetic now the object of his compassion is no longer there.

"She's good company. She'll survive," says Albinia briskly.

Lucius picks up on something Albinia has just said.

"You like her?"

"What I have seen of her," says Albinia. "She gossips beautifully but she doesn't seem mean or whining, and she can use words of more than two syllables."

"Have you just been catty?"

"No, poets are reporters of truth, so cannot be catty. And now I must go."

"Changed your mind about staying?" asks her brother with a hint of irony.

She smiles at him. "As if I was really going to stay! Didn't you want me to save you?"

"I'm extremely grateful, as always," says Lucius, and they hug before Albinia asks Lucius to whistle up her litter and escort. Lucius steps out into the street to see her off. The dark is slightly warm still but the level of humidity in the air is noticeably dropping as September plays out. The welcome cooler weather is making its way down from the seas and hills and with it the Senate is getting more crowded every meeting and the streets are getting busier in the mornings. Rome is waking up after her summer siesta, thinks Lucius, and he goes back into the dining room and polishes off the wine, while around him the slaves smile broadly and clear away. Happily drunk, Lucius falls asleep on the couch, and does not notice when Melissa creeps in and covers him with a blanket, tucking a little pillow under his head. Sweet though Terentia may be, he is content that he has managed to get away: his dreams walk over him lightly and are not remembered.

Chapter 14

On the next morning the Chief Priest's paper on the common pestilences of Rome arrives at the Consul's house and Lucius immediately decides to take his entourage for a diplomatic tour, showing off the consular face. He has a vague idea that he is supposed to be seen in public so every few days he drags his lictors and clients out for a ramble around the Forum, or one of the market-places. He stops at a new food stall and makes polite conversation with the stallholder while buying some little sausages for his lictors. They are used to their Consul's eccentric ways by now and eat gratefully, although Lucius has noticed that this does not stop them always making sure that he is carefully surrounded. Some fan out and look outward at the crowd while others stay near and look at him. It means that there is always a somewhat irregular circle of red cloaks around him. His clients get honey cakes from the baker's stall next door to the sausage seller, and the two vendors blessed by the Consul's generosity smile happily, knowing that they will sell out early and thus get the best seats in the bar for the rest of the day. Their wives who actually make the food will ensure that the next day there will be a little more stock for their husbands to sell, not just so as to take advantage of the Consul's generosity but also to ensure that their husbands are kept in the Forum and away from the delights of the bar for that bit longer. The conscientious Consul however makes sure that he works his way around all the stalls in the Forum, and given the sheer number of these, will not see the sausage seller and baker again that year.

As Lucius Sestius waits for his entourage to lick their fingers and surreptitiously wipe them on tunics, he hears his name being called and turns to face the newcomer with that half-smile beloved by all politicians. He is genuinely pleased to see Aulus Terentius Varro Murena approaching him, and apparently undisturbed by any desire to avenge his sister's honour. Lucius believes Popilia's claim that Aulus is happy to see his sister in the arms of some man other than her husband: but the new Consul has no illusions as to his personal charms. If it weren't for his promotion, he does not doubt that Aulus would pass him by without a glance. But he does not blame the man for that and is prepared to like him for his wit and ability to be at ease in a stranger's house for dinner. With Aulus Terentius is a sunburned man with the short hair and impatient fingers of a soldier.

"Meet Marcus Primus, just back from governing Macedonia," says Aulus Terentius cheerfully. After all, he only had to cope with Gauls and Germans during his stint abroad.

"Welcome, Marcus Primus!" says Lucius. "And how are the Macedonians?"

Marcus Primus smiles and says, "They're great." His brown eyes crinkle and warm up, and Lucius' mind stops labelling him as "career soldier" and gives him a new billing of "commander I would cheerfully follow into a dark forest on the very edge of the world." Apart from clearly being one of the nicest people in the world, Marcus Primus seems to have genuinely liked the people he governed. He launches enthusiastically into a description of how great the Macedonians are, and Lucius finds himself smiling and nodding and thinking how nice it is to have a Roman official who doesn't moan at him all the time. And as Primus pauses for breath in the midst of a eulogy of the sense of honour displayed by Macedonian chiefs he has known, Aulus Terentius laughs and cries, "I knew you two would get on! Lucius, Marcus and I have known each other since we were sent to the same dreadful teacher to have the Iliad and Odyssey drummed into us, and I can swear on the altar of any god you choose that he is one of the truly good people. Seriously, Marcus, Rome is lucky to have you."

Marcus Primus cannot quite accept this praise and begins to protest but Aulus just laughs and tells him to take it like a man. Lucius grins.

"Anything special happen while you were Governor?" he asks with his consular hat on.

Primus shrugs. "A nasty little campaign against a Thracian tribe just over the border. Stopped their constant raiding and reinforced our hold on the river. Didn't take too long and was cheap in men and resources. Apart from that I had a great time." He likes the word "great", Lucius notes.

"Come into a Senate meeting and tell us all about it," he offers, but Marcus Primus shakes his head. "Not my sort of thing if you don't mind. I sent in my report before I set off in the early summer, and I've just handed in my accounts to the Treasury. I'm looking forward to a couple of years of indolence."

Lucius smiles at this, for a man like Marcus Primus is never still. Lucius cannot believe he has just used the word "indolence".

"What will you do?" he asks.

Marcus Primus can't stop smiling. "I'm going to go and sort out the family estate near Pompeii. Rebuild the farm buildings, sort out the vines and drink my own wine in the shade of my own olive trees every evening. Raise my family and count my blessings."

"I give it three months," says Lucius, and Aulus laughs; Lucius wishes Marcus Primus well, thanks him for his work on behalf of a grateful Roman people, and then takes his lictors home for lunch. It is the sort of incident he encounters on an everyday basis and he pays it no more attention than he does the latest summary of repairs carried out to the city's fabric. He settles down with a sigh to read the information sent by Herophilus, determined to devote his energies to his new law. His and Piso's new law. Piso's and his... anyway.

The Lex Sestia Calpurnia has one of the smoothest possible passages through the Senate, and this gives Lucius a strange sense of satisfaction with his life. One morning as he prepares to set out for a Senate meeting, he realises that he is experiencing a feeling of belonging in Rome he has never felt. Or not for a very long time. This pleases him and he looks around as he and his entourage walk the familiar route to the Forum. His lictors step out with a mildly ridiculous sense of importance and the wind fires up, snapping their heavy red cloaks. There is a hint of rain in the air as well, and he hopes that they are not about to start the cold and wet weather too soon. He'd like to get this law through first and it shouldn't take more than a few days now that the Senate has approved. The proposal is no secret and everyone they have talked to thinks it is a good idea. Well, everyone who could be bothered to have a view. A friendly tribune has arranged an assembly meeting to ratify it and, in a few days, everything will be settled, and a good thing too.

Three days before the beginning of October, Lucius celebrates his birthday. This is unusual: Lucius generally does not notice his birthday, though his family make determined attempts. Today, not only does he receive the good wishes of his children, sisters and clients, it is also noticed at the highest level that the junior Consul of Rome is turning forty-five. There is no Senate meeting, so Lucius is in his atrium talking to clients and seeing people who want favours, when a messenger from Augustus arrives. Today there are no papers to read, no summons to the Palatine: instead, the grinning slave hands over a small package wrapped in several layers of cloth, saying "With the best wishes of the Princeps, sir, on the occasion of your birthday."

When the package is unwrapped, a small cheese is revealed: the messenger explains that this is a rare goats' milk cheese from southern Gaul, and has just arrived by the official post, so is still fresh. Lucius is astounded but pleased and the cheese takes pride of place at his birthday dinner that evening; it is delicious.

Lucius' worries about cold weather are unfounded; on the very last day of the month, the cooler weather of September disappears and there is a heaviness in the warm air. Wearing a toga remains uncomfortable and early in October, Lucius and Piso are not entirely surprised when they receive a report one morning from the Chief Priest of Aesculapius. The news is not happy. Fevers are on the rise and do not seem to be targeting just the young and the old: the famously healthy burial slaves have been affected and one has died. The Chief Priest fears that this may be a hard winter and asks the Consuls to make preparation accordingly. Lucius, sitting in his quiet little study, feels a cold breath on the spot between his shoulder blades and it is so real that for a moment he wonders if he is going down with the illness himself. Fortunately, the Lex Sestia Calpurnia has just been passed into law, and Lucius and Piso meet with the praetors and aediles to get them started on organising the law's measures throughout the city. Lucius keeps an anxious eye on the reports that come in daily: some smaller temples are turned into makeshift hospitals, rules for isolation are put up, and food supplies are carefully monitored by Tiberius. As the days go by, numbers rise slowly, and it is difficult for Lucius and Piso to judge as to whether or not their measure is having an effect. The Chief Priest of Aesculapius however is cautiously optimistic.

"Given how easily people of all ages and states can fall ill, the disease has not taken the sort of hold I feared," he reports in a quick note from Tiber Island. "My main worry now is that the river is rising with all the rains, and if the city experiences flooding then there is the possibility that the dirty water will again affect the general health." Lucius and Piso groan and send for reports on the river from the already over-worked aediles. The Chief Priest is right, river levels are rising. They must pray for a period of less rain and thank all the gods that the sewers are in a good state of repair.

When Augustus calls the Consuls and their faithful quaestor for a meeting on the Palatine Hill, they do at least feel ready for his questions and Augustus is not one to rant at them because it has been raining. Instead he listens and lets them explain the measures already taken. He praises their foresight in putting through the Lex Sestia Calpurnia and sends Tiberius off to talk to Marcus Agrippa's team of city engineers. He also lends them a small force of slaves and freedmen to strengthen the organisation of a steady supply of grain into the city, this being the first thing to go wrong when there is any sort of crisis. Now all they can do is sit and wait.

In mid-October Lucius is chairing a meeting of the Senate as October has brought round his turn again. He is thinking about the reports of illness in the city and wondering if he and Piso have got their law through in time. The Lex Sestia Calpurnia took barely a month to be ratified, but there has been hardly any time to set the machinery up and running throughout the city. Young Tiberius is working on that and co-ordinating with city officials. As he sits and thinks about this, the meeting runs on smoothly, until just before the end a nameless and faceless back-row nobody rises and asks to be allowed to address the House. Lucius is a little irritated as he has had no notice, but as he himself was nameless and faceless until a couple of months previously he invites the senator to speak.

"It has come to my attention," begins the back-row nobody,

"that when our colleague Marcus Primus recently had a letter read in this House about his activities against the Odrysian tribe while he was governor of Macedonia…" He realises he has lost control of his sentence and falters for a moment, before cutting his losses and moving on. "It has come to my attention that Marcus Primus did not explain the exact nature of his legal position."

There is a silence while the massed ranks of the Senate work this out. Lucius can see lips moving, and brows crinkling. He sighs and signals to the man to expand.

"My question is: did our colleague declare war and fight that war on behalf of the Senate and People of Rome with the full knowledge and permission of the Senate?" And Senator Nobody sits down again.

"Oh Jupiter above, a pedant!" thinks Lucius crossly: out loud he makes a point of sounding calm as he says, "We all know that it can be difficult for a Roman magistrate serving abroad to seek that permission and wait for it to arrive before moving against a threat. It has therefore been the House's policy to accept and debate and grant that permission after the fact of the matter."

"By my recollection though," oh by Hercules, the irritating man is really enjoying his moment of glory as he stands again and tucks his thumb into the fold of his toga in traditional pose, "by my recollection, such permission has never been sought or granted. Perhaps one of my colleagues can remember an occasion when Marcus Primus made this request, but I cannot."

Silence. Of course, nobody can remember something which may or may not have happened a year or so ago. Lucius beckons the clerk and gives a whispered instruction to look into this. The clerk nods and summons a minion, who scurries off quietly as Lucius announces that the matter will be investigated and the result of said investigation brought before the Senate at their next meeting. He looks at Senator Nobody who nods, satisfied, and the meeting moves on to the ending prayer to Jupiter. The meeting is over.

Lucius gives the usual summary and discusses a few points with the clerks and turns to find (how very unsurprising!) – that Senator Nobody is patiently waiting for a private word.

"My apologies for not advising you beforehand, Consul, but I was only alerted to a possible problem this morning, when one of my clients had a discussion with me. He is a veteran centurion, just released from duty, and he served in the force fighting the Odrysians last year. And while I do realise that many old soldiers are going to grumble about their commanders, this man specifically criticised Primus' high-handed attitude in not seeking clearance for the campaign. And this was not just his opinion, he had also discussed it with one of Primus' military tribunes, who was uneasy as well."

"And you just could not wait to announce it in the Senate," thought Lucius sourly. Out loud he strove to sound smooth and unemotional.

"I can assure you, er," good gods, why can he not remember the man's name? "er, that the Senate will investigate this matter."

He can't think of anything else to say to this idiot, so he nods and walks out of the House and into a blustery, rain-dotted Forum. His faithful lictors fall into line. He has long ago stopped Decius coming all the way down into the Forum him after meetings, for he has realised that he needs him more at home, working on his increased paperwork and the demands on his household. Even with young Tiberius to help, he and Decius have quite a job to keep on top of everything and this is a quiet year for Senatorial business, thank the gods. Tiberius has access to his stepfather's bureau of secretaries and accountants and the like, and the bureaucrats from the Records Office are always

FIONA FORSYTH

available to advise, but Lucius tries to keep most of his work in-house. With the help of a trustworthy freedman loaned to him by Albinia, Lucius thinks he will just about make it through these few months. He completely forgets about the query over Marcus Primus until a message arrives from the Senate clerk to confirm that there is no record that the commander Primus ever ratified his war with the Odrysians. Lucius sighs and sends a message to Marcus Primus asking for a meeting. He also scribbles a note to Piso. If Marcus Primus cannot prove that he made war outside his provincial borders with the Senate's permission, then Lucius does not have the foggiest what to do about it. Ask Primus to apologise nicely and promise never to do it again?

When Piso and he meet, there are increasingly pressing matters to discuss. The river is still rising, if slowly, and they must keep up the pressure in dealing with the new wave of disease. Piso has sent Popilia to their villa at the coast, and when she offers to take Tia and the children with her, Lucius accepts gratefully. The issue of Marcus Primus seems relatively unimportant and Lucius does not realise that Marcus Primus never replies to his note. The two Consuls are taken completely by surprise when at the meeting of the Senate a few days before the end of October, a campaign against Marcus Primus begins. The nameless and faceless senator is not in attendance – several senators have already fled the pestilence – but a much more imposing figure has taken up the attack and is rising to his feet, preparing to speak. Tall and muscular, this man looks ready to take on anything. His face is grim and the jaw is set in a line which reminds Lucius of all those statues of bygone Romans who valued determined virtue above all else.

"Marcus Licinius Crassus," murmurs Piso, who is sitting on Lucius' left. "Governor of Macedonia before Primus."

114

Marcus Licinius Crassus also holds one of the most famous names in Roman history. His grandfather was famous for two things: being incredibly rich and dying in a military disaster against the Parthians. Lucius feels a hint of sympathy which has vanished by the end of the speech.

"Fathers of Rome," Crassus begins, and the old-fashioned address signals his gravity, "I was perturbed when at the last meeting the question of Marcus Primus and his campaign against the Odrysians was brought up for us. Since then, the Consul has made enquiries and the records of the House confirm that Marcus Primus never made any application for permission to conduct war outside his province's boundaries. Now, as many of you know, I was governor of Macedonia before Marcus Primus took over. I myself got to know the Odrysians and found them a loyal and civilised tribe. I was happy to award a grant of land to them, and they always lived in peace. The tribe's traditional lands cover part of our province of Macedonia, and part of those lands lie outside our empire's boundary. This was never to my knowledge a problem. When I heard of Marcus Primus' campaigns against the Odrysians in that part of Thrace outside the boundary of the Roman Empire, I was surprised, but it never occurred to me that this was not a legitimate and approved incursion. Like all of us, I do not attend every Senate meeting, and while I could of course have read the record of Senate meetings more carefully, I did not set out to check that Marcus Primus had written to the Senate. Now it turns out that he did not. A Roman governor has declared war outside the boundary of our Empire on his own authority and this I take to be a serious matter. For this reason, I am giving you all notice that I intend to prosecute Marcus Primus on a charge of treason. I note that Marcus Primus himself is not here – again – and trust that those of you who count yourselves his friends will ensure that he finds out about his impending prosecution as soon as possible. The relevant official has been informed and will publish the date of the trial soon."

And with that Crassus sits down and there is a buzz of excitement. Lucius waits for the noise to die down and merely thanks Crassus for informing the Senate of his intentions.

After the meeting, he and Piso go straight back to Piso's house and a messenger is sent to track down young Tiberius who missed the meeting to do the rounds of the Tiber's flood defences (such as they are).

"What is this all about?" muses Piso as he and Lucius sit in his study and pour drinks. A slave slips in with a plate of snacks and withdraws: Piso leaves orders that they are not to be disturbed, except by the arrival of Tiberius.

"Some Odrysians have appealed to Crassus to help them," shrugs Lucius. "If their tribal limits overlap the province's boundary, then the tribe may well have been affected as a whole."

"We really need to talk to Primus," says Piso with a frown. "I don't like the feel of this."

Tiberius cannot see the need for worry when he joins them.

"Provincial governors are getting careless and need to have the rules reinforced. Crassus is acting as the patron of the tribe concerned and therefore will prosecute. It is what usually happens, isn't it?" he asks.

The two older men exchange glances. "Yes," says Lucius, "that was the pattern thirty or forty years ago. I suppose it just feels wrong that this is all starting up again. I thought that provincial government had cleaned up its act a lot recently. And the overall problem is that I cannot see Primus deliberately breaking the law. So, the likeliest explanation is that the letter was misplaced, or he simply forgot, in which case we are holding a major trial over a trivial matter."

"Well, it will be a short trial if that is what happened," says

Piso.

"I think Primus should just come and see us," says Lucius. "We could clear it all up and avoid the trial. I wish he had just come to see me when I asked."

Tiberius shrugs. "He has chosen not to explain himself after that first query in the Senate, and he could have done. He could have replied to your message, but again, he has chosen not to respond. Crassus has asked me to help with the prosecution, and with your permission, I'd like to. I haven't had much experience in the law courts, and it would be interesting."

"Of course," says Lucius, immediately knowing that Augustus has arranged for this. Marcus Primus' trial is a matter of concern for the Princeps, and Lucius cannot see why.

Chapter 15

Primus' prosecution is duly announced and the process of choosing the jury and collecting material begins. Lucius calculates that the trial cannot possibly start until the new year and is relieved that he won't be Consul. Theoretically the Senate have nothing to do with a public case like this, but if it goes as Lucius suspects, then all sorts of people could get involved. And he is in no doubt that challenging a governor's right to deal with a perceived threat to his province is going to be an interesting topic, considering that Augustus has just been handed provincial power as yet untested. In fact, as Albinia points out one day, it could well be Augustus who is being on trial here.

"Suppose Augustus' good friend Agrippa, while he is out in the East, considers that there is a threat from one of our client kings," she argues. "Suppose he advises the governor of Syria to invade Judea."

Lucius thinks this all too likely from what he heard of the Judeans.

"Agrippa gets his authority to give this advice from Augustus, yes?"

Lucius screws up his brow – and has to admit he doesn't know, or at least not with certainty. "But for the sake of argument, let's say that you are right," he concedes. "Do you really think anyone is going to accuse Agrippa or Augustus of instigating military action beyond the borders of the Empire?"

"Not necessarily," says Albinia. "But if Primus as governor is found guilty of treason for attacking beyond his borders rather than merely defending them, then someone could be sending a message to Augustus. Someone could be pointing out that all forms of power are limited."

"Who would do that?" asks Lucius. "The Senate have just approved Augustus' new role and there is no opposition left."

"Of course there is opposition!" says Albinia. "There just isn't an opposition stupid enough to come out into the open."

"Young Tiberius, my quaestor, asked me if I would mind him being on the prosecution team," says Lucius. "Can you really see Augustus letting him do that if this is an attack on Augustus' own position?"

"It would be a very good way of Augustus keeping an eye on the prosecution," Albinia points out. "Besides, Tiberius' father was a staunch Republican, wasn't he? Who is to say Tiberius doesn't secretly harbour Republican tendencies?"

"Well, whether Tiberius is a mole for the Princeps or a gallant Republican, Primus will be found guilty," says Lucius. "He hasn't come up with anything to refute the charges, and nobody has seen him in public that I know of. Whoever defends him is set for a failure."

"I know who is defending him," says Albinia, smugly.

Lucius is intrigued. "Who?"

"Aulus Terentius Varro Murena," says Albinia, rolling out the syllables as though the name were a line of verse.

Lucius is impressed. He had Aulus Terentius labelled as one who toed the line and it is unexpectedly comforting to find him helping a friend when it is definitely not in his own interest. He does wonder what on earth can be said in Primus' defence though. Surely they will end up having to admit carelessness. And that will look pretty feeble.

At that moment, Mentor taps on the door frame and steps inside Albinia's study. He looks serious.

"Excuse me," he says, "but you have a gentleman visitor and I'm not sure..." His voice trails away and Lucius stares. Mentor is unsure? Really?

"Who is it, please, Mentor?" says Albinia calmly.

"Aulus Terentius Varro Murena," says Mentor. "He is quite insistent on seeing you and the Consul. Do we know the gentleman, madam? Are we at home?"

"Yes, we do and yes we are," says Albinia decisively. "Please show him in and get some refreshments, Mentor."

He nods and vanishes and Lucius and Albinia look at each other with mirroring faces – curly dark hair, Albinia's greyer than her brother's, dark eyes and in Albinia's case just one eyebrow raised. Then they compose themselves to await their guest. Neither doubts that Lucius' presence is key to Aulus Terentius' arrival.

When Aulus Terentius enters, his smile is a fraction less charming and his manner is quieter than Lucius remembers. His courtesy is perfect, and he makes sure that he takes time over the greetings and enquiries over family and mutual friends. Mentor serves wine and nibbles, and does his usual vanishing trick, but an exchanged glance between him and Albinia does not go unnoticed by her brother. Mentor will make sure that a couple of slaves are hanging around the atrium, just in case.

When the pleasantries tail off there is an atmosphere of expectation and nobody pretends that this is a normal visit. Aulus Terentius does not beat about the bush.

"Firstly, I must apologise to you both. Lady Albinia, you hardly know me, and I have presumed on your kindness by coming here at all, but I needed to speak to your brother, preferably without too many people noticing. And by that I am not expecting you to do a modest matronly vanishing act, I have no right and I trust you because I trust your brother. Lucius Sestius, I owe you an apology because I followed you here."

Lucius finally feels surprised for Roman senators do not follow each other around. There is something ridiculous about the idea. He realises that Aulus is dressed very quietly, no toga, a plain tunic, and no doubt a cloak currently hanging in the doorkeeper's closet. In such an outfit, Aulus could be a high-class slave or freedman running errands, or a middle-class gentleman on his way to the gym and the baths. Nobody would look twice at him in the streets. Is he, thinks Lucius incredulously, in disguise? Even thinking the words makes him feel silly. Aulus Terentius is a highly born man and is climbing his way up the ladder of a political career, he has served abroad and is practically guaranteed a consulship at some point in the not-too-distant future. Why on earth would he feel the need to follow him, Lucius, to Albinia's house – and dressed down for the occasion?

"It is about Marcus Primus, and I must talk with you, even though I don't think you can do anything about it," says Aulus.

"Aulus Terentius, you definitely have our full attention," says Albinia, and unusually for her, she pours herself a cup of wine. She has already passed a cup to Aulus and cocks an eyebrow at Lucius to see if he would like a top-up. He shakes his head. Aulus wants to talk.

"I think that Marcus Primus is being set up," says Aulus. "When I agreed to be his counsel for the defence, I did it because he is a good man and a friend, and he had a really good defence."

Lucius is interested.

"Primus did not have any intention of declaring war on that tribe of Odrysians. The governor before him, Crassus, had found them quite harmless, Thracian of course, so not what you'd call totally civilised, but clearly no threat. The tribe's traditional lands cross the borders of our province but that had not been a problem. So, when Primus was just about to set off, in the autumn two years ago, he did not think that there would be any issue. The order to invade the Odrysians came from the Palatine."

For a moment Lucius does not grasp what he means. Then it

becomes clear.

"Augustus?"

"That is the problem," says Aulus. "Not Augustus. The Princeps was, at that time in Spain, and ill. He had sent back Marcellus however, to marry Julia. The order came from Marcellus, who was, he claimed, conveying Augustus' instructions. But Primus and I are now not so sure about that."

Lucius is aghast. Marcellus! Marcellus, the Princeps beloved nephew and married to the Princeps' beloved daughter – and practically a boy still, never mind two years ago. "Why on earth did Primus listen to a boy like Marcellus?" he asks, incredulous.

"Let me say it again – Marcellus said he was giving Primus the direct instructions of Augustus himself. What would you have done?"

Lucius says nothing but thinks that he may well have found these instructions puzzling. Augustus is not known for provoking conflict outside of the empire boundaries.

"Yesterday, Primus and I had a meeting with the Princeps, a meeting, I might add, that we have been trying to hold ever since Primus asked me to conduct his defence. We have tried to keep Marcellus' interference under wraps so as not to cause embarrassment, but we genuinely thought this would all blow over once we explained it to Augustus. After Crassus made it clear that he was going to prosecute, we had to insist on seeing Augustus: and not only did he deny that he had given the instructions to Marcellus to convey to me, which we expected, he also denied that Marcellus had given Primus those orders, which we did not expect."

"Ah," says Albinia softly, her eyes widening. "How very… unfortunate. So, Primus now has no defence."

"What about Marcellus himself?" asks Lucius. "Was he at the meeting?"

"I'm told that Marcellus is unwell," says Aulus.

There is a silence.

"Primus has taken this very badly," says Aulus. "He kept his temper with difficulty yesterday and today he won't see me. His steward sent me a message to say that Primus was ill. I don't believe that of course, but I am very worried. On the way back from the Palatine meeting yesterday he was in shock almost. He is a very straightforward character himself, and he just cannot play politics. He is taking it all personally, thinks his honour has been slighted. I am mystified myself. I thought I was rather good at understanding how our leaders operate but I cannot fathom this at all. I honestly don't see what Augustus gains through denying this. And as far as I know the prosecution itself is not connected with the Princeps: Crassus is a boring old stick and hasn't the imagination to come up with anything that he hasn't read about in an account of what his ancestors did. I must admit that I assumed that Crassus just got a bee in his bonnet about the Odrysians being treated badly and thought it his duty as their unofficial patron to make a complaint on their behalf."

Lucius looks at Albinia, who says, "The Emperor's stepson, Tiberius Claudius, has been asked to help with the prosecution. Did you know that?"

Aulus looks startled, then worried, creasing his brow as he thinks through this. "I didn't know," he admits. "Why is he involved? Isn't he your quaestor, Lucius?"

"He says he was asked and wanted the experience of helping with a big trial." Lucius shrugs. "I believe him actually. He is a fairly straightforward character."

Aulus says bitterly, "His mother isn't."

"So, without the defence of being told to do it, Primus doesn't have a hope," says Lucius.

"There's is more to it than that even," says Albinia thoughtfully. "If Primus was given instructions by Marcellus, who was conveying them from Augustus, then Augustus was acting high-handedly in not telling the Senate. And if Marcellus gave those instructions and lied about them coming from Augustus then Marcellus has at the least embarrassed his uncle. Either way, the Princeps' family don't come out of this well. Aulus, I gather you do believe Primus? He isn't making this up for some reason?"

"I don't think he is lying at all," says Aulus. "I've known Primus for years and he doesn't lie. He isn't the sort of person who needs to lie. He sees everything very clearly; he doesn't do nuance. He was always useless at rhetoric when we were studying together in Rhodes. He frustrated old Apollodorus immensely saying that if everyone just told the truth, life would be a lot easier."

"So, if you can't call Augustus as your defence, or Marcellus, what will you do?" asks Lucius. "Will you tell the court what you have just told us and risk making Augustus very annoyed with you?"

Aulus looks at a loss. He makes a half shrug, half gesture of despair. "I don't have the first idea what to do," he admits. "I don't even know why I have told you, Lucius, except that I like you and you are a Consul, and you might know a bit about the law – I just thought maybe you could come up with something."

Lucius thinks about this and cannot see a way ahead that doesn't involve upsetting the Princeps. He says so. "But I will think about it. If Primus is the sort of man you say he is, then he is being used in some way and I don't like that. And if Augustus did not sanction this prosecution then it is all going to end up a mess and embarrassing for everyone."

"Is that what the prosecution wants?" asks Albinia. And they are silent again.

Aulus sighs. "I'm going to leave it for today," he announces. "I shall go to the baths and get some exercise in, then have an extremely fine dinner with my brother-in-law. Much wine will flow, and so we shall at least laugh a lot. Then tomorrow I shall start work on my defence speech. Gods help me!"

And with that he takes his farewell.

Albinia stays seated and thoughtful, while her brother does a little prowling.

"What is going on?" asks Lucius abruptly.

Albinia frowns.

"It could just be Crassus doing what he sees is his duty by his clients," she points out reasonably.

"No, because Augustus is involved. Something is going on," says Lucius furiously.

His sister gazes at him.

"Look at it logically," she says. "Firstly, it could be that Crassus is genuinely annoyed with Primus and is prosecuting him because he thinks that Primus has broken the law. Secondly, Crassus is prosecuting Primus to embarrass Augustus – he knows that Primus' defence will make Marcellus and therefore Augustus look bad. Thirdly, Crassus has been persuaded to prosecute Primus by someone else, who hopes that the whole thing will cause an outcry against Augustus' handling of the situation."

Lucius is out of his depth.

"What on earth did Marcellus think he was doing?" he says, shaking his head.

"Being a young idiot," says Albinia. "Being a spoilt, brattish, full-of-himself idiot. Just back from Spain, about to marry Julia, thinks this means he is marked for great things and starts to throw his weight about."

"But telling a provincial governor to start a war?" Lucius can only marvel.

"And lying about his uncle's instructions," says Albinia. "He must have been confident of his own judgment – and remember, Augustus has experienced several serious illnesses over the years. Marcellus was maybe trying out his own ideas because he genuinely thought he was about to become Princeps himself."

"Oh, good gods, the fool!" and Lucius is so angry he can barely speak. After a pause he says,

"I shall have to go and see Maecenas."

Chapter 16

Maecenas lives on the very top of the Esquiline Hill. Lucius
turns left out of Albinia's and heads for the main street leading
up the hill. He is so deep in thought he walks right past the wine
shop before he realises that it is shut up. A small piece of wood
is tacked to the door. "Closed – illness" it reads, and Lucius
wishes that this Primus business had not blown up now when
he has other things on his mind. He stands still and looks around
and listens – and smells. There is no sign that the horn-workers
are overwhelmed with business at the moment, in fact he cannot
see a single open door, cannot hear the noises of hammering or
chipping and certainly cannot smell the vile smells of the
burning horn. Gradually he realises that there is an odour, an
unpleasant one, but it comes from further away, and he thinks it
must be the fires burning well beyond the city, as the number of
funerals rises. The wind must be blowing from the east and with
that reminder in his nose, he looks out for signs of the pestilence
creeping its way through the city. Even out here on the
Esquiline, far from the slums of the Subura, the signs are there:
closed shops, fewer people in the street. His lictors have no
trouble making a path for him today.

As they walk up the hill, the air clears and the houses get
bigger, with walls blocking out the unpleasant side of life in
Rome: at the very top of the hill is Maecenas' mansion. He buys
up land and houses there whenever he can, and his estates
currently include, of all things, an old cemetery which he has
covered over and landscaped. Many people think that this is
courting bad luck, what with the ghosts and the unpleasantness
of finding bones in one's herbaceous borders, and others tell
tales of the opulence of this building project, but Lucius can

only approve of what he sees as he goes up a winding private road through lawns and charming sculptures and water features. The house is no town house like Lucius' own, but more like small country villa, built for comfort and style, and without the smells and dirt of a farm attached. Lucius realises that he himself is a traditionalist when it comes to houses: he has a house in Rome in the atrium style, and an estate in Cosa which is almost entirely designed around the needs of a large farm estate. The world inhabited by Maecenas is not his world. Lucius wonders where Maecenas' money comes from, then common sense comes to his rescue. Maecenas came up through society clinging to the hem of the Princeps' toga, and along the way there would have been opportunities galore. Especially as he was always on the winning side.

Lucius has sent a messenger ahead and knows that Maecenas will be in. And sure enough the most dauntingly elegant steward meets Lucius at the front door and glides ahead of him until they come to a tiny courtyard filled with large pots overflowing with flowers still, despite the autumn cool. A few small bronze statues peek through veils of fading greenery or stand gazing at the plants in petrified amazement. It is as if Lucius has stumbled into a miniature play but the actors have frozen in shock at his interruption.

On a large basket chair sits Maecenas, a small table at hand with a plate of honeyed dates on it, and a cup made of glass – who uses glass outside? – for his wine. He smiles as Lucius approaches and waves him over to a matching chair. It is packed with upholstery and Lucius squirms about trying to get comfortable until the steward assists him by removing three cushions. Nervously Lucius accepts a glass of wine and hopes to the gods he doesn't break it. Glass is very fashionable and expensive, and he never uses the stuff. Albinia once bought him two beautiful wineglasses which had made it all the way from

Alexandria and they stand on a shelf in the dining room, for decoration only. Melissa washes them on the Ides of every month, and Lucius is waiting for the day when disaster strikes. He holds his glass gingerly then gives up and asks for a pottery cup.

"I just cannot risk breaking this," he tells Maecenas. "I have a feeling that it is one of your favourite things or a family heirloom or given to you by your best friend."

"As a matter of fact, you are right – all except the heirloom part," says Maecenas. "Augustus gave me a set of six and they are exquisite. He found them in Cleopatra's palace, so they even have a notorious history. I tried to write a poem about them, but I just cannot write I'm afraid. I shall have to get Horace onto it. He has already written a very fine poem about Actium. Have you heard it?"

Lucius confesses that he doesn't really do poetry.

"Oh dear," says Maecenas. "And what does your clever sister have to say about that?"

"I listen to hers when she gives a reading over dinner," says Lucius. "I think they are good, but I am aware that I have no taste in these matters and besides, I am biased."

"Oh, don't worry," says Maecenas. "Your sister, from the few poems I have heard, is extremely talented. If she were a man, she would be giving Catullus and Virgil some competition. As will my Horace, I think, though the reception of his lovely Odes was disappointingly lukewarm. But I think Horace is one of those poets who last. He isn't just a fad of mine. He has an extraordinary gift for metre and sheer elegance."

"Yes, I can remember Albinia saying something similar when Horace published that load of poems earlier this year," says Lucius, sheer nerves making him crude.

After a careful wince at the word "load", Maecenas nods. "And did she also comment on the role of a poet in praising the regime?"

Maecenas is too sharp by half. Lucius has no intention of repeating what Albinia said on that subject ("It isn't even as though Horace is discreet about it. There are some startlingly toadying lines – I felt myself shuddering."). However, he decides to act as though Maecenas is teasing him, for the wine in his pottery cup is excellent. He leaves the dates alone though, as licking his fingers in front of Maecenas seems just a bit too much. And he has a serious issue to discuss.

"I need your advice," he begins.

"Oh, that does sound grim," says Maecenas. "Not anything to do with Marcus Primus, I hope?"

"Well, yes," says Lucius, managing not to sound surprised. What else would he climb the Esquiline Hill for? Maecenas' views on disease control? Actually, that might not be a bad idea, for Maecenas, one must keep reminding oneself, has a great deal of experience in managing the city.

"Before you say anything, my dear Lucius," says Maecenas gently, "let me just say this to you: don't get involved. Please."

"But I'm Consul and I have been asked for help," protests Lucius. "I have at least to investigate."

"No," says Maecenas firmly. "That is just what you don't have to do. Being Consul does not mean that you are everybody's patron."

Lucius rather thinks the opposite and says so and Maecenas sighs.

"My dear Lucius Sestius," he says. "The universal patron is Augustus, Princeps, leading man of the Republic. Let him deal with Marcus Primus."

"How can he?" asks Lucius. "There is going to be a trial and Primus is going to use Augustus as his justification for the war on the Odrysians. It will be public knowledge if it isn't already."

Maecenas looks at Lucius and asks, "What do you know of

Marcus Licinius Crassus, who is prosecuting Primus?"

Lucius knows a little – with a name like that, everyone will know a little about Marcus Licinius Crassus.

"He is the grandson of the Crassus who was very rich and was an ally of Julius Caesar. Oh, and he was Governor of Macedonia before Marcus Primus."

"He was a very successful military governor too," says Maecenas. "He bears the distinction of being one of the few Roman generals ever to kill his opponent in single combat. In that respect he is far more successful than his esteemed grandfather. He was awarded a well-deserved triumph for his achievements."

"To get a triumph, he must have gone beyond the borders of his province," points out Lucius. "So why is he prosecuting Marcus Primus for doing what he did himself?"

"You are looking at the wrong thing, Lucius Sestius," says Maecenas. Lucius replays Maecenas' last speech.

"The triumph?" he asks.

"Indeed," confirms Maecenas. "To a man like Crassus, being awarded a triumph is important. Think about it, Lucius – Crassus' grandfather was killed in a spectacularly badly orchestrated campaign in Parthia. We – Rome – lost three legionary Eagle standards and thousands of men. It was one of the worst disasters in Roman history. Crassus has brought much-needed respect back to his family by his actions in Macedonia, and a triumph will confirm that."

Lucius understands that. He is Roman, after all.

"So you have done a deal with him – you are going to sign off the expedition beyond borders because Marcus Crassus deserves a triumph, and in return he is going to prosecute Primus for you. But why do you need to prosecute Marcus Primus?"

Maecenas sighs. "I am not going to explain that to you,

Lucius."

Lucius feels the explosion of frustration build up inside him, and Maecenas casts his eyes up to the heavens and says, "Really, Sestius, do you honestly imagine that we can let any old governor attack any old tribe on a whim?"

Lucius is staggered. Does Maecenas not know about Marcellus? Then he comes to his senses: of course Maecenas knows.

"Well, what about Marcellus? What will happen when Primus calls Marcellus into court as witness?"

Maecenas' smooth diplomat face is dropped, and he looks troubled. "Marcellus is too ill at the moment to worry about such things."

Lucius is surprised. "Marcellus is really ill? I thought that it wasn't that serious?"

"Marcellus has been sent down to Baiae, but he is dying," says Maecenas. "Even Antonius Musa, the doctor who saved Augustus, is having no success."

Lucius can't think of a reply. That lively, charming young man he met at dinner an age ago – dying. Even if the boy was foolish two years ago, he does not deserve that.

At last he finds a voice. "How dreadful for his family," he murmurs.

"Indeed," says Maecenas. "I'm sure you can understand that the trial of Marcus Primus is low in priority to Augustus at the moment, and he has left its handling to me." He leans towards Lucius. "On the other hand, your work to deal with epidemics in the city really strikes a note with everyone who matters. Stick to that work, Lucius Sestius. You can do real good on a big scale."

"The hospital on Tiber Island is asking for more space and more money," says Lucius, recognising an opportunity to change the subject when one is thrust in front of him. "And we need more food coming into the city. Grain prices are being pushed up."

"Why don't you use the Saepta Julia?" suggests Maecenas. "The Princeps will approve, I am sure, and it isn't as though we need a voting space at the moment. You could set up a temporary hospital there and make it a food distribution point. Young Tiberius is knowledgeable about the grain supply, and I suspect a word with the chandlers will help with prices."

Lucius immediately sees the possibilities here and unexpectedly a list of his consular concerns comes pouring out. Maecenas is sympathetic and has some good ideas. When Lucius mentions reports of heavy rain and warnings of the Tiber rising, Maecenas recommends that he should employ the specialist engineers used by Agrippa in his building schemes: Agrippa of course built sewers and aqueducts and his men know about water. They are currently scattered throughout the city on various projects, but with Augustus' blessing could be temporarily regrouped.

Lucius only remembers Primus when he is halfway down the drive and stops, realising that he was side-tracked and never got back onto this important subject – and he wonders if he should go back. A little more thought tells him that there is no point. Maecenas has made things clear. Instead Lucius goes straight to Calpurnius Piso's house to discuss using the Saepta Julia as an emergency centre.

Chapter 17

After a quick consultation by messenger with Augustus the two Consuls call a gathering of all magistrates and the Princeps, to be held in the Temple of Apollo on the Palatine, rather than in the low-lying Forum which is already showing signs of elevated water levels. On the last day of October Lucius chairs a meeting in which the Saepta Julia is turned over to him to use for crisis management. Extra funds are made available for the hospital on Tiber Island, and for the aediles so that they can employ more workers to maintain the supply of clean water – despite Herophilus' doubts, Lucius thinks this is important – and to prevent the Tiber from overflowing by making some temporary banks in vulnerable areas. Lucius and Piso point out that in the event of a serious flood the Saepta Julia will almost certainly be affected so it is decided that the temples on the Aventine will become temporary grain stores: the Aventine tends to be unaffected by floods, and is the nearest high ground to the docks where the grain-barges unload. With the exception of the Capitoline three to Jupiter, Juno and Minerva, all other major temples on hills will clear out their storerooms ready to help if needed. Travel into and out of the city will be restricted to those with approved duties such as doctors and state messengers. At the end of this meeting Augustus announces that he will be making another grain distribution to the poorest citizens out of his own pocket and a sycophantic murmur of appreciation goes round the Temple. A particularly ambitious aedile jumps up to point out that this will be the tenth such handout given by the Princeps this year, and Lucius strains all the muscles in his face in an attempt to keep his disgust from showing. He swiftly breaks up the meeting. There is a lot to do.

On the Kalends of November Piso takes over the role of Consul in charge, but the two of them spend the month working more or less side by side. Dinner parties are few and far between and the Consuls refuse all invitations as it is not the time to be seen to be indulging. Workers on the various state building schemes are diverted from their usual tasks to put up wooden shelters in the Saepta Julia, and doctors are paid to man these shelters so that those suffering from the pestilence can go for treatment. State-owned slaves assist here, as well as moving vast quantities of grain around the city, and the bakers are given a bonus to keep open and producing bread at a reasonable price. Lucius and Piso have an eye-opening and disturbing meeting with the guild of undertakers and funeral directors: as a result of which, a special squad of state slaves is loaned to the guild to manage the evening collection of bodies from the poorer areas of town and the digging of large pits at the cemetery beyond the Esquiline Hill. Lucius remembers the smell of the fires on the day that he visited Maecenas, and suggests burning the diseased bodies but the funeral directors tell him quite firmly that the pits will be cheaper and quicker.

Lucius walks round the city every day checking on supplies and hospitals alike and wonders whether he will go down with this disease: the gods are clearly on his side though. Or all this walking up and down hills is keeping him fit. He is certainly eating less, but Albinia thinks he is drinking too much. He doesn't care. Going to bed with a muzzy head is now part of his regime and he feels that it helps him forget whatever dreams he may have. Albinia doesn't nag. She has moved in with him as the pestilence made its way up the slopes of the northern hills, and her faithful staff followed her, squeezing into the upstairs quarters. On top of the Caelian Hill, his little street shivers but stays safe. The slums of the Subura are resilient but have their share of tragedy, and the public slaves wheel full carts across the city every evening.

The news from the Bay of Naples isn't good either. Young Marcellus lingers on tended by Antonius Musa, but halfway through November the city is plunged into despair when the death of their golden boy is announced. No official mourning is needed: in this, the dreariest month of the year, the rains fall and the puddles on the Campus Martius turn into small lakes and the usual fevers of winter weaken a pestilence-ravaged population. Queues for grain handouts are the only sign of life Lucius sees as he grimly tramps around the seven hills. The doctor to the rich and famous, Antonius Musa, having failed with Marcellus, offers his services freely to the Temple of Aesculapius, and himself succumbs to the illness. As he hears this, Lucius is saddened but struck by the hardihood of the doctors of Rome. Very few of them leave the city, even though they are one of the few groups allowed in and out: instead, their bravery keeps them moving around the city and risking a miserable death. Lucius has never met a doctor who is actually Roman, and he is full of admiration that this small band of foreigners – Greek, Jewish and Egyptian – displays the determination and courage of a Roman hero of old. Of course, his law has awarded them with freedom from taxes, but he doesn't think that alone explains it. One of the priests of Aesculapius tells him that it is all down to an oath that they have sworn, and Lucius thinks that it must be a powerful oath.

Marcellus' funeral is ten days before the end of November. Lucius hears the stories of the extravagant grieving that has accompanied the journey of Marcellus' ashes all the way along the Appian Way, and while he can understand that the death of a promising youngster is a tragedy, he feels slightly uncomfortable. There is something terribly unRoman about letting go like this. Like everyone else in the city, however, he risks the crowds and stands at the side of the road, unshaven, and with his shabbiest toga on to mark the final entrance of Marcellus into the city. No lictors today. He doesn't feel it is right. The women cry, and the men stand silent, and a small procession of volunteer Senators takes up the litter holding the little urn and carry it through the city. He is moved when he sees that the Princeps' sister Octavia is there, walking behind her son's ashes, with her daughters on either side of her. She is pale but tearless: Augustus' sister has played her part in her brother's plans for many years and she isn't going to deviate from the role of model Roman matron now. Lucius bows his head in admiration as she walks past. He may have many reservations about Augustus and the way he runs Rome, but at this moment, all he feels is the grief. Once the sombre procession has passed, Lucius cuts through the side streets, and arrives in the Forum in time to take up his official place with Piso and a large group of Senators on top of the Speakers' Platform. Another procession makes it way down from the Palatine: Augustus and Livia and Julia, all dressed in black, are leading the family, the household freedmen and slaves down from the complex on top of the hill, and they meet the funeral procession in the middle of the Forum. The two cavalcades do not stop but merge, and as they pass in front of the Rostra, Lucius and Piso fall in behind. The Senate follows, and then the mass of the people, thousands of men and women, risking pestilence to pay their respects.

The final stage of the journey is poignant for they are headed for the Mausoleum which Augustus has built for himself: Marcellus will be the first person laid to rest there. That huge round tomb should be filled with the older generation, nobles who have had long years of service to Rome behind them, revered ladies who head up lines of children and grandchildren, the generations stretching away. Instead its first inhabitant is a boy of nineteen, leaving a wife even younger, leaving his mother, sisters, uncle, cousins. The pestilence has produced many such scenes, but this is on a grander scale, for Marcellus, as now is clear, was Augustus' heir. The murmuring will start soon, Lucius knows, for nobody knows what Augustus thinks he is bequeathing. An empire? A monarchy? Is everything gained by Augustus with hard work, years of fighting and hard-won personal authority just to be handed on to a chosen heir, first Agrippa, then Marcellus, now what – back to Agrippa again? Lucius knows the answer: how else did Augustus get his power but through being the heir of Julius Caesar? Rome, however, is not yet ready for this to be made so clear, and Marcellus, by dying, has lit a niggling flame of suspicion.

As the family of Augustus withdraw from the tomb, the crowd parts to let them through and then goes off in various directions – most though retrace their steps into Rome, back down the Flaminian Way and through the Fontinalis Gate. Piso peels off here with a muttered farewell, and Lucius moves on to take a familiar route; Forum, Sacred Way, Caelian Hill, feeling naked without the escort of his lictors. He is just leaving the Forum when someone falls into step beside him and says, "Can we go somewhere and talk?"

It is Aulus Terentius.

They find a wine-shop open – there are few of these at the moment and Lucius wonders at the confidence of the owner. It is a long time since he has visited a wine-shop and he looks around as Aulus has a knowledgeable sounding conversation with the man at the bar. There is evidence of hard times: the list of available wines is short, no food is offered and only the barman is on duty, understandable as he and Aulus are the only customers in evidence. Lucius stands by and doesn't interfere and is relieved when Aulus chooses a nice inexpensive wine made barely thirty miles away down in the Alban Hills. Good everyday drinking. The wine is delivered with the usual jug of water and after some hurried shouting from the barman, some rather tangy pastries filled with spinach and nuts appear. Lucius suddenly feels hungry and has to restrain himself. He carefully takes one pastry and nibbles at it while Aulus does the pouring and mixing. Lucius knows that the conversation will be about Marcus Primus and Augustus, but is not surprised when Aulus begins the discussion with a question:

"What did you think of all that then?" He sounds serious and Lucius knows what the problem is.

"Augustus needs a new successor?" he says trying to keep it light. As soon as he sees Aulus' face he knows he has not managed.

"It's the sheer, bloody, in-your face arrogance of it all," Aulus speaks through gritted teeth but with great emphasis. His face is lined with anger, and no longer do charming curves make him look young and slightly sweet. Lucius stays silent and fiddles awkwardly with his wine-cup. He looks up to find Aulus staring at him.

"I can't believe that it doesn't get to you as well!" says Aulus in frustration. "You fought with Brutus and Cassius, the last time anyone stood up for the Republic, and you were there in the thick of it. You must have believed in it!"

"Of course I did," says Lucius wearily. "And I still do. But government is not static. It must change, and Rome changed because we found it impossible to keep the Republican system going. You saw the crowds out there at the funeral. They aren't going to care that Augustus is developing his family and friends into an oligarchy. Go on – go outside and tell them what an oligarchy is then ask them if we should go back to the old Republic, the one we had pre-Caesar."

"Oligarchy – where a few people will perpetuate the idea of the Republic while keeping all meaningful power in the hands of their own group." Aulus sounds angrily cynical.

"Yes, I know," says Lucius. "And who, I ask again, cares?"

FIONA FORSYTH

"Of course people care!" Aulus' voice rises again, and he takes a breath and continues quietly. "The one thing Rome cannot tolerate is a king – you know that, everyone knows that. Caesar died because that is what he was aiming for."

"And what did that result in?" asks Lucius quietly. He is having difficulty keeping calm but knows that he really doesn't want to get emotional. He has spent years keeping all this tamped down. And he has no intention of letting himself get involved in any protests. Aulus is silent and looks slightly sulky, and Lucius keeps the inner sigh off his face as he gives the longest speech he has made for some days.

"The Republic is now dead. It is no longer fit for purpose. The Senate killed it off. We let the Empire get too big, we were unable to adapt to meet the changing needs of our provinces and we were greedy and self-serving. How many handouts of grain has Augustus given this year? Ten? Eleven? He is obliged to because the grain supply is unwieldy, there have been bad harvests, there is corruption in the chain, floods have regularly affected the city and so has illness. We have farms run by slaves and we watch free men struggle for work. We have taught them to wait for help from the state and then we complain that it is a drain on the state. We overlook bribery, we don't make proper provision for tackling fires and floods, and we have allowed our armies to give allegiance to their generals rather than to Rome. We have either connived in this for years and years or been so ignorant that we deserve what has happened. So – at the moment, we need Augustus. What in the name of all the good gods do you think will happen if the Senate and People of Rome try to run themselves? Are noble, self-denying Senators going to rise up from the sewers? Will the men of Rome's slums volunteer for the army in their thousands? Will we appoint tax-collectors who don't cream off the top twenty per cent for themselves?" He stops. Aulus looks thunderous and Lucius knows that he will just get into a pointless and dangerous argument if he carries on.

Aulus starts his reply in a growl of contempt. "What I have just witnessed is the funeral of the heir. The heir! The Roman Republic is now something to be handed down from unworthy father to feckless son. What is the point of elections? What is the point of the ladder of offices? The top office is no longer available. We are asking the sons of our great families to spend years of their lives serving so that they can reach second-best. We are actually telling them that the prize is no longer worth the effort."

"No," says Lucius. "We are showing them that it was never worth the effort, because so many of us in the past couldn't be bothered to put in the effort. We let our sons down, we have been letting them down for more than a hundred years and we have created a situation which we can't unravel. So now our sons must find a way to live with that. And they will."

Aulus stares and abruptly stands up, making his wooden stool grate loudly across the floor. Lucius says quickly,

"How is Marcus Primus?"

"Resigned," says Aulus bitterly. "But he is still going to fight this. Even though he knows he will lose. Thank you for asking."

He turns with military smartness and walks out of the wine-shop, and Lucius feels contemptible. He wanders around the Forum for a bit but needs company and goes to see Marcus. Marcus takes one look and says, "You need a bath." And shouts for the water to be heated.

Bathing at Marcus' involves wine of course and it turns out that this is just what Lucius needs. He doesn't recount his conversation with Aulus, and Marcus doesn't ask. They relax and gently steam and drink wine then water then wine again. They don't talk. Marcus offers dinner and Lucius refuses politely. Instead, Marcus gives him the choice of a bed, a litter-ride home or a walk with suitable escort. Lucius chooses to walk and remembers nothing about the journey home, and indeed there is nothing to remember: Rome is quiet in the wake of Marcellus' funeral, and they meet few people amid the carts rumbling on their rounds to collect the newly-dead. Marcus goes along for the exercise and keeps a curious and sympathetic eye on his friend. He recognises the signs of disillusion and silently wishes Lucius good luck. At the house, Marcus delivers Lucius into the tender care of his household and Decius puts him to bed: needless to say, Lucius will not remember that either. Peace reigns for a short night on the Caelian Hill.

Chapter 18

When the Lady Albinia comes down to breakfast the next morning, she is informed that her brother the Consul is still in bed. The slaves think that he might be a touch unwell, and Albinia frowns and goes to see Decius.

She finds him in the study. He takes one look at her and clears the clutter currently heaped up on the reading couch. Albinia arranges herself carefully on the couch, but does not recline, and Decius realises that she is on the warpath.

"I have just had a message from Marcus Tullius Cicero, and he is worried about Lucius," she says. "Apparently, Lucius came round last night, didn't say a word, got drunk, and left."

"Yes," says Decius, carefully allowing no intonation into the word.

"Come on, Decius!" Albinia is as near to angry as she ever gets. "What is going on?"

"He went to Marcellus' funeral yesterday," says Decius.

Albinia is about to answer and stops herself to think instead. In her mind she tots up the stresses and strains of the last few months and as she realises what her brother is going through, she almost relaxes. She can see it.

"We must make sure to get him away from Rome as soon as possible," she says at last, and looks up as Decius sighs noisily.

"He has been asked to stay on and supervise the temporary measures for a little longer, while the new Consuls get their feet under the table, so to speak." Decius knows that this is not going to be well-received.

"Oh for— why can't that idiotic pair shift for themselves?"

"The Consuls for next year are very distinguished," says Decius, "but they do not have experience with this sort of administration."

"And don't want it," says Albinia, and actually snorts. Decius finds his lips twitching.

"Well, when can we drag him away then?" asks Albinia, turning to Decius as so many of the family have done for forty years.

"The end of January," says Decius. "We can work on him. And it helps that Calpurnius Piso is determined to leave office promptly and has refused to stay on."

"Very well," says Albinia and stands to go. "I think we had better wait until dinner tonight, Decius, before we get to work on him. And thank you."

She is still upset, and her determined whirling of her draperies as she strides out of the study makes this clear. Decius smiles after her and thinks that he will give Lucius a couple more hours before trying to wake him. The Consul deserves a day off.

Lucius comes to and only needs a bucket or so of water before feeling much better than he deserves. Another trip to the baths and some light reading in his study and he is ready for dinner with his sister and Decius, and Marcus who arrives completely unannounced.

Lucius can feel the three of them keeping a very close eye on him and to be honest finds that well-watered wine is all he needs tonight. After all, there will be some sort of inquisition from his sister, he can feel it, and looking at Marcus, he is certain that he did or said something rash last night. He gives in, and as a distraction tells them about his encounter with Aulus Terentius.

Decius shifts a little, and Marcus whistles. Albinia just stares at him.

"Why tell you?" she asks.

"Tell me what?" says Lucius. "He didn't tell me anything. He asked questions."

"What did he want of you?" Decius asks.

"I don't know."

"I do," says Albinia. "He wants your support. He is defending Marcus Primus and he wants you, the ex-Consul in the courtroom, sitting and agreeing. Fortunately, you gave such a lukewarm response that he didn't actually ask for it."

"There is more to it though, isn't there?" says Marcus. "He wants you to agree with him, about Augustus and the Republic."

There is a silence.

"Well, clearly, I'm not going to do that," says Lucius. "Not being a complete fool."

"Why did he come to you in the first place then?" asks Albinia. "Why not Piso?"

"Maybe he has approached Piso," says Decius.

"NO!" says Lucius. "I am not even talking about this, I'm not – I'm not…"

"Aren't you?" asks Marcus. "Aren't you tired of doing all the work to watch Augustus take the credit? Doesn't it bother you that nobody feels they can even argue with him any more or suggest an alternative? Does it really not upset you that up until a few weeks ago, Marcellus was being trained to take over from Augustus?"

"Honestly?" asks Lucius, looking straight at him. "No."

"Then why did your meeting with Aulus upset you so much?" asks Marcus. "You came straight to me. Not Piso – not Albinia. Me. You have a very small circle of people you really trust, Lucius, and any one of us would have understood your frustration, the tension you feel at serving the man who has destroyed your dream. Why me?"

Lucius cannot bear to say it

"It is because I am my father's son," says Marcus. "Despite everything he did, my father was a solid Republican. He died because he upheld the Republic. To you, I am a final last

145

Republican fling. Oh, and you know I have a good cellar and a tolerance for smelly old drunks."

Lucius has to smile. "You made me bathe first. I can't have been that smelly," he points out.

"Don't worry, you did not smell," admits Marcus. "But am I right about the rest?"

"Yes," says Albinia. "You are. Lucius betrays the Republic every day of his life and sometimes it gets to him. You were just what he needed. I see that, really I do, Lucius. But I am worried that you will feel obliged to get involved somehow with Aulus and whatever it is he plans. We all know that there is more to this than a prosecution of a governor for malpractice. Either someone is testing Augustus, or Augustus is testing us. Look – Marcus Primus' defence is going to be that Augustus, through Marcellus, told him to do something. Augustus will deny it. Then Primus will be found guilty. He will be exiled. And everyone will wonder if Augustus is covering up his nephew's mistake or genuinely made a mistake himself in giving Primus secret orders that didn't work."

Decius clears his throat. "I can see your point about there being someone who wants to test Augustus, but the other way around? Is Augustus really prepared to go to these lengths to see how much he can get away with?"

Marcus says, "Maybe Augustus actually genuinely wanted Primus to stir up the Odrysians?"

"In that case," says Decius, "I would like to know why. What does Augustus gain from such a move? Does he really want a bit more land to tag onto Macedonia?"

"I have to say I can't think of any reason there," Marcus says. "I've never heard any good of Macedonia."

Albinia says, her forehead furrowed, "It must have been Marcellus then. It must be just as Primus claims. That stupid boy! What was the point?"

"I don't see the point of any of this," says Lucius, loudly. He gains their attention. "I won't join with Aulus in whatever he plans to do, I promise. The trial is clearly going to be a complete disaster, and I want to go to the farm anyway, everyone knows I am off to Cosa as soon as I can get away. I shall miss the trial. You and Marcus can keep me up to date, Albinia. Unless you want to come to Cosa with me? It would be nice to be together with Tia, the three of us. It's been ages since we were there, all together."

Albinia smiles and shakes her head. "I'm staying in Rome despite everything. Though if the pestilence returns, I might take you up on the offer. Is the news still positive from the doctors? Do they think it is over for now?"

"Not quite over, though they are being more optimistic. But there have been many deaths and families have lost wage-earners, so there will be enough for the new Consuls to deal with. And the Tiber may still rise, of course. Flooding could be a big problem in the new year. And there are definitely going to be problems with the grain supply."

"I can't remember a time when there wasn't a problem with the grain supply," says Marcus.

During the last days of November, the rain slackens off but there are reports of heavy waters coming down from the mountains and everyone knows what that means – Rome is a city built on marshes in the curve of a large river and floods are common. The Tiber floods, on average, every four-to five years, with the last major occurrence being over thirty years ago in the consulship of Appius Claudius Pulcher and Lucius Domitius Ahenobarbus. Everyone remembers this flood, because not only was the Forum completely under water, the Circus Maximus was too. The tops of Rome's hills were crowded for days until the waters went down and the mess afterwards was incredible: the dead bodies of animals and people lay slumped in the pools

147

of standing water and pathetic drifts of ruined possessions clogged the streets. And throughout that winter, weakened buildings collapsed with no warning, their foundations of poor materials giving way months after the water had receded. There had been an outcry. There was always an outcry. Lucius remembers his father going on a quiet visit to the family's tile and brick factory and checking that procedures were being adhered to: for many people blamed the poor quality of brick and wood and concrete used in building the towers of apartments which were most hit by the flood.

Lucius and Piso know that effectively nothing has happened to improve this: every now and then a virtuous senator passes a law to improve conditions and it lasts as long as the inspection department can be bothered. Bribery is rampant in the sector which runs the city planners and builders. With a groan, the two Consuls decide that they really do have enough to do as a priority and earmark it as an urgent issue for the Senate and next year's Consuls. Augustus agrees and authorises Marcus Agrippa's engineers to look at the state of the riverbank as a matter of urgency: that is the most they can do for the moment. Piso sends his bailiff on a tour of his own city properties: like many of the Senate, he owns blocks of apartments across the city, and usually leaves them to be managed by a middleman. He orders bricks and tiles from the Sestius family factory and Lucius hopes to all the gods that Decius has kept his eye on standards over the years. On a dull but dry day, the Consuls stand and watch as the little collection of huts under the Fabrician Bridge are swamped by the river, and some of the poorest people in Rome are made homeless. There will be mutterings amongst the middle classes as the petty crime rate goes up: but by spring, thinks Lucius bleakly, many of these Tiber-rats will be dead, with a new set of the desperately poor setting up home under the bridge.

In the last days of the year, the numbers which are handed in from the Tiber Island and the various makeshift hospitals add up to some cautious good news: fewer patients are arriving, and those do not appear to be suffering from the pestilence, though a bout of breathing-related complaints are undoubtedly the last vicious flick of the whip as the illness retreats from Rome. The pestilence has left a huge mark though: the population has been weakened by ten thousand people, according to the undertakers' figures, well up on the number they would expect for the autumn of a normal year. Despite all this, there is a sense of the worst being over and the temples are busy with sacrifices of thanksgiving. Augustus' extra grain handouts have kept the poor going – and some of the less poor as well.

December's weather, after the seemingly endless November of rain, is chilly but dry. The city cautiously enjoys a breathing-space and Saturnalia comes and goes without incident, though the celebrations are muted and bring to mind those who have been lost. Lucius hands out money and disappears into his study for the day while his slaves and freedmen enjoy what the blighted city can offer. He has many reports to read for the Consuls have no real respite: the Tiber is riding high, and the waters start to spread beyond the usual low-lying areas. Lucius wonders if the gods are determined to blight every day until the end of his consulship. Augustus has started to mention expense rather a lot but nobody can see any other way but spending a lot of money: grain handouts, work to repair the Tiber embankments, relief for those affected by illness, the cost of the manpower required... There is no end yet. Still, the lawyers are kept in business as people contest the wills of the departed, and floods always bring cases of disputed property as boundaries are washed out.

Just after Saturnalia, the Consuls are enjoying a small and welcome dinner at the house of Maecenas, far above floodplains and blessedly free from illness. Lucius and his lictors walk as usual, despite the puddles and small streams running along many roads, and he secretly hopes that Terentia will be there because it would be nice to have someone who thought he was wonderful sitting next to him. And surely, she wouldn't behave too outrageously with her husband present? But Maecenas solves that particular issue by making it a small ensemble and only men – the Consuls are joined by the Princeps and young Tiberius. The dinner is held early to respect the Princeps' preference and the weary Consuls appreciate this, enjoying excellent cooking and wines and thinking with satisfaction of a decent and long night's sleep. They have reached the nuts and fruit when a slave glides in and whispers into Maecenas' ear. A small, weary smile crosses Maecenas' face as he gives a theatrical sigh and spreads his hands in apology to his guests.

"It was indeed too much to think I could give all of you a pleasant and untroubled evening – I'm afraid there is a gentleman from the temporary engineer brigade who has an urgent message for the Consuls. Shall I invite him in? Or would you rather see him in private?"

"Oh no, let's get him in here – we shall no doubt have to know eventually," says the Princeps easily. He has done very little but deal with crises for twenty years, after all.

The most senior engineer has come in person. Marcus Vitruvius Cordo, ex-army and as hard as an ancient walnut, marches into the dining room to bring a final piece of bad news: the Sublician Bridge will not last into the new year. The Sublician, stretching across the Tiber just below Tiber Island, is so old that its origins are back in the time of myths and heroes. Every child is taught the story of the time when the legendary hero Horatius kept back barbarian hordes on the simple wooden bridge, single-handedly of course.

Lucius' reverie on times of greatness past is interrupted by the Princeps leaning back and saying, "Not again! Really, don't you think it is time we built it in stone?"

The engineer advises that when the waters go down the city can rebuild the bridge in stone, but for now the old bridge must be abandoned.

"About time too," says Maecenas. "It was last destroyed the year before Actium, and we were too busy to insist on the rebuilding being in stone. I think we shall have a chance of persuading the fuddy-duddies now – twice in under a decade is too much."

And so, in a cold but brilliant dawn at the very end of December, the Consuls head up a flotilla of small boats which cross the flooded Forum Boarium, and climb the embankment to keep watch as the Sublician Bridge creaks and gasps. The bridge has been closed off for several days, so there is no threat to life: everyone has come because this marks the end of a piece of their own history. The Sublician Bridge was built when Rome still had kings, and has survived five hundred years, admittedly not without major repairs and at least two complete rebuilds, according to the wildly excited old senator standing next to Lucius. The old man is nearly the same age as Lucius' father would be, and for a moment Lucius thinks of how thrilling his father would find all this too. Then he has to listen patiently as the senator repeats what everyone has been saying for days – this is the bridge that was made entirely from wood, always repaired with wood, renovated many times of course, and there is an old religious ritual that has to be performed every time. By the Consuls, funnily enough, not a priest. Yes, thinks Lucius, and so we thought that as the bridge was about to be swept away completely, the Consuls had better be here as well. The last time he was here, it was the festival of the Argei, when straw dummies are thrown into the Tiber off the Sublician Bridge. As with so many of the city's religious traditions, nobody knows the origin of this strange ceremony, but everyone suspects that it reflects an ancient human sacrifice to the river. Father Tiber is sometimes too demanding. Lucius turns to look upstream towards Tiber Island, which from here looks like a massive marble ship dominating the river. The rays of the sun rising behind him catch on every stone line and corner, and the blue sky and pale yellow light frame the scene so that it seems like one of those landscape wall-paintings that are all the rage now – until he looks down at the river. The old senator next to him is forgotten, for the Tiber's force is like nothing he has ever experienced, and it is exhilarating. With the city wall and the Three-Way Gate at their backs, he and his colleagues stand on the newly renovated embankment which has shored up the Tiber's most dangerous curve for over a hundred years. Everyone is gazing upstream as the waters break around Tiber Island and then thunder under the Aemilian Bridge. The Aemilian's ugly but sensible stone feet dig into the water and keep solidly still, and the river churns on and vents his frustration on the stone embankment where Lucius stands well back to avoid the spray. The embankment is unaffected and with a howl the river lurches away and races on downstream. As the enthralled audience turns to keep watching the muddy yellow, foaming waters, they see the little wooden Sublician Bridge taking the force and the marvel is that it hasn't been swept away before now. The stream divides, merges, divides again and all it will take is that one chance-led funnelling of waters against one frail pier. Lucius and his colleagues wait for that moment, and groan with the bridge as the pier in the centre of the bridge snaps. The first few timbers fall so slowly, then hit the river and are whipped away out of sight and the broken bridge shivers. The river senses the imminent capitulation, and as the bridge bows down to meet the water, a whirling current smashes into it. The river has no mercy and within seconds nothing remains of the Sublician Bridge. Where will Rome's heroes make their stand now? The river roars on triumphant and Lucius turns and makes his way side by side with Calpurnius Piso to the little temple of Portunus – for the Tiber has no temple – where they will sacrifice to Father Tiber and lead the city's prayers for the waters to recede. But Lucius senses that the real sacrifice has just been made – Rome has given her ancient wooden bridge and all its associated traditions to the river and when the Sublician is rebuilt it will be in stone.

Chapter 19

The flood and the rising of the river have left standing pools of water on the Campus Martius and Forum Boarium, and Lucius worries about this leading to more health problems. The Chief Priest of Aesculapius agrees, and yet another job is lined up for the city engineers – draining the low-lying areas which are not being handled by the main sewers. The last job in Lucius' unexpectedly burdensome consulship is signed off.

On the first of January, Lucius accompanies the new Consuls up the Capitoline Hill to witness the sacrifice to Jupiter that starts their term in office. Inwardly, he feels a huge weight drop from his shoulders, even though he has agreed to stay on for a few weeks to keep an eye on the city's provision for the disease and flood crisis. Piso has had enough of Rome and makes very sure that he will not be called on for additional duties of this kind: the restrictions on travel are lifted at the start of the year and Piso retires with Popilia down to his villa down on the Bay of Naples. Tia and the children are invited to go and stay with them but decide to go back to Cosa. As soon as the weather improves Piso will make a leisurely tour of Italy, producing a report on the state of the roads, and then he considers his duty done. He doesn't want the tedium of ruling a province abroad, nor the glory of a potential war. "I shall leave that to people who trust Augustus," he says drily, and Lucius knows that Piso is thinking of Marcus Primus. That trial is due to start at the end of January, and Lucius has not seen Aulus Terentius since the funeral of Marcellus. If any gossip is circulating about the trial Lucius is careful to shut his ears.

After one meeting with the new Consuls – two men of such incompetence and arrogance that Lucius actually feels angry –

he decides that he really cannot stay in Rome for much longer. He feels more and more that he has done his part, is not needed any more and cannot bear the atmosphere of dour wretchedness. The death rate remains at a steady winter high, even though the worst of the pestilence has passed, and food shortages are grinding everyone down still further. There is enough to eat as the grain supply is running smoothly but fresh produce is very expensive and regular panicky rumours about some vital ingredient running out – oil once, more often some spice or other – lead to some unpleasant scenes as crowds gather at the shops and warehouses. He continues his regular walks and checks up on supplies, hospitals, flood levels, resenting the new Consuls' casual assumption that he will see to all this with little thanks or acknowledgment. Lucius does not see the Princeps though Tiberius visits a couple of times and once accompanies Lucius on his rounds: he tells Lucius of the scene back on the Palatine Hill – Augustus still in mourning for Marcellus and spending all day every day working to make up for the Consuls' deficiencies.

"He goes to bed exhausted every night, and spends the days complaining of the cold and damp," says the young man, and Lucius detects the merest hint of contempt in Tiberius' voice.

The Campus Martius gives up on any effort to keep the floods at bay, and as the puddles grow to lakes, Lucius organises the removal of the emergency centres up onto the Quirinal Hill, using the temples of Jupiter Victor, Quirinus and Flora. It smells a lot better on the slopes, and Lucius can even pretend that fresh breezes occasionally stir the dull grey air. He imagines the winds coming into the city straight from Cosa, but he can't go back there just yet. He makes his farewells: to Augustus via a polite note, to Marcus Cicero with the best dinner he can provide in these times of emergency and shortages.

Several days before the Kalends of February, he leaves

Rome, leaving Albinia in charge of the house on the Caelian. Only Decius accompanies Lucius and Horace as they make their way to Horace's famous farm in the hills outside Tibur. They meet up at the Esquiline Gate, and together walk out of the city. Just after the road to Tibur branches off in a determined swing to the north-east, they find the bustling complex of shops, a small tavern and the stables where they will hire horses.

"Time for breakfast?" asks Lucius, aware of the journey ahead.

"And lunch in Tibur," says Horace with a grin. "Don't worry, we shan't starve on this trip."

Bread and olive oil and well-watered wine is all that is on offer for breakfast, as the horses are made ready and Lucius pays for an arrangement which includes his return to Rome courtesy of a sister stable in Tibur. Even in winter the road to Tibur is busy, as wealthy Romans make use of their weekend estates around Tibur and so providing transport is a lucrative, year-round affair.

The journey is a smooth one. The tombs on either side of the road peter out quickly and they are soon into farmland, the smallholdings producing fresh fruit and vegetables for the markets in spring, summer and autumn. Even now in winter, they pass a few carts trundling towards the city, and there are people out in the crisp air, digging over the soil and tying plants and trees to stakes. The first cabbages and fennel are being picked, and Horace promises to introduce Lucius to a special treat for dinner one night – cabbage leaves cooked in pig fat. It is a greener countryside than his own vineyard at Cosa and Lucius enjoys the ride, relishing each mile which takes him away from the heaviness of Rome's atmosphere.

Tibur is a wealthy and slightly snobby little town, well aware of its distinguished visitors, and anxious to provide those classy touches which will appeal to high-born tastes. Horace informs

Lucius that there is a butcher in town who calls his shop "a meat emporium". At the inn, they are welcomed by a smooth and slightly damp manager who knows Horace and waves them through to "The Gourmet Room". Lucius is relieved when an excellent meal of sausage and fennel is produced and some decent wine, and the horses are rested – though to be honest this isn't the sort of journey where the horses are going to be pushed. After leaving Tibur, Horace takes a track leading north and they start climbing into the hills. When they reach the villa, it is dark: Horace has timed this journey well, as he should of course. He comes here at least once a month and spent most of October and November away from Rome, coming back only for Marcellus' funeral.

Horace is given a welcome fit for Odysseus at the end of the Odyssey by an extremely respectable pair of retainers, a couple who have worked for Horace for ten years, after being freed by a friend in Tibur. The villa is bigger than Lucius' house at the Cosa farm, and Horace is so proud of it he is comical, but it is clear that he knows he is being over the top and doesn't care. And even in January, Lucius can appreciate the enclosed garden with its own fishpond, the bath-suite, and the elegantly decorated rooms. To the surprise of nobody, Horace has a decent collection of wine too, and an impressive library. Lucius looks forward to days of doing nothing in particular.

The Sabine Farm turns out to be just what was needed – Lucius gets up when he feels like it and spends large amounts of the day reading. He misses his wanderings around the city, and there is the danger that he will get flabby again, so he usually manages a walk every day in the afternoon, sometimes with Decius or Horace, and sometimes on his own. He strolls down to the tiny village which lies on the track down to Tibur, but there is not even a wine-shop, so he doesn't stop. Hills give him no trouble, despite the wet weather, and he doesn't mind being caught out in the rain occasionally. It is a clean rain which smells of green countryside and earth, and not the foul all-pervading dankness of the city. Dinner is always simple and leisurely and accompanied by good conversation and superior wine.

One evening, Horace says something which sits uncomfortably: they are discussing family. Both Horace and Lucius had good relationships with amiable fathers, and Horace says sadly that he wishes he had children.

"Why do you never mention your children?" he says suddenly, fixing his eyes on Lucius. "Whenever I ask after them, they are away with friends or relatives or at Cosa. Do you never miss them?"

For a moment, Lucius can feel Decius looking at him, waiting for his answer. He can't brush this off as usual, for some reason.

"I don't miss them," he says. "I like them, but I'm not sure what they mean to me."

There is a silence, as two men who will probably never have children look at him, and do not understand.

Horace makes a little grimace, no more than a twist of the lips. "And there was I thinking how lucky you were," he observes, "and wondering why you didn't feel lucky. Did you feel the same about your wife?"

Lucius thinks about this and sees that Horace has asked a clever question. "Yes," he admits. "I married Caecilia because she was my friend's sister and I felt obliged. He was murdered and I felt responsible for her. And she was a perfectly nice girl, but I never loved her. I never felt I could talk, really talk with her. I feel slightly guilty that I no longer miss her, but it has been several years. I was fond of her, but mainly I am glad I had the opportunity to honour my friend. I always made sure that Caecilia was treated with respect and honour."

There was more of course. He had enjoyed her pregnancies

and their cosy evenings discussing the baby, patting her swelling belly, and watching the skin leap and twitch as the life inside kicked its impatience. He feels strangely relieved that she had not died in childbirth, for that would have been a waste and his fault. Dying of the autumn illness was beyond his reach. He feels no guilt there. He treated her more than well, and she had repaid him with an undemanding friendship and two children. He wonders what really loving a woman is like and asks Horace.

"It's fun," says Horace. And then drily, "You should try it sometime."

"I've seen Augustus look at Livia and – I don't know, to have to give in to that longing, it seems so… unpredictable. So unexpected in a man as cool as Augustus, son of a god and leader of the known world."

And while Livia is beautiful and intelligent, she is as scary as Hades. Lucius has met dangerous men in his time, and she is as heartless as any of them. In fact, she and Julius Caesar would have got on very well – or until, inevitably, Caesar tried to seduce her. Livia Drusilla does not appreciate attempts at seduction, he is perfectly certain about that. He does not say any of this out loud. Horace is looking at him, as though trying to puzzle him out.

"You live in your head too much," he says unexpectedly. "Try real living and see what happens." He points at Lucius suddenly. "There! That look on your face – you aren't going to reply directly to me, you are going to mull it over in your head then say something to take the conversation away from yourself." Lucius sees a smile on Decius' face, and in his turn points at Decius.

"Don't you grin! You are the master at keeping your feelings hidden!"

"Ah but that is part of the job," says Decius easily. "Slaves don't show feelings and freedmen find it hard to lose the habit."

"You could marry if you wanted to," says Horace.

"No, I couldn't," says Decius. "I love above my station. I worship from afar. Maybe I should write a poem about it."

Horace grins and toasts him. "Do we know your lady's name?"

"I'm keeping her a secret," says Decius, ever so slightly primly, and Lucius and Horace laugh.

"And what about you, Horace?" asks Lucius. "Albinia tells me that many of your Odes are about love, so who is your Muse?"

"Oh, so many women!" cries Horace, and subsiding nods at Decius. "Many of them out of my grasp too, my friend. But I enjoy the company of the girl who helps out when I am in residence. She is a very lovely person, and I pay her well. Her family down in the village are happy with the arrangement, and one day she will be able to marry with a decent dowry and get a good man who won't question her past. I won't use slaves like that, never that. I only want a woman who is happy with the arrangement. Otherwise, where is the fun? As I keep telling you, Lucius, I like women. I'm not sure you do. Oh…" and he holds up a hand as if Lucius had already started an objection, "… yes, I know you are perfectly good to your staff, and you have a good relationship with your sisters, yes, yes, yes, all that, but – the fact remains that you will not allow yourself to fall in love. Why? I don't think you prefer men – do you?"

Lucius is feeling very uncomfortable by now, but Decius comes to his rescue.

"Too far, Horace," he says quietly. "Some people cannot just formulate and discuss their feelings as you can."

"Oh, my dear fellow, I am so sorry!" cries Horace. "No, no, no, of course not! We shall talk about wine and when you are going to invite me up to Cosa."

And the conversation lurches unsteadily away from such

delicate subjects. Lucius locks it all away in the corner of his mind, and as usual tells himself that one day he will figure out this side to himself. He is fairly sure he doesn't prefer men though and hopes that the slave-girls he takes to bed have no cause for complaint. He certainly tips them well, he thinks. And with that, he decidedly joins in a conversation about tending vines.

Chapter 20

On the next day's walk, he is joined by Decius, and wonders if he can ever ask him who it is that he meant last night, this woman he worships from afar. Lucius knows that his sisters think him strangely lacking in curiosity anyway, but even if he were curious, he does not feel comfortable speculating too much about Decius' love life. Ever since he can remember, Decius has been there, dependable, and intelligent and kind. Even when freed, Decius had remained with the family.

They climb the ridge and pause at the top to look down over the valley and Decius says, "Back in Rome, Marcus Primus' trial will be starting."

Lucius thinks of that pleasant-faced man of action, the born military commander he met once in the Forum. He hopes that things go as quickly and easily as possible for him. "He'll get exile," he mutters, almost to himself, though Decius hears him and sighs.

"Yes. But I'd love to know what was going on there. A strange affair."

"Marcus Cicero will send us the news," says Lucius. "I asked him to let us know."

"Were you tempted to help Primus?" asks Decius.

Lucius shakes his head. "You know I would not go near that case once I realised that he was going to rely on Augustus for his justification."

"But did you believe him?"

"Oh yes," says Lucius. "Primus has no reason to lie and even Aulus Terentius doesn't get that angry over nothing. But defying Augustus, calling him a liar? That is going to destroy careers, and the Odrysians are not worth it."

"Somehow," muses Decius, "I don't think that Aulus Terentius is doing this for the Odrysians."

Lucius looks at him. "What about the motivation behind the prosecution? All that scheming that Albinia is convinced is going on – do you believe that?"

"No," says Decius. "That was all too complicated for me. I think that this prosecution is going ahead because Marcus Crassus wants Augustus to notice him. Crassus has been Consul and general and wants more and is too stupid to realise that actually he has reached the end of his career. Nobody who isn't personally groomed by Augustus and Agrippa and Maecenas will achieve anything of any note now. They will make sure of that."

***

Marcus Tullius Cicero sends greetings to his friend Lucius Sestius Quirinalis

Well, the trial of poor old Marcus Primus has been and gone and you will be unsurprised to discover that he is heading off into exile as I write. Didn't have a chance, though I must say I was impressed with Aulus Terentius who really did put up a fight as Primus' defence. It was almost fun for a bit. Right, from the beginning.

Weather's been appalling and it seemed quite appropriately miserable that we heard the case to the sound of rain drumming on the roof of the Basilica Julia. The preliminaries were over quite smartly, with a pair of genuine Odrysians providing some entertainment as Crassus paraded them around the basilica. They didn't look in much need of our help, I must say, tough buggers if ever I saw any. Anyway, the crucial bit came in Aulus' speech on the second day. The defence rested, as expected, on the plea that Primus was acting under Augustus' orders but then Aulus Terentius unleashed his surprise. I am pretty sure that only a few people knew about his charge against

Marcellus, and there were eyebrows raised all round at the thought of a seasoned general like Primus being summoned to the Palatine to be told what to do by a teenager barely scraping the bumfluff off his chin. People were cautious though – nobody wanted to be seen to believe it too easily. I heard a couple of mutters that it was quite clever, as we can't call Marcellus to confirm or deny, but then Augustus played a blinder. He hadn't been summoned of course, but at that exact point he came marching into the law court demanding that he be allowed to speak. Cheeky, I thought, but then who is going to refuse him? So, he is invited to speak by the judge and flatly refutes Primus' story. Aulus Terentius jumps up and shouts "What are you doing here? Who summoned you?" to which Augustus retorts "The good of Rome summoned me, as always," and the crowd all clap like idiots. Well, there was then a brilliant moment where I genuinely though Aulus Terentius was going to deck Augustus, but alas, he restrained himself and the Princeps left the court in a self-righteous glow.

The interesting thing was that the jury was not unanimous – so some people seem to have believed Primus' defence! Don't know what the Princeps will make of that, but it's as good as them saying that he himself lied in court, isn't it, so I imagine he isn't pleased. Anyway, Primus is trotting obediently off to the east – not Macedonia, ha ha – and if on his way he makes use of some of my villas, who's to know or care? Poor chap, I really liked him, and could have sworn that there wasn't a wrong thought in his head. But there you are, someone wanted him disgraced. And if he isn't very careful, Aulus Terentius is going to go the same way. I hope someone has a word with him soon. He has been flouncing tragically all round the city, denouncing the iniquity of it all. You would have thought that his sister or Maecenas would have got hold of him and told him to pull himself together.

But the trial has not done Augustus many favours really. The hint that young Marcellus may have felt confident enough to issue a provincial governor with orders which he said were from Augustus himself has people gossiping, despite the fact that we all stood in the streets weeping at the young man's death a couple of months ago. Nothing a Roman loves more than a gossip. But I'm tired of it all, Lucius. We are at this place in history because we couldn't rule ourselves effectively as a republic. No use carping at Augustus now.

In other news, the Tiber has started rising again and the sewers must be almost full because we are having an absolute plague of rats at the moment. Thank all the gods you and Piso managed to put something useful in place last year, but we aren't anywhere near clear of disaster yet. Yesterday a thunderbolt hit the new temple, the Pantheon. Which statue? Augustus', of course, and even better, the spear in the hand of the statue, so that the stone cracked and the spear fell to the ground, just missing a couple of children, I heard. So Augustus' power has broken in one way at least.

Written at Rome, on the Ides of February in the consulship of two of the most useless clods of earth imaginable, Marcus Claudius Marcellus and Lucius Arruntius.

***

This letter is read out loud over a late and leisurely breakfast and holds no surprises. However sorry Lucius feels for Marcus Primus, he was lost from the moment Nameless and Faceless Senator stood up in the Senate and questioned that attack on the Odrysians – or from the moment that Primus was gullible enough to think that his orders came from Augustus. Lucius shakes his head at the thought that Rome might have just lost a useful general down to the idiot ambitions of a boy. He looks up at Decius and Horace and says rather soberly, "To be honest, irritating though the Primus affair is, I'm more concerned by the

165

news about the flooding. That means more disease, and shortage of food. I really think that at this point we need to get the household out of Rome and up to Cosa. And persuade Albinia to shift as well. She can come to Cosa, and squash in with us, or go to her own place near Pompeii."

"She can come here if she wants," says Horace. "I can guarantee a very quiet life and we have room for her staff I'm sure."

Lucius wonders if this is quite proper, but knows that if Albinia decides to take up the offer, nothing he can say will move her. And she is nearly fifty, so it is quite ridiculous to worry about her and Horace. He hopes. Horace watches him, and chuckles.

"You are thinking again, Lucius Sestius," he teases. "Let me see – you were wondering whether it was quite right for your sister to shack up with a low-born philanderer like me. Am I right?"

"You are way too free with my thoughts," says Lucius and throws an olive which pleasingly hits Horace on the chin.

"Children, stop teasing each other," says Decius, but there is lightness about his face that has just settled there. Decius is happy to go to Cosa, it seems. His mystery woman maybe? She is taking shape in Lucius' suspicious head. He just hopes it isn't Marcella, the wife of the vineyard manager, Titus. That might prove awkward. He finds that he has missed what Horace is saying and apologises.

"Thinking again," says Horace with a sigh and shake of his head. "I was asking if you wanted to get started tomorrow – go back to Rome and sort out your affairs, and then travel to Cosa. If so, I might come back with you and just take a sniff at what is happening. I need to see Maecenas soon anyway, and he can put me up for a couple of nights I'm sure."

"Don't you have a place of your own in Rome?" asks Lucius

surprised. He has always assumed... Why didn't he know?

"No, I stay with Maecenas," says Horace. "Otherwise his mansion would only be half used most of the time. I have a nice little suite which he keeps for me. Pet poet, and all that."

He sounds a little bitter, a most unHoratian moment, and all Lucius has to do is raise his eyebrows. Horace sighs dramatically.

"It's your fault, Lucius Sestius. Your brand of thinking is a disease, clearly, and now I've caught it. As we move further and further from the Republic, I'm finding that I need to write about it. I have praised Augustus for what he has achieved and that is fine but – now I feel the gap where my freedom used to be and I want to mourn it, just a little. But I don't want to rock the boat because I'm so comfortable here and I'm lazy." He tries a smile, but it doesn't work, and he carries on. "There are so many good things to come out of what Augustus has done and I don't mean to deny them at all. And I know that I owe Maecenas everything I have, and I cannot deny that this results in an obligation. But surely, I can grieve for what I am losing at the same time? You see, I have an idea, a plan for my next set of poems, and I must write them. But I shan't publish them unless I can get the balance exactly right. Oh, bother you, Lucius! This is all down to you. Always worrying, always wanting to be a Republican, but unable to find your way back. It's rubbing off on me!"

He jumps up from the breakfast table and says abruptly, "Take no notice of me, I just need a walk and a think." And with that he is off, and they hear him calling for his hat and cloak. Decius blows out a sudden surprised puff of air.

"I did not expect that," he observes.

"Me neither," confesses Lucius "Some interesting poetry coming up, I think..."

"I have never seen a poet being inspired before," says Decius solemnly.

Lucius grins. "Actually, if you think about Albinia, you never see her mid-inspiration, do you? Her poetry appears at a dinner party, and otherwise she hardly ever talks about it or what inspires her."

"Really?" says Decius in surprise. "You honestly don't know what inspires your own sister?"

"No, she is a very – well, her life is like a bookcase. She keeps everything labelled and in its place. And the compartment for me is not even next to the compartment for her poetry."

"It might be if you ever showed a moment's interest in it," says Decius. His tone is not sharp, it is not a reproof, just an observation. But Lucius suddenly feels abashed.

"I don't – you're right. I never show any interest in her poetry, not really. And yet she and Tia are the most important people in my life," he says wonderingly.

Decius sighs. "Yes, and they do know that, but only because they pay so much attention to you. They wouldn't guess it from your attitude towards them. Your sisters are so intelligent and funny and loving, and you don't notice." Now Decius sounds annoyed, and Lucius is struck by this. Something important is being said. "You've never even had a conversation with either of them about why they don't marry, have you? Do you actually know?"

Lucius is definitely on the back foot now. "They would tell me if they wanted to," he begins.

"No. No, they wouldn't. And lucky for you, neither of them can get married, so that lets you off the hook."

"I don't understand," says Lucius and tries to sound less whining than he feels.

"Albinia is still mourning her husband, dead nearly twenty years now. She can't get over that. She has written no love poetry since he died – or none that she has shown to anyone. She would love to have had children and seeing yours is actually painful for her though she cares for them of course. And Tia has been in love for years, but she can't marry the man, so she doesn't talk about it."

"Tia?" Lucius is bewildered. "Well, I thought she was just…well…"

"Yes? Just? Just what?" says Decius. "Or do you really mean "I have never thought about Tia, in the same way that I don't think about anyone too much because I am so careful not to let myself care." Is that what you mean – master?"

This is shocking: Lucius cannot remember the last time Decius called him "Master". In fact, he has not sure that Decius has ever actually addressed him as such before. It is all wrong and he feels angry and slightly queasy. Something has been said that should enlighten him, but he has missed it, and it was important.

"What is this all about?" he asks. "I have upset you, I see that, and I – I would never knowingly upset you. But I don't know what is going on."

Decius is silent for a while and then says "I'm sorry too. But really I do think that you could take a more active interest in the lives of your family."

Lucius knows this is true. But he doesn't know how to go about it.

Horace returns in time for a bath before dinner, in an excited and affable mood.

"I think I have it," he announces, as he wallows in the warm water. "It is all about the place of liberty in our society now. What are we free to do? To be good citizens? To serve in the army? To make an honest living? All these of course. But what is different now, is that we have freedom from civil war, from political tension – and so freedom to think about life and what it means, to be philosophers. I'm going to write about my new freedom."

"No more wine and women?" asks Lucius.

There will always be wine and women, and beautiful young men, and dancing and song…" says Horace dreamily. "But I shall let the younger poets deal with all that. Propertius, Tibullus – they can swoon and sigh and be frustrated and camp out on the beloved's doorstep and kiss the ground he or she treads. I'm too old for all that."

"You're about my age," points out Lucius.

"My point exactly," says Horace. "You gave up on all that so long ago you're practically shrivelled up."

"The bath water is getting cold," says Lucius quickly, and Horace smirks.

"Your heart, Lucius Sestius!" he cries. "Your heart is cold and hard and shrivelled. It isn't a heart at all, it has turned into a walnut. An old, pickled walnut which nobody will ever try to crack open."

Much splashing then ensues, and Decius makes no attempt to join in, thoughtfully towelling himself dry and padding off back to the house. He has supervised the packing, but wants to check, and has no desire to get drawn into an argument about Lucius' heart. He does not know why Horace has chosen this visit to needle Lucius about his emotional dryness but finds it interesting to watch. He even found himself joining in, hence his own unusual bout of honesty at breakfast. He finishes the last-minute arrangements, and as the afternoon draws to a close, Decius takes a walk around the February garden, and finds it cold but lovely still. They will come back here, he is sure. And Horace is sensitive enough to make sure that Decius gets an invitation in his own right.

Chapter 21

Back in Rome, Albinia is immediately intrigued at the thought of escaping into the hills to write with Horace, and it is so clearly writing in which she is interested that Lucius feels relieved. He loses none of his slight scepticism about Horace's new interest in philosophy though. He leaves Albinia sending messages to the poet, who is, as he said, staying with Maecenas on the Esquiline Hill. That evening she comes to dinner with him, and announces that she will set out for the Sabine farm in two days, with Horace letting her enjoy the peace on her own for a while before he leaves Rome and joins her. She has also brought a letter for Tia and presents for the children, books of course. Lucius is giving himself just a day in Rome before setting off for the coast. He will take just Decius and they will sail up to Cosa. A couple of the slaves will bring Melissa and the rest of the household and a wagon up via the roads and it will take them much longer. The roads will be dreadful after the long and wet winter.

And so the next morning, which is cold, rainy and miserable, Lucius and Decius head down to Rome's port, Ostia, and spend the afternoon warming up again in the city baths, and an interesting evening in the common room of their tavern as they wait for their ship to sail. Decius cannot help letting slip that this is the Lucius Sestius who was Consul last year and brought in all those wonderful ideas about grain supply, health care and flood control which all but saved the city... An embarrassed Lucius tries to correct these claims but the crowd at the inn are having none of it and he is plied with drinks and questioned until he can barely speak. Of course, what most people want to know is "What is the Princeps really like?" and Lucius is quick to realise that he cannot praise Augustus highly enough. He finds it fascinating that the people in the inn reduce the complexity of ruling an Empire to a set of gut feelings: there are too many slaves and foreigners, wages aren't high enough and nobody wants another civil war. Well, unless, Augustus tells them that it is necessary of course. Looking round the audience, Lucius reckons a good third of the people present are foreigners, but presumably these are the right sort of foreigners, ship's captains, merchants, and other people who pay harbour taxes and spend money. Several other men may well be slaves, but do not draw attention to this of course. Lucius does quite enjoy being praised for his work as Consul, and as he leaves the inn, he overhears the landlord saying "Now that you see is typical of the kind of person Augustus gets working for him, not too proud to have a drink…"

Lucius Sestius, man of the people, boards the coast-hugger that will take him to Cosa, and sleeps like a baby in a corner rigged up with a canvas awning. He does not notice the boat slip away just before dawn.

A day later, they spot the tiny island offshore which is the first landmark that tells them they are really close to Cosa: it is at this point that every ship's captain gives the order to start in towards the shore, for the waters and reefs around the island form a ragged skirt of green and must be avoided. The land has always been in sight, but now the mountains begin to stand out from that thin strip of sort-of-grey, and gradually the shore seeps up until you can see lines of dull sandiness and green. Cosa itself is invisible at first, huddling inside the cliffs, and its grey stones emerge slowly until the rocky little promontory is topped with a small crown of walls and towers. As they creep along the wrinkled cliffs on their left, the shore ahead looks smoother and smoother, layering itself up to the foothills in the distance, while Cosa peers down and shrugs her rocky shoulders.

As the ship lands him at the harbour, it is the most beautiful morning, chilly, a little damp but with a silvery sunlight which makes everything sparkle. The town itself, perched on the white cliffs, looks completely out of reach. Cosa was built for defence and its walls still rear up impressively, but Lucius knows that it is a town on the wane. For two hundred years his family have lived in Cosa, and invested in its port and fishery, and he still has a large stake in a factory making amphorae: but the town itself is no longer a military town, and the wealth lies in the hands of himself and two or three citizens who have bought up large tracts of land to the east. They are building villas there, and grow vines and make wine, just as Lucius does on his family estate. There is still one important industrial complex just inland from the harbour: an inner lagoon holds the fish which are turned into sauce in a workshop which lies between the lagoon and the amphora pottery. This ensures that fish sauce from Cosa makes its way all over the Empire and has done for a hundred years: but Ostia, Rome's port, is growing and beginning to monopolize the import of goods to Rome. Soon all of Cosa's produce, oil and fish sauce and maybe even wine, will set off on a mere day's journey to be delivered into the hands of the big boys in Ostia. Lucius knows that he will still make money from his investments, but he won't have the satisfaction of being a direct supplier to towns as far away as Gaul. The Ostia giants will bargain hard and demand quantity rather than quality, smaller producers will fail, and Lucius' profits will shrink. The town of Cosa itself on top of the hill is already physically separate from the sources of its wealth and gradually it will dwindle as all attention focuses on the large farms and the harbour. Lucius does not need to go near the town to reach his home, heading off to the east and the hills. He hops over the Aurelian Road and quickly strikes the track leading up to the villa.

The path is wide enough for two carts to pass each other and lies between a small grove of olive trees and a row of dusty cypresses. Ahead he can see the first little tower in his rather fancy wall. There was a time when that wall, surrounding the villa and the farm buildings was useful, but now it is a remnant and of no practical value at all. Cosa and its surroundings do not come under attack any more, though some of the townspeople still remember the pirates who attacked in the year after Lucius was born. These pirates didn't do too much damage, finding the trek up to the hilltop town with its thick walls rather daunting, and after discovering that Cosa was in the process of churning out amphoras of fish sauce at that time of year, went on to more lucrative opportunities. Fish sauce has a smell that in itself is a powerful deterrent. But up here on the beginnings of the slopes which surround the area, there are only the smells of new green growth and wet soil, and Lucius breathes in the air of forest and stone and thinks for some reason of Rome. Surely he isn't missing the city already?

As he approaches the gate, the slave on duty notices him, springs up and dashes back to the house. The welcome is familiar: Lucius can hear the calls, as Tia shouts for the children, and he is heartened by a clear "Hooray!" from Celi.

"Nice to be home and welcome, eh?" says Decius beside him, grinning hugely. Several dogs, originally guard dogs but so spoiled by the children as to be useless, rush up and demand attention, closely followed by Celi, Publius (who walks rather than runs with a look of almost painful dignity on his face) and Tia. Last of all comes Publius' puppy Argos, who is practically grown now, but like his owner is of a philosophical turn of mind and makes his way everywhere by going from smell to smell, each smell requiring consideration. Eventually, he will arrive at the gate, look around and discover that everyone has gone indoors. And this is the dog Publius has chosen to train to hunt wild boar.

The farm celebrates the return of the master by the heating up of the bath water, followed by an early dinner, and Lucius goes to bed clean, fed and happy.

When Lucius gets up the next morning, he wraps up because he knows that first thing, Titus will be expecting the master of the farm to come and inspect the vines. This is an important part of the Sestius family fortunes and Lucius knows his duty. He leaves the villa and strikes off towards the cluster of buildings which lie beyond the kitchen garden. Slave quarters, storage barns and the wine press lie in an impressive block of practical brick and tile, but tucked behind these is a small and impeccably-maintained cottage, one storey high and with its own regimented patch of herbs and vegetables growing unabashedly in front of the door in a south-facing garden. Lucius knows enough to go to the back door and when he ambles into the kitchen, he finds Titus sitting at the big, scrubbed table with an air of expectation. A loaf of bread is in front of him, along with a dish of honey and another of olive oil, and Titus' wife, Marcella, stirs something on the range.

Everybody nods at everybody else: Titus and his family are freeborn, have lived in Cosa for generations and don't go in for bowing and scraping. The farm and its well-being are the most important thing in their lives, and no matter who owns it, the vines are theirs. Titus' father worked on the farm for nearly fifty years before he died, and Titus is training up his own teenage sons to take over from him. Lucius greets Marcella, enquires after the sons ("They need to knuckle down a bit more") and knows better than sit down: he grabs a hunk of bread and dips it in the oil.

"Come on," says Titus and together they leave the cottage and walk around the back of the farm where the straight lines of trellised vines march down the slope towards them.

As they approach the vines resolve into individual plants, their arms intertwined to the end of each row. Brown earth forms paths between each row, but again this breaks up into colours and lines, clods of earth in an irregular mosaic, with little clumps of grasses dotted through the miniature hillocks. Out of this tiny landscape grow the vines like huge trees overshadowing everything else. And then they are at the first row and the scale shifts and the vines are no taller than him. Titus leads off straight to a trailing arm which he carefully lays along the trellis and ties up with a long blade of grass. Lucius can hear him muttering about checking the whole lot himself if he has to, and he is off down the row, prowling, pouncing on each vine that displeases him. Leaves are briskly scattered on the ground and as Lucius follows the air becomes filled with a scent of torn greenery, a clean scent that makes you want to rub your skin with the leaves. And right at the far edge of the scent is a sharp sweetness, barely there, but promising much.

"I want to try a new vine," says Titus, over his shoulder as he coaxes a tiny cluster of the leaves.

"Oh?"

"First on its own, then, if it works, try a cross," says Titus.

"Where will you get them from?" asks Lucius.

"A friend on the Alban Hills, near Fregellae. He has some crosses with a Falernian, no less, been working on them for years and reckons they are ready to move north now. He's charging their worth, mind. And there's the cost of getting them here. A wagonload from Fregellae is going to set you back a bit. But If you can see your way…"

"What are the chances of them failing?" asks Lucius.

"Pretty low, I'd say," says Titus, wrinkling his nose and gazing south towards the Aurelian Road, as if watching out for the wagon from Fregellae. "He's already done the hard work by grafting the Falernian, so they are used to the soil not being as rich as down south. We have good land here; we know it produces decent vines already. The soil isn't brilliant, but it does drain."

There is a silence. Titus waits patiently, staring towards the south and Lucius looks at his marching ranks of vines and imagines one more row with that promise of Falernian magic.

"I like the idea," he says at last. "Put down some figures for me and I shall think about it."

Titus nods and the two of them continue down the row, turn and work their way up the next. Titus no longer does any of the real work himself, but Lucius can see him taking notes and storing up a list of instructions for the boys. Later on that day, there will be some serious knuckling down.

Several days later, the Rome staff and the wagon arrive, and the noise level on the farm increases considerably. Melissa joins the house staff seamlessly and the male slaves help out on the farm, thus making it the easiest spring anyone can remember. Sergius takes the opportunity to tidy up the outbuildings: the female slaves embark on a complete wardrobe refit for anyone who comes near. The children enjoy a new curriculum, and to Publius' huge delight, Decius gives him some lessons in philosophy and rhetoric, which leaves the tutor free to concentrate on Celi's knowledge of world literature. She is not mightily impressed by this as he insists that she polish up her Greek: she finds the Odyssey fun though and regales the family at dinner time with her own slant on Odysseus' adventures. She is highly critical of Odysseus himself, finding him sly, deceitful and selfish.

"And nowhere near as brave as a hero should be, really," she explains earnestly while her brother sighs.

When asked who her favourite character is, Celi goes immediately for the wicked enchantress Circe, though she is annoyed that the character fell in love with Odysseus quite so easily.

Lucius himself finds time weighs on his hands, though he gets out onto the farm quite a lot as a replacement for his walks around the hills of Rome. Titus won't let him near either the delicate stuff, requiring knowledge of vines, nor the dirty stuff, unsuitable for the master of the house. This leaves Lucius with riding, driving the cart when allowed and not much else. For the first time in his life, he finds he has time to devote to writing letters. His mild curiosity about how Rome is faring in his absence is assuaged by gloomy missives from Marcus Cicero, while Albinia and Horace send witty two-handers from Tibur: as he reads these Lucius can almost see the two of them falling over themselves with glee at their own cleverness.

The evenings are spent very comfortably after dinner with long discussions about the farm, the vines, the future of wine in Gaul (Titus is a bit dubious) and whether they should give olives a serious go. And every morning Lucius can look over the rows of regimented vines marching up the slopes above the Aurelian Road and dream of making a fortune when the new stock from the south produces the wine to end all wines. Life is good, and he allows himself to slow down.

***

Letter from Albinia to her brother, Lucius Sestius Quirinalis, written on the third day of March, in the consulship of Marcus Claudius Marcellus and Lucius Arruntius.

Well, I hope you are getting better weather than we are! For the first week I was here it was pretty good, but Horace brought the rain – a remark which he would like me to point out is most unfair as the rain comes from the east and he came from the west. And there you have our life together. I'm living with an irritating younger brother all over again. There are some perks though – he really does have an excellent wine list, and

UNLIKE SOME, he does not say "Uh?" when I introduce any subject more intellectual than drainage. And we have been working and the atmosphere for writing is perfect! He is going in a new direction at the moment, and already his confidence is riding high. We threw together a little philosophical jewel for you by the way...

Lucius, you are the true judge of my musings –

What am I now to say about you being in Cosa?

That you're crafting a wine, something to blow all my scribblings out of the water?

Or are you slipping silent through green woodlands,

Pondering that which is worthy of your wisdom and virtue?

You aren't just flesh, you have a heart –

and the gods gave you looks, and wealth and the ability to enjoy life.

What more could a doting nurse wish for her sweet chick? –

You have wisdom, the power to say what one feels,

health, a way of life you can enjoy and afford.

And still you live between hope and worry, between fear and anger –

so treat every day's dawning with the conviction that it will be your last.

An hour one did not hope for is welcome – and when you need a smile,

come and visit me!

I'm sleek and shining and looked after – a pig from a philosopher's herd.

I hope you recognise yourself. He said that the line about you having a heart was especially important. We are currently working on a poem for Maecenas to keep him sweet while Horace stays away from the city. I don't think Maecenas will need much soothing though, rumour has it that everyone who can is leaving. The pestilence is back. And the really bad news is that it is also in the Bay of Naples area – all those rich fat cats going to their villas for the winter have taken the disease with them, and it sounds grim. We are staying put here for now but I'm thinking that we are still too near Rome. What is the situation up in Cosa?

***

Lucius does not like the sound of that – are people really worrying about where to go in Italy to escape the pestilence? He looks for Decius to tell him, but cannot find him, and has to wait until dinner. No news has reached the farm about pestilence in the Cosa area, but Lucius decides to go into town the next day.

On horseback, Cosa is a few minutes down the track, and so Lucius and Decius set off at a leisurely pace the next morning in a fine drizzle which requires a couple of Titus' wet-weather all-over cloaks. Lucius thinks they look like two large anthills on horseback as they make their way down the track. Progress is slow: Lucius' mount is the inappropriately-named Alexander, an all-purpose nag whose ambition is to stand still for the rest of his days. By the time they get to town, Lucius has had enough and decides that his research should begin in the nearest wine-shop, while Decius, rolling his eyes, trudges off to run errands for the household.

Lucius of course knows all the wine-shops in Cosa, as he supplies them with a small amount of each year's harvest, no matter how enticing the demands of his other markets. Local business should be respected, he thinks, even as he watches Cosa quietly sink into oblivion. Maybe years in the future young Publius will have to take the decision to pull out of Cosa altogether, but Lucius will not give up on the little town yet. And so when he walks into the Tavern at the Gate, its owner Aponius brings over a jug of wine and some bread and olives straight away, and settles down for a proper analysis of local news, while the kitchen-boy runs out into the rain to see to the horses. Aponius has lived in the area all his life and started work at the tavern for his uncle when he was a teenager. He took over when arthritis persuaded his uncle to retire and there is nothing about Cosa that uncle and nephew between them do not know. The most important thing is that there have been no obvious cases of the pestilence like that rampaging through Rome, but then, very few visitors at this time of the year, so who knows? And, talking of which, there was a small group of Romans staying at the villa of the Domitius family.

"Why is that news?" asks Lucius idly, eating one of Aponius' olives and wondering for the hundredth time whether or not he should really expand into olives on the farm.

Aponius hefts one elbow up onto the table and holds out a hand so that he can mark off all the reasons on stubby fingers.

"One, the owner of the villa is not with them, two, there are only four of them, three, one is definitely top-drawer and four, they have told the housekeeper not to tell anyone they are there."

"Well, that was stupid," says Lucius, his mind whirring away at olive trees.

"Well, yes and no, because the housekeeper hasn't told anyone. Her husband on the other hand comes into town every third day and gets pissed at that table over there and tells anyone who will listen everything about his incredibly boring life. Including the pain of four more horses to look after even though they are very nice horses."

"They didn't come by sea?"

Aponius raises an eyebrow and sighs. "No, Lucius Sestius, they did not come by sea. Which, if they came from Rome, is another strange thing, because I can't think of any reason you would actually want to take several days over a journey which could take you one day, and at this time of the year. Not very good at this whole being mysterious without anyone noticing,

181

are they?"

"So, what are the theories?" asks Lucius beginning to get interested.

"Got to be running away from something, right?" says Aponius grinning. "Take your pick of: they've seduced the Princeps' daughter, they just managed the most daring robbery in the history of the city, or they are being prosecuted for patricide."

"All of them?"

"No, only one is a real toff, says Felix – Felix being the housekeeper's husband."

"Who doesn't like horses," says Lucius.

"Who doesn't like work," agrees Aponius. "He reckons the others are protection. A couple of slaves, big ones, and an ex-soldier."

"Why have they stopped here?" asks Lucius. "Sounds as if they should be ploughing on if it is that serious."

"Well, you have two options there," says Aponius. "Either they are lying low and waiting for updates from Rome, or they are totally innocent, and the housekeeper's husband is a pile of horse-dung."

"You are very bored here in Cosa, aren't you?" asks Lucius.

"You are not wrong there," says Aponius. And they clink cups and take a drink.

And Lucius suddenly has an intuition. He knows someone who is probably not welcome in Rome just now, someone who might feel the need to get away quietly. He mentions the gossip to Decius on the ride home, not mentioning his suspicions and certainly not mentioning Aulus Terentius.

"A Roman in Cosa," points out Decius on the ride home, "is not news. Everyone here has been fully Roman for hundreds of years."

"They still love being curious about a stranger here," says

Lucius.

"You mean Aponius is the nosiest man in Italy," says Decius sceptically.

Alexander plods on, and Lucius shrinks down inside his waterproofs and still manages to feel wet and cold all over. The Domitius villa is several miles beyond his own farm, and he is trying to avoid thinking about going there, while knowing that he will have to, if only to make sure that he is wrong about the unknown visitor.

Chapter 22

Letter from Marcus Tullius Cicero to his friend, Lucius Sestius. Written at Rome, on the Ides. Of March that is. Is it really only the Ides? This is turning into the dreariest spring ever. Weather is foul, illnesses everywhere, and I can't even go to Tusculum because apparently the pestilence is there as well. Hope you haven't been caught up in it yet, but it might be worth your while thinking about getting some supplies in. Food's getting scarce. We've already had the usual riots, demanding that Augustus become Dictator to deal with the situation. Actually it was quite funny, because this time the rabble really got organised and someone actually worked it out in advance – they descended on the Senate House in full flood, surrounded us and demanded that we pass a resolution calling upon Augustus to save the day. Those useless Consuls thought this was a brilliant idea, passed the resolution without even counting hands, and steamed up the Palatine to offer the Dictatorship to Augustus. I didn't bother with that part, no point. He refused all right but took a special commission to provide more grain. He's appointed a whole raft of fairly sensible lackeys to get it sorted and young Tiberius is in there of course; he seems to be good at that sort of thing. Anyway, no public festivals or feasts while the crisis is going on. At least the worry over food is giving us something other than the pestilence to talk about. I'm not really sure why I'm sticking it all out here but I am. I'm not ready to die from starvation yet. If things get really bad, I might visit you…

***

Lucius goes looking for Decius again and is more determined this time. They both go and find Sergius and do a stocktake.

Fortunately, anyone who has lived in Italy over the last twenty years knows how to conserve food, and the barn doors still have bars and a lock. The great vats of wine are carefully covered, and the covers tied down, though Titus worries about not letting the air get to them. The slave at the gate is allotted a friend to keep him company, and the fencing around the farm is carefully checked and repaired, especially around the small flock of goats and the cows. There is nothing new here: whenever there is unrest in Rome, the farms of Italy check on their own self-sufficiency. Italy has not been able to keep Rome in grain for years, but each town and village and farm does its best to feed itself. Italy does not get much support from Rome, thinks Lucius.

Spring is coming which lifts the mood. Titus is out every day coaxing the buds along his trellises, and on his walks Lucius sees the farm coming to life. As is prudent, he has decided to put more land under wheat this year, and Decius has decided that he has the time to devote special care to the gardens and orchards around the villa, to ensure that a good supply of fruit and vegetables come in. The green shoots of the wheat carpet the large field to the west of the villa, while the smells of herbs and flowers and greenery begin to infiltrate the air.

Lucius does not, however, forget the four visitors at the Domitius villa. He does not rush off immediately but waits a couple of days and just goes without telling anyone. Well, not quite anyone. He leaves a half-written letter to Marcus Cicero in his study.

The mid-morning journey is short and lovely, going up the valley at just the right moment in spring. The light is perfect, though it is quite chilly still, and the surrounding gentle slopes are carpeted in green, all shades from the dark shiny ivy to the pale shades of the grasses. The sun is warming the land and awakening the scents of life, the smells of the juices flowing in earth and stem. Little pockets of mist swirl in the folds of the hills, and lines of vines and olive trees swoop down the hillsides. Lucius doesn't hurry but lets Alexander the horse plod along as his master looks around and notes the differing stages of the farmlands. He is automatically checking that nobody is ahead of his own estate, no wheat taller than his, no vines with lusher foliage.

A little hill of startling symmetry marks the villa of the Domitii, a hill of gentle fir-clad slopes. It is a slightly darker green to everything around it and is so perfectly proportioned it looks man-made. The villa lies at the top of this hill, surveying the slopes of vines which stream down to the road. Lucius finds the track and turns up to the villa. Like his own there is a wall around the central buildings, and long before he arrives, a scurrying around the main gate shows that he has been noted and messages are being sent up to the house. He is welcomed at the gate with no surprise, the slaves immediately using his name, and he is escorted through a beautiful formal garden to the front door of the house where Aulus Terentius is waiting for him. Aulus has the strangest look on his face, embarrassed, almost coy, as if he is about to laugh self-consciously and confess to some social faux pas. They meet awkwardly, neither speaking and for a long moment Lucius has a terrible urge to turn round and get out as quickly as he can. He is conscious that all around them, people are watching – the slaves working in the garden, and two men he doesn't recognise standing just in the doorway. Clearly, they all think that this meeting matters. There is no sign that any of the Domitius family are in residence, and he cannot see the family steward whom he would recognise, he is sure, even though he cannot remember the man's name. How on earth have the Domitii got involved in all this?

"Oh, don't look so grim, Lucius!" says Aulus with an

unconvincing smile. "Come in and have a drink."

And the visit takes on the trappings of normality, being led through the hall and into a comfortable room which isn't quite a study nor a dining room, though it has couches and a desk. It is very… cushiony. Small tables are dotted all over and there are already plates and cups laid. Someone was sure that a visitor was going to arrive. They have barely settled into a couple of chairs in silence before slaves arrive with food and drink and water for washing hands and feet. It is altogether too much fuss for a mid-morning snack for a casual visitor and Lucius can hardly stand the tension inside him. He must speak, to cut the bands of worry tightening his jaw, but forces himself to wait until everything is served and the slaves have slipped out once more. Every time the curtain across the doorway is pulled back to let someone in, he catches a glimpse of the two men, clearly on guard duty. They will listen in to everything, he has no doubt.

Silence falls again and he cannot hold back.

"What has happened?"

"I thought you would find out soon enough," says Aulus. "Slave gossip was it?"

"Sort of," says Lucius. "Your housekeeper's husband is a chatty drunk, and I know the owner of his favourite bar."

"Ah, that would be Felix, is it?" says Aulus. "And to think I puzzled over whether or not to send a message to you. I decided not – I thought it might be too direct, maybe embarrass you. I should have thought of the bars. You supply them all, don't you? This place only produces for the estate and sends any surplus to the family's Rome place. Do you send any of your wine to Rome?"

Lucius thinks this awkward attempt at chat is a waste of time. Instead he gets straight to the heart of the matter.

"What have you done?"

Aulus hesitates and doesn't answer the question immediately.

187

"It was the Primus trial of course," he says. "I couldn't believe how stupid the whole thing was. You know what happened with the trial, I suppose?"

"I heard," says Lucius. "You had a defence, but Augustus came in and trod all over it. You must have known he would. He wouldn't allow you to use the late lamented Marcellus to tarnish the family image."

"It was all true as well," says Aulus ironically. "Certainly, can't allow that. You know what bothers me?" He isn't interested in a response to this so Lucius gives none. "The really irritating thing is that it is hardly that important is it? Marcellus, it turns out, acted like the arrogant little shit he was brought up to be, and interfered in matters beyond his capabilities, and that is all! Primus should have checked before he carried out those instructions and went after the Odrysians. But Primus is the sort of person who cannot imagine why Marcellus would lie about the orders coming from Augustus himself, so he obeys. And when he comes back to Rome and discovers he is being prosecuted, he doesn't know what to do."

Aulus pauses to refill wine-cups and adds water.

"He came to me one morning, just after we had met you in the Forum that time – remember? He was in a state, didn't understand what on earth was going on, asked me to explain, and I realised that he was just going to be sunk. Augustus was going to deny it all, and Primus was not important enough to save. And it made me so angry, Lucius Sestius, so angry. A good man being scrapped just like that to save the image of Augustus and his family. Because of course nothing was going to be allowed to smear the beloved Marcellus. And I began to think of Julius Caesar."

Lucius begins to feel cold.

"So, I found myself thinking about why Caesar was killed, the threat of tyranny he represented, the feelings of panic this instilled in people like Cassius and Brutus. You were young then, you remember it well, you know why it happened. Trebonius and Brutus and Cassius – they weren't bad men overthrowing a government for their own ends, they weren't assassins paid to carry out something evil. They were doing it because they couldn't allow Rome to become a kingdom, a helpless land in the grip of one-man rule. It won't work, it never works. The tyrant cannot be benevolent, he always ends up selfish and arrogant and abusive."

There is a silence. Lucius agrees with everything said so far. He remembers well the assassination of Julius Caesar and the decision he made in its wake. He remembers the mess of feelings and complete lack of rational thought which led to that decision. In a blur, two years of sailing, marching and one horrific campaign bypass his brain, and several years of dull exile in Sicily and North Africa are summed up in one bright picture of sand and heat and a shimmering palm tree.

"The tyranny is working at least, and you are ten years younger than me, a different generation," he hears himself say. "And what else is there?"

Aulus Terentius gazes into his wine-cup and says, "We could restore the Republic."

"And Augustus?"

"He has to go," says Aulus.

"And how would you do that, without setting off another civil war?"

Aulus has no answer.

"What are you doing here?" asks Lucius.

Aulus sighs. "Augustus found out. I'm running away. I think I shall try Gaul. I thought you might help."

"And how did you find out that he knew?"

"Oh, that was nasty. Terentia told me, she was given a message. Poor thing, she was terrified for me. That was unforgivable."

"Terentia?" Lucius can hardly believe what he is hearing. He tries imagining Augustus or Maecenas telling Terentia state secrets. Even though Maecenas is her husband, to use her – really?

"It wasn't Maecenas," says Aulus, tracking Lucius' thoughts.

"Augustus?" says Lucius, boggling at the sort of pillow talk that would let Augustus mention that her brother was planning to kill him… ("…and so, darling, I'm going to have your brother arrested…").

Aulus smiles and shakes his head. "No, not the Princeps. I'm not sure that Augustus, son of the God Julius, could lower himself to that. No, it was Livia."

And Lucius is not surprised by this at all. His mind goes back to that first dinner party, to the upright woman whose home was run in so exemplary a fashion, a background for her perfect hostess' manners. Of course, a model wife, who wove her husband's tunics for him, should never be prepared to engage in such a distasteful task, but there was something hard in Livia. She would not baulk. And he remembers Marcus Cicero's analysis – "Livia is as scary as a snake."

"I was surprised too," says Aulus lightly. "She came round on a visit one morning and announced it to Terentia quite calmly while nibbling on a honey-cake. My poor sister. I'm sure that Livia was there with Augustus' full knowledge of course, but she will have enjoyed the opportunity to upset her husband's mistress."

"Then Augustus wanted you to be warned," says Lucius and takes a moment to review this idea. "No, he wanted you to run."

"Yes, so much easier to organise a trial when I'm not there," agrees Aulus. "Even if I present a risk so small as to be pathetic, I must be shown up for the cowardly traitor I am."

"And is Terentia safe?"

"Yes," says Aulus gazing into his wine-cup. "Or at least, I am fairly sure she is, having acted her part. I decided to head north and east, so I told her to go down to her villa on the Bay of Naples. I'm sure Maecenas won't mind. She won't cause any trouble."

"And you?" asks Lucius curiously.

"I'm not ready to commit suicide yet," says Aulus briskly. "Too much fun to be had in this world still, so I'm going to run until I'm forced to stop. I thought southern Gaul, and then maybe Spain. Augustus still hasn't really tamed the far corners of Spain."

"I can lend you a ship," says Lucius, surprised to hear himself. "We can get you to Massilia. Then you can go north or south to Spain and disappear."

"Thank you," says Aulus and manages a very slight grin. "I hoped you would say something like that." He pauses, looks down at his wine-cup and flicks his eyes up at Lucius again. "Come with me? To Massilia?"

Lucius hears the invitation and sees the flash of laughter in Aulus' eyes.

"No," he says. "I'm not with you, I don't agree with you. But if you're caught, you'll die, and you don't deserve that."

He sighs. "Aulus, how does someone like you get involved in this rubbish? You know the Republic is gone. When did you start caring about that?"

"When did you stop?" asks Aulus, and immediately shakes his head, clicking his tongue in annoyance at himself. "I'm sorry, that was childish. We all work out our own ways, don't we? Terentia is five years older than me, and I can remember her getting married to Maecenas. Must be fifteen years ago now. We were all a bit disappointed, but Augustus arranged it, so we went along with it. My mother was the most upset. She knew that Maecenas wasn't the right person, but my father said it was a good idea, put us right in the centre of things. My father hated Mark Antony, so we naturally were on the side of whoever was leading the opposition to Antony. Great way of choosing which way to go, isn't it?"

"It's how many of us chose," says Lucius. "I hated Antony too."

"And it turned out well for us," says Aulus. "Maybe even for Terentia, but I don't know. She doesn't have children, but Maecenas is generous with money, and it isn't as if he treats her badly, you know?"

Lucius nods but thinks that Maecenas probably barely thinks of Terentia, and when she does come to mind it is only so that she can be used as a messenger. That sort of casual neglect is cruel. He remembers Terentia flirting up at him and wriggling on his dinner couch and he cannot help a smile. Aulus sees and smiles back, suddenly flashing an image of his sister across his face.

"Yes, she liked you. Probably still likes you. You should visit her when this has all died down. Maecenas won't mind. Nor will Augustus – I expect that his feelings for her have disappeared now, if he ever had any. Augustus won't associate with the sister of a traitor."

The word has been uttered and it still doesn't suit Aulus, even hanging there in the air, spoken almost defiantly by Aulus himself. In his head Lucius takes the word, examines it and puts it alongside the face on the couch opposite him. There is no fit there.

"I don't see you as a traitor," he says quietly. But he does think that Aulus is nearly as unfeeling towards his sister as are her husband and lover, and once more he pities Terentia.

Finally, although Lucius has not asked, Aulus tells him about the actual plot. It isn't a plot really, not by anyone's standards, and it is the least important part of this conversation.

After the trial and conviction of Marcus Primus, Aulus in a mess of disappointment and outrage went on a self-destructive quest for justice. He went round legal experts first, looking for a new strategy or a loophole he could exploit. He was summoned to a conversation with the Consuls, who explained to him that this was not a good thing and he should stop. Marcus Primus was already condemned and disgraced and on his way to a life in exile. End of the episode. But Aulus Terentius decided to exploit the connections his sister's marriage had brought and went to rant at Maecenas. He got nowhere there, and complained loudly to anyone who would listen, ending up getting drunk and loud at a dinner party: his remarks were of course reported on to the Princeps who decided to put a stop to it all.

"He invited me up to the Palatine and gave me the sort of telling-off you get from your mother when you are seven. I lost my temper," says Aulus. "I told him he would never be free from the fear of a dagger in the dark."

"A dagger in the dark?" exclaims Lucius, barely able to refrain from laughing. "What have you been reading, for pity's sake?"

Aulus laughs. "I know. Unbelievably melodramatic and stupid. Augustus suggested I left Rome. I stormed back home, sat in my study and started shaking as I realised what I had done. I've seen enough of Augustus over the years to know when I had completely blown it. And the next morning was when Terentia came to pass on the message. And I came here."

"Does Domitius know you are here?"

"The elder Domitius, Gnaius, does not. He is too in with the Palatine gang, so straight and loyal. But I know his son, Lucius Domitius Ahenobarbus, he is a friend and tried to calm me down. When he saw I wasn't in the mood he said I could come here if I needed a safe place. He gave me a letter for the staff.

That was before I threatened Augustus though, he might not be so generous now. Still, the people here know me, and I have no intention of staying much longer. I've brought some bodyguards with me, nobody else."

"What about money?" asks Lucius.

"I took the emergency stash I kept hidden in the house in Rome and visited my bankers for letters of credit. I have enough. And nobody questions anyone who leaves Rome in a hurry because of the flooding and illnesses going around."

Lucius thinks. "At the moment, all you are guilty of is saying some very unwise things."

"I threatened the Princeps," says Aulus. "That goes beyond unwise. I'm not going back to apologise and hope for forgiveness."

"But have you actually conspired with anyone else against him?" asks Lucius

"No, of course not," says Aulus, almost impatiently. "That isn't going to matter though."

"Augustus is very keen on mercy," points out Lucius. "You see a prime example in front of you. Marcus Cicero and I were pardoned under the post-Philippi generosity."

"We are beyond Philippi now, Lucius Sestius. I am going to be charged with treason because I have conspired to kill the Princeps. It doesn't matter that it didn't happen like that and it will all happen in absentia. That is who Augustus is, Lucius. He is completely ruthless and will use any means, regardless of who gets hurt. He will even use an ex-mistress, why not? Poor Julia, she will be the next sacrifice."

"Julia? Augustus' daughter Julia?"

"Of course, Augustus' daughter Julia. Keep up, Lucius. You'll see – she won't be allowed to be a widow long; she'll be married off. My money is on Agrippa."

"Agrippa's married and old enough to be her father," objects

Lucius. Aulus just looks at him and he shakes his head. "Aulus, let's not get off the point. You are sure there is no chance of making things up?"

"None," says Aulus and presses his lips together tightly to make it clear that nothing else can escape.

Lucius sighs. "We had better get you away to Massilia then," he says." How interested in finding you is Augustus likely to be?"

Aulus shrugs. "He told me to leave Rome. I've left Rome. Why should he pursue me?"

Lucius looks at Aulus and can't see anything unspoken lurking.

"I was just wondering if there was anything else. If Augustus was likely to discover something to make him change his mind."

Aulus sighs.

"If Augustus decides to change his mind, I'm sunk. I'm hoping for Terentia's sake he won't. I think Maecenas will help me there."

The conversation moves onto Gaul, and they swap notes on what they have heard about travelling north into Gaul from Massilia. Lucius decides not to supply Aulus with names of any of the merchants he has had dealings with in the past. He feels slightly uneasy about Augustus' attitude to Aulus. Despite his own encouraging remarks about Augustus' reputation for mercy, he remembers some strange stories regarding the Princeps' behaviour during the turbulent years of fighting various opponents. The general reputation for mercy which Augustus has been careful to cultivate is all very well, but Lucius feels that he is taking a slight risk himself in giving Aulus this minimal amount of help. Still, he is last year's Consul and riding high, and has little to lose: surely it can't be much of a risk?

Chapter 23

Lucius rides back down the valley but sees nothing around him this time. His mind is calculating. His family may not have the fleet of ships it once owned to distribute pottery amphorae full of wine and fish sauce, but he does have two little coast-huggers, the Swan and the Nereid, who spend the spring and summer months hopping back and forth between Cosa and Massilia, and all ports in between. They are currently beached at Cosa and no doubt their usual crew have been up to see Sergius and arranged their terms and wages for the season. He must check that. If past years' patterns are kept, the ships will be checked over and repaired by now, and the stocks of amphorae will be ready and waiting. If Titus can be persuaded to make a shipment ready there should be nothing unusual about a trip to Massilia in the near future. He will advise Aulus to take just one of his bodyguard with him and send the others back to his own estates somewhere, not back to Rome, just in case they have been missed. Probably a good idea for Aulus to move from the Domitius villa and find an inn in Cosa: Lucius doesn't want him to stay at his own villa. Maybe the innkeeper Aponius will find a room and not make a fuss. By the time he rides up the track home, Lucius thinks he has it all sorted. It will take a few days, and he hopes Augustus isn't madly keen on hunting Aulus down. He arrives back at the villa and nobody has noticed that he was gone. Or rather, nobody has needed him. This is as it should be, he thinks contentedly and he strolls to his study, calls for a snack and decides to finish his letter to Marcus Cicero.

***

Letter from Lucius Sestius to his friend Marcus Cicero at Rome. Written in the valley of Cosa, quite a few days before the first of April, don't know exactly how many, I shall ask Decius. He'll know.

You will be glad to know that the vines are doing well, though Titus assures me that some sort of blight is due to hit the whole of Italy in May. I haven't the foggiest where he gets this information from, I think he makes it up and speaks it out loud as a way of averting the Evil Eye. I wish he wouldn't worry so much, he is beginning to look old, and though I know he is over fifty, it seems strange that every year his vines renew their youth and he goes on aging. Good gods, what a pretentious sentence. Take no notice of me, Marcus. I must have spent too much time with Horace.

As you can probably tell, I feel very comfortable this spring away from the city, despite the rather worrying reports people like you send me about disease and famine and goodness knows what. I hope you are taking care. Gallio (the children's tutor, as you will have forgotten) desires me to offer you the advice to heat all water thoroughly before you use it to drink or wash. It is an idea he has picked up from one of his Greek philosophers and the logic behind it makes a sort of sense to me – apparently the heat burns away any nastiness in the water. I suggested that one just strains the dirt out of the water, but that won't kill off the invisible nasties. According to Gallio. I wondered about the existence of nasty stuff one cannot see, but Gallio quite rightly pointed out that disease is itself invisible until the symptoms start. Enough of such cheery stuff.

You must come to us if things get worse. We have had no sign of disease here thank all the gods, and we have plenty of food. One of the joys of the countryside, you just grow some.

Any news of where Marcus Primus has ended up or what he is doing? Or is it bad form just to ask? You may be interested to know that I am dispatching a special order to Massilia soon, found a new strain of vine up in the valley and it is looking just right for Gaul. Yes, I know you have no interest in vines, Marcus, but this really is an interesting one. And please give my regards to Terentia the wife of Maecenas if you see her.

***

Marcus is not the most subtle person in the world, but he has survived the last two decades and can pick up a hint. And if he doesn't it won't particularly matter. But Lucius does think it would be kind to let Terentia know that her brother is well away and safe. He is sure that even someone who embarrassed him at his own dinner party deserves that consideration, and he cannot help feeling sorry for Terentia with her luxurious and loveless life. She is very pretty, after all.

At dinner that night, he receives yet another message from Titus that he is not coming but having an early night. Lucius makes a note that he must drop in and have a proper chat with Titus soon.

The next morning Lucius gets busy. He strolls down to find Titus in the fields and asks about sending a load of last year's wine to Massilia. Titus regards him suspiciously.

"Well, the big vat is almost ready I suppose but I'd like to keep it going a couple more weeks really. Can this wait?"

Lucius tries to sound casual.

"I really could do with this load being ready in three days," he says and sees Titus' eyes widen, and realises he has utterly failed as far as being casual goes. He changes tactics.

"Titus, this is not about the wine and I apologise," he says quietly. "I just need you to get a load of wine decanted into amphorae and loaded into the Nereid and ready to sail – as soon as you can. And without making a fuss. Can you do that?"

Titus' eyes remain wide for a long few seconds, then he blinks and nods. "Of course, boss," he says. And Lucius cannot tell whether Titus has really accepted this or not. But he does trust Titus, so he smiles and goes back to the house, confident that it will all happen. It is only then that he remembers that he was going to ask about Titus' health and has completely forgotten. Never mind: he sees Titus nearly every day.

Back in his study, Lucius thinks and counts the days on his fingers and writes a swift unsigned note to Aulus Terentius. And in an unusual burst of confidence he summons Publius from his studies.

When his son appears in front of him, Lucius takes a long look and smiles. His son is a slight boy but has beautiful posture – thanks to Helice! – and a face where the lines of manhood are waiting to emerge. Slightly chubby cheeks are being eclipsed by chin and forehead, and Lucius realises that he can see his son growing up into a man of character. Publius stands patiently, and eventually coughs and says, "You called me, Father?" very politely, but clearly prompting Lucius into action.

"I'm sorry, Publius," says his father. "I was just thinking. But I have a task for you, and I don't want you to be offended or ask why one of the slaves can't do it."

Publius looks surprised as if such a reaction would never occur to him.

"It is very straightforward," says Lucius. "I just want you to ride up the valley to the villa of the Domitii and give this note into the hands of a man called Aulus. Ask at the gate and I'm sure they will take you to him, especially when you tell them that you are my son."

Publius has been looking at him all through this and answers immediately, "Yes, Father." The boy asks no question but takes the wax tablet and turns to go straight away. Lucius feels a rare moment of pride. He fights down the urge to go after his son, watch him give the order for a horse and stand by him as he mounts, ready with further and unwanted advice. Publius is a good rider, knows the way, will take a slave and Argos the dog with him, and will carry out the simple errand perfectly. Lucius sends up a thought or prayer to his own father thanking him for a secure childhood and a constant stream of encouragement.

As he sits in his study and thinks of all this, Tia comes in.

"Are you too important to talk to at the moment?" she asks on seeing his distracted expression.

As always Tia knows what to say and he laughs.

"No, I'm never that important," he says smiling at her, and thinking how lucky he is to like both his sisters. "Although, I am glad to hear that you show the proper respect for your elders."

Tia sniffs and tries not to smile but fails.

"Young Publius looked almost as important as you when he ran out of the house," she observes. "I gather you have had a meaningful father-son conversation?"

"I gave him an errand," says Lucius.

"He likes it when you notice him," says Tia and her lips pinch back just a little. She has never thought Lucius pays enough attention to Publius, and she is probably right.

"I notice him a lot," says Lucius, embroidering a little. And forestalling her comment he says quickly, "I know I don't say things to him, but I honestly think he doesn't mind. And the older he gets the easier it is to talk to him. I'm trying, Tia. Really."

Tia stands with her mouth open, robbed of her comments. She laughs.

"Oh, all right, Lucius! I believe you. And I shan't nag. I was going to ask you if we should try and persuade Albinia to come and stay. And she could bring Horace of course." There is an evil grin on her face as she utters this last sentence. Lucius has been wondering the same thing. About Albinia and Horace that is. The invitation idea is a good one so he agrees that he will write to Albinia straight away.

"I'll help you," says Tia and draws up a stool on the other

side of the desk. She looks at him expectantly, so he takes the next clean wax tablet and they spend a happy hour arguing over what they say to Albinia to persuade her and Horace to leave the comfort of the Sabine farm and journey to Cosa.

"To ward off the plague and disease
We ask you to Cosa – pretty please!
It's proving quite sunny
And we have some money
So Horace and you can be at ease."

***

This disgraceful piece of doggerel is dispatched immediately, and the authors congratulate themselves on their skill at composing what must be an irresistible plea.

Young Publius reports back to Lucius' study just before dinner time: he has delivered the message straight into the hands of Aulus and there is no reply, although he got tipped generously, and now doesn't know whether to be offended or pleased.

"Do you think he thought I was a slave?" he asks anxiously.

Lucius listens to his son's beautifully enunciated question and shakes his head.

"My guess is that he knew exactly who you were and wanted to give you a present," he says. Publius holds out the coin.

"It's a denarius, so I think you are right, Father," he says seriously. "May I buy a book?"

Lucius agrees and suggests Publius write to his aunt Albinia for some recommendations.

On the next day, Lucius sets out on Alexander the horse to amble down to the port of Cosa. He doesn't take anyone with him, and he leaves a villa full of quiet industry, Tia sorting out the household, the children at their lessons, Decius doing accounts and Sergius down on the farm. Titus is still in the cottage: this is unusual for him, but he is tired and looks grey around the mouth and eyes. Lucius has been down to see him as he promised to himself and is worried. Marcella is her usual brisk and capable self but as Lucius leaves the cottage she goes to see him out, and as soon as they are out of the door whispers, "He has been tired recently, but I have never seen him like this. Do you think it could be that plague from Rome?"

Lucius doesn't think so. The pestilence is swift to hit a person and they are horizontal and visibly failing within hours. Titus says there is nothing but tiredness. Lucius promises Marcella to send a doctor – there is a decent one in Cosa, a Greek in semi-retirement who lives near the forum in town. He is also the father of the man Lucius wants to sail to Massilia with a cargo of wine and a couple of passengers, so it is at least convenient. He leaves Alexander at the stable just outside Cosa's gate, and once inside and past Aponius' inn, it is a short walk to the house Lucius seeks. The doctor is a Greek freedman, Publius Larcius, and his son, also Publius, is one of Lucius' most valued staff. The son started work on the Nereid when he was in his early teens and now in his thirties can captain either ship. Lucius needs him to be available in three days' time to sail. In the meantime, he will have to supervise the loading of a few hundred amphoras of wine which will start coming into the port from the villa tomorrow morning. It is all a bit of a rush job of course, so Lucius has decided to lie and tell Captain Larcius that there is a big festival coming up in Massilia, and they have received an urgent plea from their merchant contact there. Of course, when Captain Larcius and the Nereid arrive in Massilia nobody will be aware of having sent a letter, but Lucius will send Decius on the journey to explain, hold some negotiations and sell off the wine. He doesn't see why he shouldn't make a profit on this unexpected journey. Decius can make the rounds of a few more traders in Gaul and find out how many people are in the market for a pleasant if not-very-special wine from the loveliest valley in Etruria. Lucius' plans take wings. On the return journey, Decius and the Captain can stock up on pottery. The Gauls make some lovely shiny redware that still manages to undercut anything coming from southern Italy. He has a little cup in his study that he likes very much, a present from his wine merchant in Massilia. Lucius went on a voyage there about ten years ago just out of curiosity and was sick for the whole journey there. Not on the journey back, curiously, and he did have a lot of wine in him. The cup is one of the most perfectly proportioned things he has ever seen; from a smooth lip around the top it bellies out slightly, then in again to a much smaller foot. Lines incised into the clay mark the changes in direction of the little cup's curves, and a simple pattern, stars alternating with ears of wheat, march around the fullness of it. Lucius keeps expecting the pattern to show signs of wear, but it hasn't yet.

Wondering about the prospects of importing that redware from Gaul into Italy takes Lucius right into the walls of Cosa and up to the door where Larcius senior and junior share a house. They keep one maid – Lucius suspects she is more than that but doesn't ask – and it is she who answers the door and shows Lucius into the room used by Larcius senior as a study-cum-consulting room. Doctor Larcius doesn't have many patients: the people of Cosa are hardy and don't believe in paying money for a doctor to tell you that you are ill. But this suits the doctor for he really doesn't want to be dragged away from his books for too long. He is researching for his life's great work – a treatise on the digestion and its disorders. He is enjoying a quieter life than the one he led in Rome where even as a freedman he was always at somebody's beck and call. Once his wife died, he saw no reason to stay in the city and decided to move to Cosa. His one child, a boy of about ten, flourished in the small-town environment and loved being near the sea and ships. By the time he was twelve, the boy was slipping down to the port at every opportunity and the father realised reluctantly that there was no point in educating him in oratory or medicine or anything but sailing and so entrusted his son to the Sestius family's ships and crews and prayed every day to Neptune for the safety of all sailors. Lucius knows that if he tries the usual small talk preparatory to the main business, Doctor Larcius may well tell him all about the latest revolting alimentary condition he is reading up, so quickly explains his business; the doctor pours some wine and calls for his son. When Lucius leaves an hour or so later his business is done, and he feels pleased with himself. Doctor Larcius will pop in to see Titus the next day, and Captain Larcius will start getting the Nereid ready to sail to Massilia with a cargo of wine.

Chapter 24

The Swan and the Nereid are short and full-bellied ships, oak-framed and with a variety of planks as each winter several are replaced with whatever is handy – mostly pine, and cypress, Lucius knows, in the way one always has known something. Until the sailing season starts again in March, on fine days the paint is touched up, and the planks caulked with tarred wool. Rough edges are smoothed, and there is always a debate over whether or not the rudders will last another year. They usually do. The sails are checked and mended and the spare sails checked and mended, the rigging replaced, the anchors polished. Lucius does not know why anchors need polishing, but it is done anyway. When the weather is too bad to work on the ships, the crews take any work going around the port, the fish farm, the pottery which makes amphorae to carry wine, olive oil and fish sauce. There is never quite enough work to keep everyone occupied throughout the whole winter, but nobody starves, because the Sestius family are good employers and look after their own. A matter of common sense, Lucius' father always used to say. You want to keep your ships' crews from season to season, they have too much valuable knowledge of the coastlines to waste by driving them away through indifference or penny-pinching.

The Nereid is Lucius' favourite ship: there are only two left from the modest fleet which had carried Sestius amphorae around the Mediterranean in Lucius' childhood. He is lucky that after the Civil War has taken its toll on his family's finances he has two ships left, and luckier that the Nereid is one. There isn't much to choose between the two, the Swan is slightly longer and has a gracefully curving swan's neck at the stern, repainted every winter, as salt spray, sunshine and superstitious caresses from the crew wear away the white paint over a summer. But the Nereid has always been Lucius' favourite, ever since he was told the story of the mermaid. It had been on the beach at Cosa when he was about seven, watching the crews carrying out the winter repairs on the fleet. One old man had been carefully painting a picture on the side of a boat, and when Lucius went up to ask what it was, he found himself entranced. The half-woman half-fish creature seemed to swim gracefully along the side of the boat, the coils of her elegant long tail curling up behind her like a perfect wave, while she lifted her human half out of the water and gazed steadily ahead, a small and secret smile on her face, as though she could see that she was nearly home and someone was waiting for her there. The man realised Lucius was beside him after a while, and stopped painting, taking a careful look at the small boy and enjoying the rapt study of his work.

"You know who this is, master Lucius, don't you?"

"Is she the nereid? Like the ship's name?" asked the child. "My tutor says nereids are sea nymphs and that they are goddesses. I didn't know they had fish tails though."

"Not all of them do," said the old man.

(Lucius wishes he could remember the man's name. He was one of the few people who still spoke Etruscan in Cosa, a language now dead and gone, just like the speaker.)

The painting carried on, and delicately the man picked out little scales along the creature's tail with tiny V-shaped flicks of the paintbrush. The boy Lucius was absorbed. When the man had finished the tail, he paused again and carried on talking.

"This however is our special Nereid, and the boat was named after her because we saw her on our first voyage, me and the captain, ten years ago now."

"You saw a sea nymph?" asked Lucius, impressed.

"Oh yes," said the man, and carefully touched up the Nereid's eye, making it gleam wickedly. "You see all sorts of things at sea, dolphins of course, you'll have heard of them, and I've seen fish with wings jumping out of the water and trying to fly. But they always fall back in. I don't think they get their wings dry enough to fly, you see, not before they have to go back into the sea. But they keep trying."

"Can I come with you one day and look for flying fish?" asks Lucius.

"You'll have to ask your dad," says the man. "Sailing is dangerous work."

"But you are safe because you saw her, the Nereid. What did she look like?"

"She was beautiful," says the man promptly, and falls into the rhythm of a tale often told. "She was sitting on a rock, drying her hair, running her fingers through it, and she didn't take any notice of us at first. We were going a fair old rate, and the captain knew to give her room, not to go too close, and as we backed off a bit, she looked right at us, and she smiled. And that's when we knew we had to call the ship after her. And ever since then, the goddess has looked after us, and that's why we paint her on the ship – to show her our respect and thanks. We know that we belong to her, and the Nereid is the luckiest ship in Cosa."

Nowadays, the Nereid does not appear quite so big or impressive, but the picture is repainted every winter and the sea nymph has certainly taken her responsibility to them all seriously. The Nereid is indeed the luckiest ship in Cosa, and everyone knows it.

Loading the amphoras of wine is the most important part of preparing to sail: the Nereid and the Swan are sturdy little ships, but a cargo must be stored properly or any ship can capsize. The loading has to be done out in the bay, with smaller boats laboriously rowing the wine-jars out to the ship standing at one of the off-shore piers. A special net is lowered and packed, and the precious wine drawn up the side of the ship. To Lucius' eyes the process seems remarkably smooth, but the port-workers do this every day during the sailing months. He can't hear the noise from the shore, but he imagines that there must be some chinking as the amphoras shift in the net, and maybe the odd curse. Each amphora is passed smoothly in a chain of men and disappears down into the belly of the ship, where several veteran packers will stand them upright and wedge them with wool, old sacking, and bits of wood. Once the floor is covered with amphoras the second layer can go in, tightly tucked upright between the necks of the layer beneath. Four layers and the belly of the Nereid is full. With calm seas the amphoras will hold their position: in a storm there is a risk of amphoras breaking and the whole elaborate construction can shift. If that happens the ship will list and be prey to waves swamping her. The packing of the amphoras is vital, and when it is done, there is much scrutiny from the shore, to check that the ship rides well in the water. Only if Captain Larcius is satisfied will the Nereid sail, and he has been known to order the ship repacked from the beginning.

On the day the Nereid is due to sail, Cosa and her little port are looking like a picture painted on a villa wall to show the delights of seaside living. Lucius and Decius ride down through fields and olive groves and spring flowers dot the roads. Lucius notices that the flowers of spring are mostly white and yellow and wonders why. Albinia would know, he is sure. As they approach the port, the few rocks frame a bay of sparkling water where graceful ships dance slowly round their moorings and the smell of the fish farm is almost subdued. Aulus and his silent henchman are already there on foot, waiting their turn to be rowed out to the Nereid, and while Decius strolls over and strikes up conversation to his fellow passengers, Lucius makes no move to speak to them. He finds a willing hand to hold the horses, and strolls along the wharf as he has done many times before. There is no reason to be there at all really, but he stays to watch as the group of men is rowed out to the Nereid and climb up the side of the ship. One bag is all that Aulus takes with him, and once it is hauled up, the ship starts to look busy. People climb around doing things with ropes, Aulus and Decius disappear, and the ship's captain gives an exaggerated wave to the shore. Without thinking, Lucius waves back. He takes one last look at the ship and turns for the short ride up the hill to the town. Behind him, the sails catch, and the Nereid does a delicate dancing turn and cuts her way across a bay sparkling with sun-bright waves. Lucius makes Alexander climb the steep track up the cliffs to Cosa's side gate and zigzags slowly through the streets, leading Decius' horse, until he reaches Doctor Larcius' house. There is nowhere to park the horses, but an obliging urchin bargains with him to take Alexander and friend and have them waiting at the usual stables. The urchin has freckles and a missing front tooth, so Lucius allows his frosty heart to thaw for an expensive moment.

Once more the housekeeper ushers Lucius into Doctor Larcius' study, and wine is poured. The little statue of Neptune has been moved from the shrine in the corner to the doctor's desk, so Lucius respectfully pours a drop of wine into the dish in front of it.

"This is an important voyage for you," states the doctor calmly. "More than usual I think?"

There is the hint of a question there but not so much that Lucius can't ignore it if he wishes. But he finds himself relaxed and trustful and he nods at the doctor before drinking.

"And every voyage is important for you," he says and gestures at Neptune. "He was on the shrine when I last came, now he is closer to you."

209

"He keeps me company while my son is away," says Doctor Larcius. "You, I have no doubt, will do something similar when your Publius flies the nest."

"I can't even imagine that," says Lucius, "and yet it is such a normal part of life. Your son grows up, you arrange a career and marriage and he moves on. It is like a map laid out in front of me – and him. The same thing will happen to my daughter, except that she will leave my house forever and at an earlier age." He really cannot imagine Celi ever being old enough to get married and hasn't a clue who she will choose. He has no doubt that she will choose, despite Roman traditions which lay down that he as stern paterfamilias will make all important decisions for his family.

Doctor Larcius says nothing but in a very undemanding way and Lucius enjoys a moment of just sipping wine and looking at Neptune. The small bronze statue is full of movement and power: Neptune himself rises out of a wave, brandishing his trident above his head, and one arm is stretched out balancing the god as he takes aim at some unknown monster. The god's hair and beard are being blown back by an imaginary wind, but there is no doubt that he is the master of his environment and that water and wind will calm at his command. Lucius thinks of his ship and crew, and of Decius, and trusts in the god.

"I wanted to ask you about Titus," he says at last to the doctor. "I know that you must be discreet and respect his privacy, but I am concerned about him."

"Well, Titus himself has no issue with your knowing my diagnosis," says Doctor Larcius. "When I left him earlier this morning, he said he would tell you about it. So, I shall leave that to him."

"You visited this morning?" asks Lucius in surprise.

"I have visited him every day since you asked me to come and look him over," says the doctor.

Lucius absorbs this and comes to the conclusion that this is bad news. He sighs and empties his cup. The tranquil moment is over. He asks Larcius for his bill so far, and pays the amount asked, noting that the doctor has been very generous with his time.

When he gets home, he calls for Tia and the two of them walk over to Titus and Marcella's cottage. It is midday but they find Titus lying on a couch, covered in a blanket and looking as though he has no blood in his veins. Marcella has dark smudges under her eyes and is strangely gaunt as if she were a patient here as well. Titus tries to sit and manages it very slowly with Marcella fussing around him and tucking a pillow behind his back, as Lucius and Tia sit uncomfortably and wish that they wouldn't. But this ritual is necessary for Titus, so they wait patiently, aware that they have time that Titus does not.

When he is comfortable Titus looks at them and suddenly grins, a most unusual expression for him, for Lucius nearly always sees Titus in terms of a serious conversation about vines.

"Not much to say, Lucius Sestius, is there?" Titus' voice is tiny, and he stops for breath every three or four words.

"I wish..." begins Lucius and lets the sentence trail off. This is for Titus to manage.

"My grandfather went the same way at the same age or thereabouts," says Titus and the story comes out creaking with laboured breath.

Titus has been slowing down since the winter and Doctor Larcius says that his heart is inexorably giving up. He still has some weeks to live and has several requests for Lucius – to look after Marcella and let the boys take over from him, so that the family is secure. Lucius says that Titus barely has to ask. Titus next makes the formal request that Lucius look after his will, and Marcella gets out a small wax tablet, already sealed.

"And don't worry about food, Marcella," says Tia. "I'll make sure that the kitchen sends down enough for you all every day. You won't have to cook. And do you need any other help? Send your laundry up to us."

"I'd like it if someone came and read to me," says Titus. "Dying is very boring." They smile and Lucius assures him that he can have all the readers he wants. What sort of literature would he like?

"Anything," says Titus and wheezes a little laugh, "except Cato the Elder on Agriculture."

Lucius promises that he will provide more interesting reading than this and the visit comes to a natural end.

Back at the villa, Publius is given the task of organising a rota of readers and of choosing material to read to Titus. Publius and Celi are fond of Titus and his family, having run in and out of the cottage at will all their lives. Lucius doesn't want them to stop now and explains that it will be greatly appreciated by Marcella if they go and support her.

"You don't have to do anything special," he promises. "Just be kind. And if you think you are in the way, make an excuse and leave. But I don't think you will be."

The children look solemn but go straight to their schoolroom to consult with Gallio about reading matter and soon, as Lucius is going out into the garden, he sees Publius walking briskly down the path to the cottage, with Celi skipping beside him.

It is ten days after sending the letter to Albinia that she and Horace arrive at the villa. Lucius welcomes the distraction of wondering what has happened to Aulus Terentius, and worrying about Titus, and as always when Horace is around people laugh a lot more. The poet is especially good with his children notices Lucius. Publius respects Horace's superb range of knowledge on almost anything ever written, and at dinner, the boy has asked permission to recline next to their guest so that he may quiz him on his philosophical views. The dinner is punctuated with laughter and Publius' light voice asking questions. After the fruit has been eaten, and the children have gone to bed, Sergius and Decius excuse themselves. Lucius apologises for his son's intense interrogations, but Horace is amused and brushes the embarrassment away.

"Lucius Sestius, you have a son who thinks, really thinks and how old is he? Twelve?"

Lucius thinks.

"Thirteen in the summer. And Celi will be eleven."

Horace waves the years past in a vague manner.

"They are wonderful children. They have manners and intelligence and are kind. Utterly delightful to talk to."

"Kind?" Lucius echoes his guest. Are his children kind? He thinks they probably are, but he has no idea how Horace knows this. But Horace is an observer.

"They are unfailingly polite with your slaves, Lucius. And they listen to Helice and respect Gallio – they are both freed, aren't they?"

Lucius nods. Gallio came freed and Lucius himself freed Helice after a few months of seeing the way she interacted with the children. He is glad he did: he has never enjoyed the thought of entrusting his children to slaves, irrational though this thought is.

"Well, the way that people treat their freedmen is important," says Horace, son of a freedman, and always mindful of that. The conversation stutters and moves on to poetry. Albinia and Horace have been working hard this spring and are eager to tell Lucius and Tia all about it. Horace's new work is taking on a philosophical slant now and though he explains why to Lucius, Lucius does not feel that he ends up understanding. Any more than he understands why these poems are going to be called "Epistles".

"I'm preparing for retirement," says Horace. Albinia laughs

heartily.

"You are moving on, that's all," she says. "You are observing more, and thinking more, so your poems are reflecting that. And you are too happy to write love poetry."

Abruptly, Tia stands and excuses herself. They all look a little surprised, but she adds that she has things to do. It is palpably a lie, but Albinia lets it go and merely blows her a kiss as she leaves. Someone else to check on in the morning, thinks Lucius.

"That one you sent me," begins Lucius and sees his sister wince. "The poem you said you had both written – is this one of your new Epistles, Horace?"

"I think it will be," says Horace comfortably. "If Albinia lets me take the credit. Did you like it?"

"Sort of – but all that about me living as though each day is my last – well, to be honest, that was annoying. I've been through phases like that in my life, where I really thought the day could be my last, and it wasn't much fun. I mean, I didn't really appreciate anything just because the thought I might die was there, hanging over me."

"But what you need to do," says Albinia, "is actually live. You aren't a risk-taker, Lucius."

"I'm done with risk-taking," says Lucius. "I like having a nice boring life now. And I appreciate it."

"Ah but is it inspiring?" cries Horace, waving his wine-cup around. "Do you appreciate things unless you are aware that they might be lost to you?"

Lucius thinks this is a remarkably stupid question but realises that he is being goaded. Horace and Albinia always seem impatient with him nowadays.

"I can appreciate things," he says. "You don't have to write a poem about everything, you know."

Albinia looks at him with eyes comically narrowed.

"Go on then," she says. "Write a poem. Write a poem of

appreciation."

Lucius has had enough. He sends for a wax tablet, and feels his temper rising as they wait. In a fit of righteous indignation, he writes:

I don't see the point.
People tell me that it is clever.
Sometimes, I can see the patterns, and special words.
And, yes, it's clever. I see that.
But clever isn't important.
When the leaf on my vine uncurls,
I see the life streaming through to the tip.
I feel the life coming up through my feet
from the earth under me.
That is important. And needs no words.
***

He tries to read it out loud but can't. He hands the tablet to her instead and feels ridiculously awkward and stupid as he watches her read, her lips moving, a tiny murmur.

Albinia sighs and hands the tablet to Horace.

"And without words, you could not describe this. This important thing in your life."

"But I don't need poetry to say it!" Suddenly it is crucial that she understands him. "What I said there about the life running through the vine – I don't need to say that at all, not out loud, not in a letter or a poem – it doesn't stop happening, it doesn't stop being important just because I don't use words to describe it. Even If I didn't appreciate it, it would still go on being important."

He can see her getting interested, eyes gleaming. Horace looks up but is not ready to join in the attack, yet.

"So, don't important things need to be said, described, celebrated?"

"They are already, Albinia, that's the thing I don't get about

215

poetry! I don't need to say that the vine is important, it will be important, it will keep growing anyway – I don't matter!"

"Ah!" says Albinia, almost a sound of pain. "At last! That is your problem, dearest brother – you don't think you are important! Now who told you that, I wonder?"

He stares at her. "That isn't what I meant, and you know it!"

"Oh Lucius, don't be angry. I'm sorry you felt so needled by me that you actually said something personal and revealing, and I shan't tell anyone else of course. Nobody will make a poem out of your feelings, I promise. And Horace promises too, don't you? And I need to go to bed, so I shall leave for tonight. Be good, both of you. I'll pop my head in on Tia, check that she is all right as well."

She unfolds from the couch, and steps over to Lucius, a little stiffly, and with one knee cracking comically so that they both laugh. Albinia is getting old, he realises. She drops a very light kiss on the top of his head, and waves as she turns and leaves the dining room. He is left, as usual, with a wine-jug and a cup, and so he makes use of these to push the whole conversation deep down inside wherever it is one stores one's memories. As he swallows the wine, Lucius pictures words vanishing down his throat to become mangled along with the food and wine in his stomach, and hopefully to vanish. He hopes he never feels obliged to write a poem again. The little wooden tablet lies on the table, but the words are easily disposed of – he holds the tablet over the lamp until the wax is soft, and then he smooths the warm wax. The words are gone. That is how important words really are, he thinks, feeling smug. He has forgotten that Horace is still there and is watching him, until the poet sits up and says, "Don't worry, Lucius, by the time that Epistle to you is published it will be about someone else. Goodnight," and trots off. Another conversation where Lucius hasn't quite followed what people are trying to tell him and he feels exasperated by it all. And there is something wrong with Tia, and he doesn't know that either. Lucius sighs, drains his cup and wanders out into the garden to smell the darkness before he goes to bed. He finds his son already there and the two of them sit companionably on the bench near the front door without speaking for a while.

Chapter 25

April is a beautiful month in Etruria, the first half spent watching the growth of flowers and crops and vines with increasing excitement, the second packed with festivals giving thanks and praying to the gods for every aspect of agriculture. With Aulus safely away, and visitors to distract him, Lucius feels a burden gradually being lifted and he drinks less – according to Albinia anyway. She and Horace take walks and write and visit Titus and Marcella, and though Lucius watches quite carefully there really seems to be nothing more to their relationship. Tia joins them on the walks and scolds Lucius for making his watchful eye too obvious.

"You really don't need to worry!" she says earnestly. "And to be honest, if they were getting romantically involved, why would that bother you? Are you scared that Albinia will fall pregnant and disgrace the family name?"

Lucius feels himself redden and says of course not.

"She is happy," says Tia. Lucius looks at her.

"Are you?" he asks.

"As much as one can be," says Tia, and then sits up very straight as she looks firmly ahead, and adds, "I miss Decius."

For a moment Lucius is a bit confused, then as he is just about to say "Yes, I do too," something inside his head shifts and he realises. "Decius? You? Really?" He can't think of anything else to say.

Tia laughs. "Yes, me, Decius, really. I'm glad that we have succeeded in being discreet anyway."

Lucius looks at his sister and thinks how well she is looking. Oh well...

"I see why Decius was always so keen to get back here any

time we went to Rome," he observes.

"Oh, Decius knows his duty," says Tia and looks at him anxiously. "He really does you know. He will always put his work first. You don't have to worry that he or I will let you down."

Lucius has not even thought this and says so. In fact, it doesn't bother him at all, instead he feels quite pleased for the two of them. He hastens to say this as well and Tia's smile is his reward. She hugs him and leaves the study in haste, quite possibly wiping her eyes. He will talk to her again later, though he doesn't think that there is any issue about their relationship which she and Decius won't have considered. They can't marry of course, so if Tia does get pregnant it might be awkward. He wonders what on earth to say to Decius – as Tia's brother, should he demand to know Decius' intentions? Ask why he hasn't been told before? Check that Decius is taking – er – precautions? The last thought makes his mind boggle and he hurriedly decides to get Albinia to check with Tia. Albinia of course will know so probably so does Horace. Actually, the whole villa probably knows and just doesn't worry about it. So maybe that is what he should do. And Decius won't be home until May probably, so he has time to let it sink in. He goes to bed whistling a song which he belatedly recognises as a very rude marching song he learned on an early foray into war, more than twenty years ago. The Fifth Legion, Julius Caesar and North Africa are now consigned to history, but the jaunty little tune makes him smile still.

Several days of rain mid-April keep everyone inside and constantly gazing out of the windows. Lucius is always being told that rain at the wrong time is a terrible thing for the crops, but it must rain sometimes, he reasons to himself. The farm gets out the ancient covered wagon and patches up the holes in the awnings so that Doctor Larcius can come and visit Titus in relative comfort and without getting soaked. The kitchen spends the time getting ready for the feasting which will accompany the various festivals: Fordicidia, the festival of fertility, the shepherds' festival Parilia, Vinalia for the vines and Robigalia the most practical of all, which asks the gods for protection against all the blights and insects which attack plants. For their farm, the Vinalia is the biggest and best, and already people are wondering how they can celebrate with Titus ill. But even if Titus is ill, there are several mighty feasts to be prepared and Sergius hires in a couple of women from Cosa to come and help out around the house and with the nursing at Titus and Marcella's cottage. Titus is still well enough to give brief orders and the wine for each festival is carefully chosen. Lucius and Sergius make a note of the animals and produce which will be used in the rituals – incense, wine, a very young calf for the Fordicidia ("Optional," says Lucius decidedly, "We don't have a calf to spare"), a lamb for the Parilia, a puppy for the Robigalia ("Yuck," says Celi. "Do we have to?"). Each festival has its own peculiar rituals and for some reason nobody knows, at the Vinalia a whole jar of last year's wine is poured into the stream which runs down the middle of the valley, watering the edge of the lands owned by the Sestius family. Despite the weather, and Decius' absence and Titus' illness, the excitement is growing.

The people of the Sestius farm keep the festival of Fordicidia relatively quietly: cows and their unborn calves are sacrificed in Rome, and larger towns may consider a sacrifice, but cows and bulls are expensive. Towns like Cosa are content with special prayers, echoed in the villas which march up the valleys of Italy. Lucius' farm has a small herd of cows and he and Sergius and the herdsmen gather to pray over them, and incense is burned on a fire. The day moves on without fuss for everyone, and when a rider approaches the gates there is no stir, though the gate slaves send a message to the house and meet the rider as they have been told. Once they find out that the rider is one of the crew of the Nereid, another message is sent to the house, at a run. Lucius is in his study, when Sergius hurries in and says with no preamble, "A letter from Decius has arrived. One of the crew is here delivering it, so something's up."

Lucius starts up out of his chair and takes the letter, saying, "Tell Tia please." He has barely unsealed it and opened it before Tia arrives and they sit side by side on the couch to read it.

To Lucius Sestius Quirinalis at Cosa, greetings from his freedman Decius Sestius.

I write in haste to tell you of a very strange event, and I am concerned.

After an uneventful journey, we arrived at Massilia and unloaded our cargo. I negotiated its storage in the usual warehouse and started to make the rounds of our Massilian friends. We stayed at the same inn you and I stayed in years ago and nothing has changed – including that frightening landlady. She has grey hair and few teeth, but her scowl is as charming as ever. I sent my companion to enquire around the barges going up the Rhone, and we got transport sorted easily. But when I woke the next day, he and his bodyguard had gone. I have spent a day looking for them and can find no sign. This now the sixth day before the Ides of April. I shall enquire further of course, and let you know what I can.

***

Lucius is immediately concerned. Decius' normally elegant prose is stilted and would alert the suspicions of a Vestal Virgin, if one of those revered ladies ever took up postal interception. If Aulus Terentius has disappeared, there are three explanations – he has met with an unhappy accident, he has slipped off without letting Decius know which seems unlikely, or he has been deliberately targeted. And the only person who would deliberately target Aulus Terentius is the Princeps.

He looks at Tia. "We shall just have to wait. Decius will find out and send another letter." She nods. But she is not happy. If Augustus has pursued Aulus to Massilia, then he will know how Aulus got there, the connection with the Sestius family and the names of everyone on board the Nereid. Waiting patiently will be hard.

On the day of the festival of the Parilia, everyone struggles out of bed early, long before sunrise, and gathers at the main sheep field. The sheep have all been herded to the far end of the field, and the people crowd around the empty sheep pen, weaving garlands and branches of greenery in and out of the bars of the fences. Inside the sheep pen, several of the farm hands are engaged in a solemn and not very effective sweeping of the ground, making exaggerated curving loops in the air with the brooms. The fire is lit, and one nervous-looking shepherd wraps a very small lamb in a blanket and faces the fire. He visibly tells himself to do it, the lamb struggles and bleats and, in a panic of pressure, man and lamb leap over the bonfire, jumping so high, the crackling flames are left far beneath them both. Everyone cheers, the lamb is sent running back to its mother at the end of the field, and the crowd turns to watch for the first sliver of sun to rise above the hills to the east. A quick dab of dew on the face and a prayer for shepherding success, then the ritual drink is handed around by the kitchen staff who have brought down an amphora of the traditional brew, an utterly revolting mixture of milk and wine. Every year, Sergius looks for ways to make this more palatable, and the addition of honey and cinnamon almost does the trick, but few people drink more than the obligatory mouthful. A few lads, cheered on by their friends, jump the bonfire and Publius looks up at Lucius with a look of doubt on his face: Lucius assures his son that this is by no means a necessity. The farm kitchen puts on a magnificent breakfast, and everyone goes home afterwards for a nap, before struggling out in the afternoon to do the bare minimum of work. The next day is busy in preparation for the main event – the Vinalia.

Titus is failing but towards noon on the day itself, he is carried out of the cottage on a couch and brought to the side of the stream, where last year's wine is handed out to everyone to sample. Lucius leads prayers to Venus, Jupiter, Bacchus and to the divine power of the stream: a jar of the finest wine they own (as judged by Titus) is poured into the stream, and everyone crowds the banks of the stream to tip in the lees of their own drinks. The majority then troop off to the villa where a huge feast will be served on tables set up in the main garden, and the party will go on all day. Lucius helps take Titus back to the cottage and leaves a small group of friends there with their own amphora to have a quiet celebration. He spends the afternoon wandering around groups of people, talking to slaves, family, friends and neighbours, and gradually getting drunk, which is practically the rule at Vinalia. He knows through bitter experience that he must not fall asleep in the afternoon and goes off with a cup of well water to wander up and down his rows of vines until his head clears. He tries not to look at the garden as he makes his way back to the house, comforting himself with the thought that a very bad-tempered Sergius will ensure that a massive clear-up will put everything back to rights the next day.

Titus dies – fittingly enough – late on the evening of the day of the Vinalia, festival of the vines, and his funeral, quietly prepared long before, takes place the next morning. The entire farm is hungover as they build a pyre and burn his body, and Lucius finds it worth a smile that even Titus' funeral is dominated by thoughts of wine. The ashes are cooled with wine as is the custom and will be buried, not in a cemetery, but on the side of the road from Cosa: Titus' wishes were clear about this. Lucius plans to plant a single vine on the grass verge. That will be after the Robigalia, the festival which everyone forgets is happening until the morning itself when there is a scramble in the kitchen to come up with one more meal, and Sergius remembers that they never sorted out a puppy for the sacrifice. Lucius dislikes this ceremony and a priest from the temple to Jupiter in Cosa usually gets summoned to carry it out for them. The priest arrives complete with a puppy he prepared earlier, they pray, and the puppy is sacrificed with a chilling little whimper. Celi struggles not to cry. A meal brings the series of celebrations to the end for this April. The gods have had everything they need to bless the farm for the year. On the next day life will return to normal, though in Rome the festivity goes on: in a few days, the games in honour of the goddess Flora (yet another deity concerned with fertility) will begin. Lucius doesn't think his small community can cope with more eating and drinking. And Titus' illness and death has cast a shadow over them all: the people of the farm and villa are quite glad to get back to work, while Marcella and her sons need time to grieve. Lucius is pleased that Celi has decided to make a point of visiting Marcella every day, and he and Sergius draw up an agreement which gives Marcella and her sons the right to live in the cottage indefinitely. He makes sure that there is a clause in the agreement whereby Marcella will still be able to stay for the rest of her life, even if the boys leave. Lucius privately thinks that Marcella will not remain a widow for long: she is at least ten years younger than he is and she is an attractive woman, a good homemaker. Someone will appreciate her, and Lucius wonders if Sergius will put in a bid after a decent time has passed. It would be a good match in terms of status and age, and Sergius would gain two stepsons. In Cosa, Lucius thinks, things have a way of settling back into an ordered tranquillity after times of upheaval.

He goes into the town to pay the bill for Titus' care to Doctor

Larcius on the day after the Robigalia. Plodding back on the faithful Alexander he is in the haze of not-really-thinking-about-anything which is produced by one cup of un-watered and excellent wine. The good doctor has accepted the payment of his modest bill and they have toasted Titus in fine style. Lucius has just turned up the track which leads to the farm, when he hears a shout behind him and turns to see a horse and rider galloping up. To his amazement, the rider is Decius, unshaven, dusty and looking as though he hasn't eaten for days. This is clearly not the time for niceties, and as Decius draws up beside him, Lucius asks quickly, "Are you all right?"

Decius nods briefly and says, "Aulus has been killed, I think on the orders of the Princeps. I left Massilia five days ago, but the official courier has probably already reached Rome and Augustus will know about our part in helping Aulus to escape."

And with that, the horse stumbles and Decius slides off in an inelegant flurry of limbs, and sits on the ground, managing to hold onto the reins. Lucius jumps off Alexander who stands still of course: never any need to hang onto Alexander's reins. Lucius drags Decius up from the ground and with one arm around his shoulders starts to half-drag him towards the gate. The gate slaves have spotted them, and one comes running to help while another vanishes, no doubt to get help from the house. As Lucius and his slave get Decius through the gate, he sees Tia running from the house in a panic, her skirts kilted up, her feet bare. She calms down as she comes up to Decius – one quick look satisfies her that Lucius is fine – and then she takes over, giving directions and calling for water, wine and a blanket as she escorts them through the garden. They take Decius straight to his own room and lie him on his couch. Tia gives him a little wine and water, and wipes his face gently, then shoos everyone out. As Lucius leaves the room, she is sitting by the couch with Decius' hand in her own and looking strangely

225

content.

Sergius and Lucius retire to his study and Lucius relays his own instructions, which have tumbled into place in those brief few minutes of watching as Decius is tended. Lookouts are placed at the boundaries of the farm, and on the Aurelian Road itself. Lucius has no doubt that a summons from the Princeps is on its way, and while he has no intention of disobeying, he does want to be forewarned. He spends the afternoon gazing out of the study window and making lists of instructions to cover as many eventualities as his scurrying brain can conjure. The hope that Augustus will not ask him for an accounting of what he has done to assist Aulus is held up for examination in the clear sunshine and found to be lacking in substance. Horace finds him there as the sun is beginning to slide into the evening and announces the intention of dining with "an old friend" in Cosa. Lucius looks at him.

"You have an old friend in Cosa? You've never mentioned that before!"

"I have just heard that he has moved there," says Horace with the shocking confidence of a professional liar. Are all poets so good at untruths?

"Do borrow Alexander to ride down there," says Lucius graciously. Horace laughs.

"I shall walk, thank you," he says.

Lucius watches the poet leave a few minutes later, accompanied by one of the farm boys equipped with a torch for the return journey. He blesses Horace for his diplomacy, and summons Sergius to give some instructions regarding dinner.

Decius is recovered by dinner time and he, Lucius, Albinia and Tia have a quiet meal on their own in the summer dining room, running the risk of cold food against the advantage of greater privacy. Once the food has been brought in, the slaves are dismissed, and they serve themselves as Decius tells the story of Massilia.

"You got my letter saying that Aulus had disappeared, didn't you? I'm sorry about that, it was very difficult to say exactly the right thing, and I thought there was a risk, if Aulus had been captured, that he would give my name and details and any letter would be read. But I knew that if I acted quickly, there was a good chance a message would get through to you, so I got one of the crew of the Nereid onto a ship going back to Ostia and we paid the captain to stop at Cosa. That was several days before the Ides of April. I spent a couple of days looking for Aulus, checking with the people he had seen about travelling up the Rhone, and then heard a story about an upper-class Roman who had been arrested and taken to the house of a local magistrate. I found the official concerned and made enquiries – discreetly, and through his clerk – but he denied all knowledge of the rumour. I also got the landlord of my inn to keep an eye out for people hanging around or maybe asking questions, so I decided that I could risk watching the magistrate's house for a bit and sure enough, on the third day after I sent the letter to you, I saw a group of slaves leaving the magistrate's house with a cart, loaded with some sacks and spades. I got a couple of small boys to follow them and to tell me if and where they left the town and that is exactly what they did. I knew which town gate they would use coming back, found a bar to prop up nearby and saw the same group return, minus the sacks, just as night fell. I didn't think there was any point in looking for a grave, but I am firmly convinced that Aulus Terentius is dead."

A silence, not exactly surprised, but sadly accepting, follows this and for a while they let Decius eat. He continues,

"I decided to carry on watching the magistrate's house for a little while, and it was a good decision for the next morning a carriage drew up outside the house and I saw the man who got into that carriage. Lucius, it was Maecenas. I think Augustus sent him to Massilia in pursuit of Aulus and that he condemned him and had him executed – his own brother-in-law."

There is a silence around the table. Decius takes the opportunity to refill his plate and cup, and Lucius finds himself listing all the possible scenarios involving a cart, some sacks and a couple of spades.

"Did you ask again about the arrested man?" asks Albinia, doubtfully.

"No," says Decius through a mouthful of bread. They wait patiently.

"Maecenas left Massilia on the next day." Decius picks up his cup and resumes the narrative. "He made his way in the carriage to the docks, so I knew he was on his way back to Rome. The Nereid was also waiting in the harbour of course, and we sailed the day after Maecenas. Unfortunately, once we hit the coast of Italy, the wind turned and so I had to ride the last part of the journey from just south of Populonium. I reckon that Maecenas will only just be reaching Rome.

Albinia stares off into the distance and says, "And given that he will have sent Augustus a letter via official courier, we must assume that the news has already reached Rome, and that Augustus knows that we helped Aulus Terentius to get out of Italy."

Lucius says, "You didn't. I did."

"What help did you actually give him? And who did you tell?"

Tia leaps in to defend him.

"He didn't discuss it with anyone but Decius, Alby. Nobody else was involved."

"Except the sailors of the boat you lent him – you lent him one of our ships, didn't you? Which one?"

"The Nereid," says Lucius.

Albinia smiles. "Good. It's a lucky ship."

Lucius looks at her in surprise. "You approve of what I did?"

Albinia gives a short "Huh," of bitter laughter. "Yes, I approve. I would have done exactly the same, and so I am glad that we did not invite Horace to this dinner! He is too close to Maecenas to hear this conversation. If the Princeps told Aulus to get out of Italy, then of course you were right to help him. That Augustus had him followed and killed is utterly disgraceful. But I am afraid that it is quite clear that we cannot trust Augustus one whit and must prepare for the worst. Lucius, how do you feel about exile?"

"Been there done that," says Lucius almost flippantly, and after a silent moment, he and Albinia laugh. Tia does not. Tears are running down her face and she holds Decius' hand. Decius' face has one deep crease between his eyebrows, a sign of the utmost concern. He has not yet shaved, and he suddenly looks older, a very respectable uncle at the family table. He says quietly, "The alternative to exile is suicide."

Lucius has prepared for this. "Exile it is then," he says decidedly. "And though I shall miss Cosa, I shan't mind exile at all. As long as it isn't too cold."

"And we shall come with you!" cries Tia, her voice attempting humour and failing miserably. She swallows a little hicuppy sob and says, "I mean it, Lucius. I want to come with you."

Lucius says into his wine-cup, "That is kind, but you can't all come. I need someone to stay to look after Cosa and the children. If Augustus lets me keep it of course." That brings another moment of silence as they all look at the prospect of being poor. Traditionally, exile also means loss of property.

Albinia says, "Well, whatever happens I can look after the children very well on my income, so no need to worry about that. As for the rest, we shall just have to see. I suggest, Lucius, that you send the Swan away as soon as possible, with a few choice pieces in her. She can go to Massilia and wait there for a message telling her what to do."

This is a very good idea, and if the Swan catches the Nereid on the journey, all the better. More ideas arise and are examined: should Albinia take the children away tomorrow morning? Where should they go? What about Horace? Should they warn Sergius about what may happen?

"He will guess, even if you don't tell him," says Decius. "Everyone on the farm will have an idea by now."

"I would like to tell Horace, if you don't mind," says Albinia. "He might feel that it would be wise to go back to Tibur."

"I don't suppose there is any chance that Horace might have known that Maecenas was off to Massilia?" asks Decius, and Albinia looks angry for a moment, before thinking and calming. She shakes her head and says, "I'm sure I would have noticed a messenger arriving with a letter from Maecenas for him at Tibur and he has received nothing since he came here at least."

"The trial took place while we were with him at the Sabine farm," says Decius. "Then he came back to Rome with us and stayed with Maecenas."

"Maecenas would have had to have left Rome before the start of April if he was in Massilia in time to catch Aulus Terentius," says Lucius. "I doubt if informing Horace of his proposed travels was high on his agenda." He pauses to think about the timing. "Aulus left Cosa long before you and Horace arrived."

Albinia suddenly looks upset and says, "Horace was really keen to come here when we got your letter inviting us – you know the one with that absolutely awful bit of verse that you both thought so funny…"

Tia leaps in with, "You are beginning to talk nonsense, Alby. Horace has nothing to do with any of this, and the idea he would spy on us for Maecenas is ridiculous. Put it all out of your mind and let's get thinking about what we do now."

By the end of the evening they have decided on some small actions – nothing too big, nothing to arouse anger in the Princeps. They can squirrel away some money, some small items, but if Augustus decides to seize Lucius' estate there must be something to seize. Lucius packs a small chest with books and a couple of favourite bronze statuettes from the desk in his study. He looks at the busts of Brutus and Cassius and decides to leave them: Augustus can certainly have those!

Tia puts her small collection of jewellery in with his treasures and Decius bundles together a collection of papers which he says are important. Decius speaks firmly and nobody raises an objection. Despite all this, the chest remains only half-full and they gather around looking into it and thinking how strange that nearly every physical thing Lucius values is there. To fill the chest, the collection is topped off with a toga, some boots, and Lucius' cloak that he keeps for walking the farm in winter. While none of them say anything out loud they are all thinking of Britannia, that strange and grey land beyond the civilisation of Gaul, a land where it rains nine months of the year and is misty for the remaining three. Lucius cannot remember where he read that, probably in Julius Caesar's accounts of landing there. But it may turn out that this is the only land where having an item of clothing like a toga, with its yards of wool, is useful.

"Horace has written a poem about Augustus conquering Britannia," says Tia, echoing their thoughts.

"Nobody wants to conquer Britannia," says Decius, and daringly puts an arm around her shoulders.

"Perfect for me then," says Lucius. And he calls for Sergius to arrange for the chest to be taken down to the Swan and stored with a minimum of fuss. Sergius will also arrange for the ship to be loaded as quickly as possible with something – anything – and to get ready to set off as if on a perfectly normal voyage. If necessary, Tia and Decius can sail too, while Albinia will guard the children. And then, to allay the gloom, he invites everyone into the garden with their wine-cups and a new jug of last year's finest. They watch as a bobbing orange light carried by one of the kitchen boys heralds the return of their house guest, and a slightly wobbly Horace floats along the road and joins them. His dinner with his imaginary friend has gone well, and nothing is spoken about Augustus or treachery or exile. It is a beautiful evening, slightly cool, but with that lovely dark blue night sky that looks soft and deep, as if you could bounce on it and wrap yourself in it. Lucius does not think about the future. He finishes the wine, says goodnight and goes to his own room where he sleeps well. He is not afraid.

In the morning, there is an atmosphere. First of all, there are fewer people around than usual. Decius and Tia go down to the Swan, and many of the slaves are on patrol duty. Gallio and Helice have wisely decided to take the children off for the day to climb hills and look at plants and such things. The whole villa is waiting, and it is not easy to keep going. Lucius cannot think of anything else he needs to do, but Decius and Tia have left instructions for Sergius and the man is in and out with any number of requests and queries. Lucius finds the myriad lists he made yesterday come in useful, and since everything seems under control, he considers setting off for Rome now, rather than waiting. But even as he thinks this, there is a shout outside.

Chapter 26

The slave who has been watching the Aurelian Road runs in just before noon to say that there is a carriage and a group of mounted soldiers accompanying it. Lucius wonders if Augustus himself has arrived but it is no surprise – indeed it is almost appropriate – when the carriage stops at the gate and Maecenas gets out.

"Lucius Sestius!" says Maecenas a little too cordially. "I decided to come by carriage this time, but never again. I have no idea why we rave about our roads so much; I felt every bump." He turns to the ornately armoured soldier who stands at the head of the little group and looks steadfastly anywhere but at Maecenas. "Officer! How long did that dreadful journey take us?"

"We set off yesterday morning, sir," says the man through gritted teeth.

"So we did," says Maecenas. "And I have been travelling for simply weeks, it seems, so now I need a little rest while I explain things to Lucius Sestius. You and your men can get some food and look after your horses and suchlike."

The man stiffens but turns round and yells unintelligible orders to his men. Lucius has not planned on actually having to entertain his visitors but how like Maecenas, he thinks, as he leads the way into the house and asks Sergius to serve light refreshments as soon as possible in his study. He knows that Sergius will also send food out to the soldiers. He is taken aback when the officer marches into the house behind them, hand on his sword-hilt and a look on his face which says that he will carry out his instructions even when he is asked to look after an idiot like Maecenas.

233

Maecenas once more settles himself in Lucius' study and says as he looks around idly, "I was last here nearly a year ago, wasn't I? To offer you the consulship. I think Cicero would probably say "O tempora! O mores!" at this point, wouldn't he? The times have definitely changed."

Lucius sighs. He really finds it hard that he must put up with being arrested by Maecenas: Maecenas going down the route of civilised affability is making Lucius' teeth ache.

"Do I take it that as soon as the horses are refreshed, we shall be going back to Rome?" he asks.

"Oh yes, of course," says Maecenas. "You need to see Augustus and explain why someone like you thinks it a good idea to help Aulus Terentius escape."

"You didn't find it in your heart to help your own brother-in-law?"

"No, because I am not a fool," says Maecenas. "Once someone starts plotting against Rome, then he has severed all family ties. Don't you think?"

"Barely a plot," says Lucius. "And Augustus himself told him to leave Italy. I was just helping him to do that."

"Dear me," says Maecenas accepting the wine-cup Sergius offers in silence. Lucius takes his own cup, and Sergius nods and leaves the room. Nobody bothers offering the cavalry officer anything.

Maecenas sighs and says, "I can see that dear Aulus was not entirely open with you, Lucius Sestius, so let me tell you what has been happening in Rome while you have been happily rusticating. Make yourself comfortable."

Lucius bites his tongue at such rudeness but finds silence in his wine-cup.

"Aulus no doubt told you it was all to do with the dreadful unfairness of the Primus trial," begins Maecenas. "And it may well have needed that to get the idiot moving, but he has been showing signs of dissatisfaction for some time. It is the reaction of a man with little talent to a regime which only promotes people because they deserve it. Aulus thought when I married his sister, that this connection and a respectable family name would see him to the consulship and beyond, and he stopped thinking that he had to work for his rewards. I'm afraid it hasn't worked like that for a very long time."

"You made me Consul," points out Lucius.

Maecenas sighs. "And we got a good few months' work out of you, Lucius Sestius. Augustus thought you had the capacity for hard work, and I thought you would be sensible and not make trouble and we were right. You and Piso put in some excellent reforms around the city – just what we hoped for. What we aren't going to do is promote a lightweight with the avowed intention of pimping his sister to get what he wants. Oh yes, we all know about Terentia, let's not pretend we don't. I hope Augustus enjoyed her. It's all over now of course, and the poor little thing was desperately upset for a week or so. I expect she has moved on by now though. You know, I'm sure there was a good reason why I married her at the time, but I really can't remember what it was. And what with her hopelessly stupid brother, I suppose I should divorce her now, but that will just bring more tears and expense."

He pauses to refill his cup.

"Where was I? Oh, Aulus and his ridiculous plot. Well, yes, we realised he was going to go off the rails in a big way soon, so we hauled him in and the stupid man admitted that he was beginning to go round collecting like-minded, disaffected has-beens. Only a handful took him seriously and he admitted he didn't even try you. But the handful had begun to meet, and a man named Caepio was a little worrying. I thought he had it in him to have a serious attempt at an assassination. When we intercepted some letters that Aulus wrote off to one or two military types in his old legion we decided that it couldn't go on. We hauled him in again and gave him a dressing-down and sent him off home to decide how he was going to play it. We hoped he would do the decent thing. When he left Rome, Augustus decided to observe and let him make his way to Gaul. He met up with Caepio, then we lost the two of them, but we had worked out that Massilia and Gaul were the likely destinations, so we had people go and start looking there. Lo and behold he turns up on one of your boats! So, our people got rid of him and sent the information they had gained back to Rome. Augustus has done you the courtesy of asking me to accompany you back to Rome to see him and explain yourself."

Lucius notices that not only does Maecenas say "We" a lot, but that there is no mention of Maecenas' own involvement at Massilia. Maybe admitting that he was present at Aulus' death is too uncomfortable, despite Maecenas' air of detachment throughout his narrative.

"Do you know what the Princeps has in mind?" asks Lucius, more out of curiosity than anything.

Maecenas sighs. "He isn't happy. Don't expect a full pardon. I assume that you were expecting something like this to happen, so as you haven't already committed suicide, I also assume that you have decided to take your chances. Worth the risk I'd say. A trial of some sort is inevitable, but you may be exiled."

Suicide is honourable of course, but, like Maecenas, Lucius is betting on exile rather than execution, given he hasn't actually plotted against the Princeps himself. This is going to be a tedious and unpleasant time in his life, but he thinks he will get through it. He hopes the children will not be too frightened.

As he thinks this, he hears voices in the corridor and Publius and Celi run in, followed by Gallio, who is looking alarmed. Celi runs straight up to Lucius and flings her arms around him while Publius stands in front of Maecenas and glares. The room is suddenly crowded, and Lucius cannot stand or indeed move as Celi wraps herself around him.

Maecenas looks up at Publius' scowling face and says with an air of infinite superiority and a lick of scorn, "Young man, you are in my way."

Publius cannot get any closer, but he stays firmly planted in front of Maecenas and folds his arms across his chest in an age-old gesture of defiance. And before anyone can say anything else, the calvary officer has moved out from behind Maecenas' chair and hits Publius with an open-palmed slap on the side of his head which sends the boy flying. Publius does not have time to unfold his arms before his head hits the edge of Lucius' desk with a sound halfway between a crunch and a thud, and his body bounces off the desk and down to the floor. For an instant nobody moves, and all their attention is focussed on the boy as they wait for him to move, cry out – but Publius lies still.

A few ghastly seconds of hot disbelief and denial race through Lucius' mind, then he takes Celi and shoves her at Gallio, barking, "Get her out!" He pushes the officer out of the way and falls down beside Publius, hesitating to even touch the boy – then as some ancient army training comes back he holds the back of his hand in front of the mouth, grasps the slight and limp hand. Over and over in his head run the words, "He's dead, he's dead, he's dead."

Lucius is alone, unable to see anything but his son's body and aeons pass as he kneels there looking at the face with its skin so soft and young, faint hairs on the upper lip – really? Publius was growing a moustache already? But it is down really, he wasn't going to get very far with that. Gently Lucius strokes the fine, fine hairs and marvels at the way Publius' mouth has relaxed into the buttoned-in corners and rounded bottom lip of a cherub. He is just a little boy still.

An arm goes around Lucius' shoulders and a gentle voice

tells him to get up, so he stands and lets the voice take him to another room where he is made to sit and a cup of wine is pushed into his hand. He can hear people talking, exclamations and sobs. Far, far away Celi is wailing unrestrainedly. Someone nearer is saying "Hush!", but he doesn't know who is saying it nor who needs to hush. Maybe he is crying but he doesn't think so. He isn't feeling anything. The cup is empty and there is a muttered conversation as it is taken from him and refilled. The voice tells him to drink up and he does, feeling the ache of weariness settle behind his eyes. Maybe sleeping is the answer and he lies down and feels the darkness wrap around him as his mind builds walls to keep the light at bay.

As he awakens, he can hear whispers rise and fall around him, and gradually he realises that they are real and that several people are having an argument.

"And I am asking you to wait a day!" hisses voice number one, light but intense. Albinia.

"I can give you a day but no more," says the second voice, not so familiar.

There is a pause and a sniff of disgust from Albinia, then she whispers again, "Then with your permission I shall go and make the arrangements. Please don't feel you have to stay here and guard him. I'm sure that if you stand outside the door you will catch him if he tries to escape." Steps and swishing, then she halts and says in a tone of such anger, "Please come out of the room – now. I don't want you to be the first thing he sees. I shall ask Horace to sit with him, if you really feel someone should be in the room all the time." After a while, the second person follows her through the door, and Lucius thinks he hears her say, "When did you lose all your humanity?" and then he remembers.

He cannot help groaning out loud and another person comes through the door and says "Lucius?"

He opens his eyes and sees Horace sitting down on a stool next to his couch. Horace takes his hand and Lucius clutches at him. "My son?"

"I'm very sorry, Lucius," says Horace, and his eyes are indeed swimming with tears. "Publius must have died immediately. His head – he cracked it against the desk. It was an accident. I'm so sorry."

"An accident?" Lucius tries to sit up and has to take it slowly. What had Albinia put in that wine? "I've been asleep— how? How long?"

"Just a couple of hours," says Horace. "Albinia is looking after everything."

Looking after everything. That means his son. Publius is being washed and dressed and laid out in the villa's entrance hall. Flowers will be being picked to put around him, and someone will be arranging a funeral. They have only just said farewell to Titus. How will they handle another death, another funeral pyre? Lucius feels panic and rage and grief well up inside him, and he turns to bury his head in his pillow, shaking and howling his sobs out into the material while Horace crouches down beside the couch, arms around him.

As the sobbing exhausts Lucius he slides into a half-sleep, and while aware that Horace is holding him and people are talking around him, he also knows that Publius is lying on the family's ancient funeral couch, on show in the entrance hall. He sees the small figure, covered by a sheet which is tucked in under the feet and comes up as far as the face. The body is so much shorter than the couch and the skin of the face is now so white and Lucius aches even in his dreaming state to see the eyelids flutter. The little mouth is pale and dry too and the lips are slightly parted: Lucius thinks, "I must put in a coin for the ferryman." He knows exactly which coin, but when he tries to go to his desk to fetch it, he finds that his limbs will not move.

He is still asleep and doesn't know how to wake.

Albinia has changed places with Horace as he enters reality once more and she squeezes his hand gently as she sees him opening his eyes.

"Brother," she says softly.

"Albinia," he says, "have you put a coin in his mouth for the ferryman?"

Albinia strokes his hair back from his forehead. "No, Lucius dear. I thought you would want to do that."

And with her help Lucius gets up: on legs surprisingly shaky at first, he hobbles over to his desk. At the back of a drawer is a small wooden box which rattles as he takes it out, and his hands shake so much he gives the box to Albinia to open. When she looks inside, she nods and takes out one small silver denarius, a coin barely bigger than her fingernail. The two of them then slowly walk out of the study and along the short corridor to the entrance of the villa, where, just as in his dream, Lucius sees his son lying on a couch, feet towards the door as is the custom. A soldier stands on either side of the front door, and Lucius hopes they are at least embarrassed. There is no sign of their officer or Maecenas, and Lucius doesn't bother to ask where they are. His gaze is fixed on his son. The couch and boy are covered in cream draperies, but Publius' face is one shade paler even than these, and his dark hair seems stark against all the light colour. Lucius looks at the coin in his hand, a denarius minted far away in the East in the year before he fought at Philippi, when the Princeps was barely twenty and he himself just twenty-five. On one side of the coin are the instruments of sacrifice, and on the other is a portrait of Liberty personified. Sacrificing Julius Caesar according to Brutus had brought freedom back to Rome. Now Lucius' son has been sacrificed but they still will not find freedom. He places the coin gently between the lips, and says, "Safe travels, Publius. Pay the ferryman and see what is on the other side."

A stool has appeared next to Publius' couch and Lucius sits on it and tells the story of the coin on Publius' lips.

"I was travelling, first with Cassius, then with Brutus – we went all over the East, raising troops and money, because we knew that we would have to fight at some point. And we decided to mint special coins to pay the troops we raised. I was put in charge. I decided that we would mint on the move – take everything we needed wherever we went so that we could put coins out, get the message out, in every place we stopped. Coins do that, you see, Publius. You put images on them so even people who can't read get the idea. We found a man who had been in charge of one of the provincial mints in Cilicia, and persuaded him to head up the operation, and one day I sat with him and together we designed this coin. He drew the design, but I thought of the theme. Freedom. It was all about freedom. So, we put a portrait of the goddess Liberty on one face of the coin. And to get that freedom, Brutus said, we had had to make a Caesar our sacrifice, so I decided that the instruments of sacrifice should be on the other side, an axe, a tripod, a cup. I thought I was being clever. I was very young, Publius. But freedom is important, and I really thought that it was worth the sacrifice. I see now that it isn't. I'm so sorry."

He sits with his son, as the household slip in and bow their heads and pay silent tribute. Even Marcella with eyes already red comes along, supported by her sons one on either side, and Lucius looks at them all and thinks that between them, he and Marcella have one complete family. How strange life is.

As evening falls, two unexpected arrivals slip into the villa – Decius and Tia have come back from seeing to the Swan in Cosa harbour. Lucius is heartily glad to see them, though Tia is beside herself with grief, and quickly retires to her own room with a maid and Albinia. Decius sits next to Lucius and gazes at

Publius' body with a look of such hard, icy anger that Lucius for the first time wonders what he himself looks like.

"We did wonder about sailing with the Swan, as you suggested, but in the end, we decided not – we thought maybe later, when we knew about what was going to happen," says Decius quietly. "So, we just left the harbour and went to Larcius' house to tell the doctor what was happening – some of it anyway. The Nereid should be back soon, and I thought he would appreciate knowing that. We stayed with him, then a messenger arrived. Sergius had sent him to go all around the harbour and the town until he discovered where we were. He told us that a detachment of soldiers and a carriage had arrived, and Tia insisted we come back. They told us at the gate. The Swan is waiting for two days in case we need her, then she is going on to Massilia and your chest will be left at the inn there. There are a couple of soldiers in the courtyard by the way, but they had no chance of stopping Tia."

"I don't know exactly what is going to happen now," says Lucius softly. "I think they will surround the villa to make sure I don't make a run for it, then take me to Rome as planned. I can't see them delaying that much, so will you prepare for the funeral please? Wait as long as you can – then hold it without me."

"Of course," says Decius and there is no need to talk any more. The light fades completely, and lamps are lit. Tomorrow friends and neighbours will start to arrive and a smell of cooking reminds Lucius that someone must make sure that people are fed. He is not hungry, but he will at some point eat. Decius will make sure of that. And sure enough when little bowls of soup are served to those keeping vigil in the hall, Decius makes Lucius take one and watches while he spoons soup into his mouth and makes no demur. And finally, when he is almost slipping off the stool with fatigue, Decius takes him to his room and puts him to bed.

He wakes at dawn and when he starts to get up, he nearly treads on a bundle of blankets next to the bed. Closer examination shows that this is Celi, and Lucius wonders at what time in the night she eluded Helice and came in here. He is touched as he looks at her peaceful face and carefully steps over her. Once dressed and washed, he walks into the hall and bumps into a frantic-looking Helice. He explains and she nods in relief and runs off towards the corridor – "Let her sleep!" calls Lucius after her, softly, and Helice nods as she skitters down the corridor. Gallio has taken the stool next to Publius and as Lucius draws near, he sees that the old tutor – when did Gallio become old? – is reading to Publius. It is in Greek, and Lucius listens and recognises it as Plato's dialogue Meno, which discusses the nature of virtue. Publius' shade will be pleased with that. Gallio sees him, reads to the end of the paragraph and gets up. He bows to Lucius and steps away, saying, "I shall finish reading it to him later, sir."

"Thank you," says Lucius but does not sit. He is making his farewells. He knows that soon Maecenas will enter, and he will be taken away. He sighs and moves away, and sees Albinia and Tia hovering, and goes over to hug them.

"Celi is still asleep," he says. "Helice is with her and I don't want to wake her. When she does wake tell her I love her very much and nearly trod on her this morning. Whatever happens, tell her everything – don't cover things up. She will have to know eventually. If the Princeps confiscates everything, let him. We have enough between us to cope. Decius knows where there is a little put aside for emergencies and…" He stops as Albinia lays her hand on his arm.

"I have enough for us all. Don't worry, Lucius. We have got it all arranged. Once you have gone, Horace is following you to Rome, and we shall give him several slaves and some horses so that he can send messages to let us know what is happening. And of course, he will be able to see Maecenas, maybe even Augustus, if he thinks that will help."

"It won't," says Lucius. "Tell him not to try. Augustus has already decided and nothing Horace can say will change his mind."

And with that, Maecenas comes in through the front door and stands just inside. He does not need to say anything. Lucius looks around at his family and smiles at them just in case this is the last time he sees them. Sergius comes hurrying up with his cloak and in complete silence Lucius is escorted to the courtyard where what looks like the entire staff of the villa are waiting to one side while the soldiers, already mounted, line up at the other. The carriage stands in the middle, looking lumbering and impractical. Lucius does not look back or to the side but marches straight up to the carriage and gets in. He ignores Maecenas. The soldiers line up on either side and the procession moves away. Lucius gazes out of the small window and ticks off the small and unimportant landmarks of his land as he leaves it – the old wall, supposedly built when the Etruscans were ruling this land, the dovecote at the end of the drive, and the small group of cypresses which is the first thing you see when approaching the track from the Aurelian Road. He knows he may not see them again but is too numb to let that get near to him. All he is doing at this moment is existing.

Chapter 27

The journey to Rome makes no impression on Lucius as he dozes, wakes and dozes again, occasionally thinking of Publius, occasionally noticing the tears running down his face. At one point he dreams that Maecenas has put a blanket around him, and even though he wakes to find it true, it means nothing. One must keep an animal safe and happy before it is sacrificed after all. He is given excellent wine in copious quantities for the same reason. He knows that they travel through the night, and once they reach Rome, they are transferred into a litter as the carriage won't make it up and down the narrower streets. The streets are crowded and festive, and once when Lucius peers out of the litter, he sees that everyone walking through the city is dressed up in their finest. Maecenas takes a brief look and says, "It's the Floralia."

They make their slow way to the Palatine and are marched into the large room with the desk in the middle. And there sits the Princeps, working away at a pile of wax tablets, his secretaries hovering. No flowery garlands or bright tunic for him.

As soon as Lucius and Maecenas walk in – the soldiers have peeled off, most staying outside in the square in front of the Temple of Apollo with just a couple coming into the house and standing on either side of the front door – the secretaries whisper and scurry off. After a few moments, the cavalry officer also comes in and takes up his station just behind Maecenas. Augustus arranges the desk in front of him and makes room for his clasped hands to rest in front of him. He nods at Maecenas and Maecenas takes Lucius' arm and brings him forward to the two chairs standing in front of the desk, facing Augustus. They

245

sit and a cup materialises at Lucius' elbow. He takes a sip. Well-watered wine. He could do with a snack as well: he cannot remember when he last ate, though he has a vague memory of soup drunk a long time ago. He clutches at the cup and waits.

"He looks absolutely terrible, Maecenas," says the Princeps. "Anything I should know about?"

Ah, thinks Lucius, so Maecenas hasn't dared send a messenger with that news. Interesting.

Maecenas clears his throat. "I'm afraid there was an accident. The son – just a boy – he fell and hit his head. I'm sorry to say that the lad died immediately. Naturally, Lucius Sestius is in a state of shock and grief."

Augustus' eyes narrow slightly, and he says nothing, then looks at the officer. The man comes forward and stands to attention and looks straight ahead as he recites a wholly truthful account of the death of Lucius' son. At the end – it doesn't take much time to tell the story – Augustus nods slowly, and murmurs "A tragedy. How terrible."

"But an accident," says Maecenas, far too quickly.

"Yes, yes," says Augustus. "I understand that. But – what to do now? Look at him – he is in no fit state for anything. I'm going to have to think about this. Take him home – to your home, Maecenas, and keep him there until I have had a chance to think. I'll let you know what I decide."

And the audience is over. After a short pause, Maecenas gets up, takes Lucius' arm again and leads him back out into the square. Once more they climb into the litter, and Lucius falls asleep as they wend their way through Rome and onto the Esquiline Hill to Maecenas' house. There Lucius is put to bed and made to drink something by a worried-looking Greek who, it turns out, is Maecenas' private doctor. He really must stop sleeping, he thinks as he drifts off, and is quite pleased with himself for finally having a real thought.

He wakes up to find Horace sitting next to him, and for a moment thinks he must be back in Cosa. Looking round the elaborately decorated room though, he remembers. His head is filled with clouds, and he is too hot, but he is in the house of Maecenas, on the Esquiline Hill, in Rome. It is the Floralia, and people in bright colours are dancing and watching shows and chariot races, while back in Cosa, his son is lying in state in the atrium of the villa and the family tomb on the old road leading out of the northern side of Cosa is being prepared. Perhaps Publius will be cremated tomorrow, his ashes will be laid next to those of his grandfather and he will be safe. Lucius for some bizarre reason, after all he has been through in life, is alive, has outlived his own son and that seems almost beyond belief. Nothing Horace can say will surprise him.

"Hello," he says cautiously. "What is going on?"

"We don't know," says Horace, admirably resisting the temptation to ask questions about how Lucius is feeling. "All I do know is that you are to be kept here in Maecenas' custody until Augustus decides what to do with you. And Maecenas is worried."

"Good," says Lucius, and sits up. A tiny spark of energy is lighting up inside him. Just enough to ask questions. "What day is it? I've lost all track of time. Is it still April?"

Horace has to think about this, and his lips move as he calculates.

"Tomorrow is the Kalends of May – last day of April today."

"It's unlucky for weddings, May," murmurs Lucius.

Horace says gently, "You have had a terrible shock, Lucius, and I need to take care of you. Will you let me?"

Lucius thinks and says, "Yes."

So, Horace takes him off to the small but luxurious bathhouse attached to one wing of Maecenas' house, and Lucius is massaged and scraped and washed down. His teeth are cleaned, his nails trimmed on both hands and feet, but he draws the line at a shave, saying firmly that he is in mourning and must grow his beard. Horace vanishes as Lucius is being dried. When he returns to his room, a pile of fresh tunics in sombre colours are waiting for him, and a table crowded with jugs of wine, water and olives, oil and a plate of bread. He drinks and nibbles and looks around wondering what to do next. A slave appears to clear the plates and Lucius asks for Horace, just as the poet comes in, laden with scrolls and some wax tablets.

"Reading matter, just in case," says Horace. "And we can write back to Cosa and tell them what little we know as long as Maecenas reads it through first."

"In case I say something nasty about Augustus?"

Horace shrugs. "Who knows? I'm sorry, Lucius, I feel completely in the dark at the moment. We are genuinely at the mercy of powers beyond our control, and that sounds such a cliché I shudder at using it. But at least we can tell Albinia we got here safely. Well, sort of safely."

"And Maecenas is happy with your being here?"

The slave leaves the room, with the food plates but leaving the wine and Horace pours himself a cup. He checks Lucius' drink and tops it up, neat wine, no water. And sits down with a sigh.

"I don't know about happy. But he sees the value of having me around. I can do all the stuff that involves having to talk to you, so he can keep at a distance. He is worried about what Augustus thinks about the way this has all been handled." His voice goes quiet and Lucius leans forward to hear. "We must be careful about what we say, Lucius. We must make sure that we cannot be overheard to say anything in the slightest bit tactless, critical, anything at all. We can assume that not only do Maecenas' slaves report back to him, but several of them will be working for Augustus himself. I am here as a sort of go-between, a friend of Maecenas and Augustus, and your friend too. You can trust me though I realise that you have no proof of that."

"You're a friend of Augustus?" says Lucius. "Are you sure?"

"No, I'm not, am I?" says Horace with a small smile wobbling on his lips. "I'm a pet. But I have my uses and at least this means I can be here to – well, just be here."

And Lucius is glad of this. He has decided that he does trust Horace, or at any rate, cannot be bothered to regard him as a spy. It just doesn't matter.

"I think Maecenas has being gently going downhill in Augustus' estimation for some time and now this happens. It may well be time for him to retire." Horace speaks with little regret. "And he is too close to this latest threat. His Terentia is an unhappy woman and no longer willing to be tossed about like a triagon ball between Augustus and Maecenas, I think. What they have done to her between them… and her brother was happy enough for her to, well, have an affair with the Princeps. It must seem to her that every man in her life betrays her in some way. And when they used her to get Aulus to run, then hunted him down – well, I do not know how she can bear to live with Maecenas after this."

Lucius thinks of that dinner party, Aulus amused and good company, Terentia flirting outrageously. His son was still alive then, and at that point Lucius hardly thought of him from day-to-day, except to envy him for being safely away from Rome in Cosa.

"I don't think from what I can recall of the meeting yesterday, that Augustus is pleased with Maecenas. Were you there? I can't remember."

Horace shakes his head and waits for Lucius to continue.

"But why am I here, do you think?" he asks. "I'm surely going to be executed or exiled or something – but to be kept in

Maecenas' house? Why?"

"Augustus is not going to kill you," says Horace. "I'm sure of that. The complication is Publius' death. Augustus was not ready for that. I think that he wants to handle things differently now."

"Doesn't look good to kill a child, then drag the father to Rome to be executed, does it?" says Lucius.

"Something like that," says Horace, and his mouth creases up as though he is on the verge of tears.

The two of them spend the rest of the day writing to Cosa and pretending to read in the comfort of Lucius' quiet guestroom. Maecenas' staff is extremely well-trained, gliding in and out with barely detectable murmurs checking that the two men have everything they require. Visits to the latrine confirm that there are always a couple of soldiers on guard, one at each end of the short corridor, but this is of little interest to Lucius as he has no intention of trying to escape. Soon he will know what is to happen to him and he waits with no expectation. His mind is gradually clearing and flashes of pain grip him every now and then as the memory of Publius haunts him. When this happens, it is so physical he has to curl up and just wait for it to pass.

Towards evening there is a change in the air, a loud and hurried conversation that gets nearer and Horace and Lucius know that it is time to go. They stand and begin to check sandal straps and look for cloaks, but it turns out that the Princeps has come to them. For the first time, Lucius thinks, "He is not going to have me killed."

And yes, it turns out that Horace was right: Augustus will not be putting Lucius Sestius through a trial and execution or even "killed while trying to evade capture" which is no doubt the official explanation for Aulus Terentius. Lucius stands through the few minutes of this visit and studies Augustus' face as the important information trickles through. Horace can give him details later. For the moment, he wants to study and fold into his memory the face of the man. The calm expression with the tiny crease of concern in the middle of the forehead. The eyes, still clear and grey, the complexion smooth. Augustus does not betray the passing of time. The golden hair (never really golden of course) is faded to sandy brown, but Augustus is still comparing well with the boy portrayed on all his coins. The Princeps cannot afford to grow old.

Sometime later, Augustus says, "Do you have any questions?" in that way that schoolteachers do when they clearly expect the answer, "No". Lucius has no questions. The Princeps leaves.

Horace gives a sigh and sits down.

"I know you don't feel it right now but… I do think that is the best we could have hoped for."

"What is?" says Lucius. "I wasn't really listening; you'll have to tell me."

Horace looks sharply at him but does not comment on this. "Sit down," he says. "Let's go over it." And with cups of wine, they do.

In return for his son's life, Lucius is being sent to Spain. Spain? Why on earth…?

He is allowed to go back to Cosa, under guard, and he can arrange his own transport to Spain from there. A bright young man in Augustus' employ will be his secretary and will report back to the Princeps on his behaviour. In Spain, he can carry out an inspection of the roads or some other useful task, and he can write some recommendations for the governor. He will stay there at Augustus' pleasure. None of his belongings, property or money is confiscated, but he cannot claim any expenses and must fund his own lifestyle in Spain.

"Spain?" says Lucius. "I wonder why Spain?"

Horace shrugs.

"You don't have any contacts there, do you? If he had sent you to North Africa or the East, well you've been there before. He wants you in alien territory and treading a dead-end path."

"Roads?" Lucius sighs. "I really did do too good a job last year, didn't I? Showed signs of being able to organise stuff and get things done."

"I don't suppose for a moment anyone will care what you do in Spain," says Horace. "Well, as long as – you know…"

"Oh, I shall behave," says Lucius. "I can't think of anything else to do." He pauses. "It all seems very – anticlimactic, you know. Will he keep his word? Won't he just have me killed on the journey?"

Horace thinks. "I can't see what he would gain. He said he would have your appointment announced in the daily reports, so it would look really bad if you then were killed on the road. Or in the province. And when it comes down to it, Lucius Sestius, you have two things going for you – you didn't conspire against him, and he likes you."

"Likes me?" Lucius is completely taken aback. "Gods above, why?"

Horace suddenly smiles, and claps Lucius on the shoulder. "The gods above know, Lucius Sestius, but I agree with our Princeps there. Now – let's bathe, eat and sleep and go back to Cosa tomorrow."

Lucius shakes his head. It is all so – strange. It certainly isn't happening to him. They set off down the corridor to the baths, and Lucius suddenly wonders where his host is.

"Is Maecenas around?" he asks. "Should I say goodbye and thank you?"

Horace looks down his nose and fails to hide a tone of disgust as he says, "Maecenas has decided to visit one of his many country houses. I don't know exactly where he has gone, and he left no message for you. Come to that he left no message for me either. He really is not covering himself with glory, is he? He has been my patron for fifteen years or more and I am beginning to wonder how loyal I need be."

"It is for life," Lucius reminds him. "He hasn't hurt you, and he will look after you. You were the person he needed to…" and he waves his hands around vaguely "…to look after me when…"

"Yes," says Horace disdainfully. "He ran away from that responsibility as quickly as possible, didn't he?"

They have reached the baths and undressing in the little changing room while an impassive slave takes their tunics and folds them neatly. Another slave hovers ready to follow them into the suite of warm and hot rooms, armed with little flasks of oil and a couple of strigils for scraping them down.

"I thought we had to be careful," Lucius says after a little silence.

"We do," says Horace shortly. "I should not have said anything. He is my patron. I owe him everything."

And on that note, they go to bathe, each thinking about the shifts in the relationships around them. Lucius finds that losing Maecenas from his life makes no difference: Horace is disturbed at how much distance has now emerged between himself and Maecenas. His loyalties, so carefully guarded and developed in one direction, have swerved, but he must keep up appearances. Horace is a poet of the middle class, always on the side of the powers-that-be. He has a sudden yearning to go to Spain with Lucius Sestius, and quickly dampens it down. Horace does not do adventure.

For once, Lucius does not sleep well, and he awakens a grumbling Horace early. A new squad of soldiers has arrived, and their officer actually introduces himself: he is a career soldier named Vibius Cornelius and he makes an attempt to appear human. Either that, or Lucius has no reason to avoid knowing anything about him.

"They definitely treat you differently," observes Horace as they walk through the streets. "You aren't a criminal, they call you "Sir" and Vibius can look you in the face."

As Lucius cannot remember anything about the last troop of guards he had, he takes Horace's word for it. Vibius Cornelius certainly seems pleasant and efficient and isn't responsible for the death of his son. He breathes sharply, and keeps walking, one foot, another foot, until the pain dulls. He tries to distract himself by looking around him: his picture of Rome is still shaped by disease and floods, but all of that has disappeared. Today, the festival of the Floralia is still in full swing and provides a veneer of spring colour and joy. Ropes of flowers, now wilting, hang from every shrine and temple and many houses too, and most of the people they see have flowers in their hair. They have all spent the last few days watching plays and are looking forward to the races which will end the festival in a couple of days' time. The idea that a wave of the pestilence has swept through Rome over the winter and is now spreading over Italy seems ridiculous. Romans are quick to pick themselves up and carry on, thinks Lucius, and almost smiles. He needs more time before he can do that.

Chapter 28

He rides up the track to the villa, seeing the landmarks he left pop up in reverse, cypresses, dovecote, wall, and at the gate to the courtyard is Celi, running towards him, her arms and legs moving furiously, punching through the air to get to him. He left her sleeping because he didn't know how to wake her, and he guesses that this may have been a mistake. So he jumps off the horse and runs towards her, and gathers her up and has to be careful not to squeeze her too tightly as he breathes in her innocent smell, of freshly-washed skin and hair, with just a trace of olive oil and herbs. Before he knows it, they are both crying, her sobs shaking her whole body while he lets the tears slide down his cheeks and into her hair. He holds her until she starts to hiccup gently and then carries her across the garden and into the house. In the entrance hall, Publius is still lying on the couch and he is glad that they have waited for him. Lamps burning sweet-scented oil are placed around to ward off the inevitable odour of decay, but Lucius does not worry about smells. He walks over to the stool at Publius' side and sits with Celi still curled round him. They look at Publius for a little while in silence, and then Celi says,

"We can have his funeral now, can't we? Helice and Gallio have told me what happens, and I promise I will be able to watch and do everything properly without letting him down. But I really want to be there."

"Of course," says Lucius. "Shall we do it today, now?"

"Yes," says Celi, determinedly. "Decius has already organised the pyre and the tomb. Do you know, I didn't know we had a family tomb, Father? I must have walked past it on the way to Cosa, but I have never been, even on the days for the dead. We always pray for Mother here and then you go off to the tomb and leave me behind. And I wasn't allowed to Grandad's funeral either."

"Well, you aren't going to be left out or left behind anymore," says Lucius. "Not unless you choose."

"Why would I choose that?" asks Celi.

"You are growing up," says Lucius. "You may want to do things differently. Soon, I must leave to go and do some work for the Emperor in Spain. You might want to stay with Aunt Albinia or Aunt Tia here."

"No, I shall come with you," says Celi decidedly. "I can see Spain then." And so it is decided.

The Sestius family tomb lies on the lower slopes of Cosa, next to the track up to the north-east gate. The procession from the villa to the cemetery is substantial and augmented by four soldiers and takes a very long hour. When they arrive, the pyre is ready. Publius' body is laid gently on the top, and Lucius begins the customary speech as the sun begins to set and the evening birds sing. The boy he describes is both like his son and completely different: but this is the nature of funerals. A tradition must be followed, and the dead are different from the rest of us, he thinks. Slightly less traditionally, he ends the speech by reading a poem written by Albinia:

My brother's son and light of our house,
lie quietly in the cool earth.
I shall plant a tree and, as it grows,
think of you, and how you grew.
A sapling still, you left us,
and left us tears and aching hearts.
Dear little boy, light of my house,
lie quietly in the soft earth.
***

Once the flames have taken hold, he takes Celi and steers her away, thinking that this is enough: it is the right decision and she makes no complaint. Despite her bravery it has been a hard thing to go through, and the little girl in her is beginning to show. Her face is dirty with being rubbed and tear tracks shine endearingly through the smut. Once they cross the Aurelian Road, the road up to the villa seems a struggle but she refuses to be taken up on one of the horses. She is flagging by the time they turn off onto the track – cypresses, dovecote, wall, thinks Lucius. As they cross the garden the front door opens and light flows down across to them as a line of the house slaves come to meet them with lamps, and Celi is embraced in a golden glow as she is led off to bed by Helice. Lucius decides to stay in the garden, and in the dark, he wanders around and smells the warmth and sweetness of the night flowers and herbs and listens to the sounds of his people going about the end-of-day routine. Horses are led into stables; shutters are closed, and the lamps are gradually extinguished until there are just a couple still burning in the entrance hall. The front door has been left open for him, and he slowly goes in. Just inside, he almost starts to see Decius waiting there to close the door, hand him a small lamp and wish him "Goodnight". He claps Decius on the shoulder, takes the proffered lamp and wanders off down the corridor to the family quarters. He checks on Celi – fast asleep and with Helice nodding in the corner – then goes into Publius' little bedroom for the first time since… and his mind veers away. There isn't much at first sight – a couch, a table and a stool, a chest for clothes. Lucius sits down and puts the lamp on the table. He looks around the room slowly, adding it all up. Couch, blankets neatly folded, a scroll on the table. There are a couple of shelves on the wall, holding the things a twelve-year-old boy has decided to treasure. In the corner of the room is an old wooden ball, long abandoned, but never thrown away. Lucius picks up the scroll, expecting Plato, and finds some of

Albinia's poems – she must have had them copied just for Publius. He finds this touching and uplifting. He must remember that his sisters are as grief-stricken as he is, as Celi is, but he can't honestly say that he has noticed anyone but Celi since arriving back from Rome. He must try and look after them all. Getting up, he wanders over to the shelves, and the toys and treasures emerge out of the shadows: a wooden soldier, a top, a small wooden box containing shells. There is also a little pile of wax tablets and pens, and he wonders if Publius too wrote poetry. It would not surprise him, but every leaf has had the wax smoothed over a myriad times and so Publius' voice is unheard. He must ask Albinia if she knows. Still carrying the scroll of poems, he leaves and finally makes it to his own bedroom. The lamps shows him that a small cup is on the table and a wax tablet lies open next to it: picking up the tablet, he reads "Drink it – H". He smiles and it must be the first times in a while because his face feels as though it is stretching unnaturally, cracking the layers of dust and ash. The cup holds an un-watered, rich, sweet wine, just a few mouthfuls. Lucius sits at the table and sips it slowly, letting the day come to him and sink into his mind. He need make no effort at this moment. After a while, he unrolls the little scroll and looks through the poems, wondering which ones Albinia has selected for his son. There at the top is one of his favourites, "A poet living in Rome":

Mine is one of the little hills.
I look down a gentle slope and the words
spill out of me and down the hill,
running to get to the Sacred Way
and parade themselves.
Lines slink around my feet
and trip me, vanishing when I look down.
I follow them, chasing, calling,
and pass the little house of Cinna.

My neighbour is a lawyer, precise,
And lives to make everything tidy.
The doorway is recently swept and washed,
Even sprinkled with dried rosemary.
Cinna has prepared his house as neatly
As he parses his rolling clausulae.
The Temple of Tellus looms on the other side,
and I dash through its shadow. "You can't avoid me,"
says the Temple, "for I am Mother Earth."
I whisper a prayer in iambic tetrameters
And hurry on, trying to catch up with the paragraphs
now happily gambolling at the foot of the hill.
I round them up and speak firmly to them
And they fall into dutiful crocodile lines.
As I walk at their head, I sort them out,
Swapping places for some, making others
Stand up more smartly or walk a little
Slower. A turn around the Forum –
And my lines are neat and pinned,
Each wriggling word brushed.
My poem is done. I head for home.
***

Lucius can remember Albinia writing this, years and years ago when she lived on the Velia in the centre of Rome with her husband the always genial Apuleius. He knows why Publius would have liked it. The description of the liveliness of the words, like naughty schoolchildren, has always appealed to him too. He keeps that image in his head as he gets ready to go to sleep.

Lucius leaves Cosa on the Nereid in the middle of May. With him come Celi, Gallio, Helice and Sergius. Oh, and some minion of Augustus. Lucius isn't ready to learn his name yet, as he is only a spy from the Princeps. Lucius has other things to consider. Tia and Decius are to manage the Cosa estate – not confiscated by the Princeps – and Albinia is to see about the sale of the house on the Caelian Hill in Rome. Lucius needs money and inspecting roads in Spain will not be cheap. The province is huge and heavily militarized so the roads are important and numerous and while Lucius will not be expected to pay for the repairs, he will receive no pay and no expenses. He will need a house while he is out there, and staff, and he promises Sergius that he will look for some investment opportunity out there, a farm, a pottery, maybe even a mine. The house in Rome is dispensable as Lucius cannot see himself ever visiting the city again. When he has inspected roads in northern Spain for several years, no doubt he will be allowed to come back to Italy and live quietly in Cosa, producing wine and making amphorae and tiles. He really should consider farming olives.

Epilogue – nearly a year later

Lucius Sestius Quirinalis, special adviser on roads to the Governor of the Roman province of Tarraconensis, stands on a hill overlooking the Atlantic Ocean. It is a steep climb to the top of the rocky hill, and the wind has already whipped the sweat from his face. As he stands on that drizzled and gusty promontory, Lucius loses all sense of time. There is no warmth in this place even though it is spring, and no flowers even once you leave the track and start to climb. Little jumbles of rock poke their heads out of the scrub and heather, ready to catch your foot, and providing a painful landing should you trip. The Atlantic growls at the foot of the hill, and the grey cliffs are ceaselessly beaten by waves which are unimpressed by Rome and Augustus. For a few moments there seems no point to this trip. Everything is grey – the rocks are darker grey than the sea, the sea is darker grey than the sky, and that is all the variety there is. But as he looks and turns from north to south and back and realises the enormity of the expanse of the ocean… then the experience leaps into being. It is like nothing Lucius has ever known, and he has stood and looked at the sea many times in the course of his life. This sea is the angriest he has encountered, the waves rearing up to show mouths of grey water yawning at him through the white sprays of foam, and it goes on forever. He strains his eyes to pick out the point at which the horizon limits his view, and even when he has seen it, there is no indication that the water itself has stopped. It is quite clearly marching on and on and Lucius wonders if the ocean ever ends at all. In Alexandria, where the great scholars and philosophers gather, some of those minds argue that the world is curved rather than flat but that does not seem possible here. The sea is everything, and it is only when he hears the faint whinnying of the horses down on the track that he is startled back into his world. The young engineer, the special adviser sent by Augustus to accompany him on this tour, shivers and asks with unaccustomed shortness, "Can we go now?" Lucius looks once more at the sea and says, "How soon is now?" trying to turn his strange feeling of timelessness and void into a frivolous comment. A shiver runs through him, rippling from shoulders to toes, and he turns quickly, saying, "Sorry, yes, let's go." They pick their way between the outcrops of stone, reach the track, and mount their horses again.

Ambling along in silence suits Lucius. The engineer is a quiet individual which is why Lucius picks him for these forays into the western reaches of Tarraconensis. He does his best thinking on these journeys, as he considers such matters as how to handle Celi's moods or remembers Publius' enthusiasm for training the puppy to hunt wild boar. But today, he thinks of something else – the Princeps has sent him a letter and Lucius is beginning to work out a wonderful idea for dealing with it.

Caesar Augustus to the curator of roads Lucius Sestius in Tarraconensis, greetings.

Now that the whole of Spain lies under Roman rule, we have it in mind to mark our achievement. We therefore order you to commission and set up three altars in Tarraconensis. These altars should be to the Guiding spirit of the Princeps, and the Goddess Roma. We expect that this commission will not take long and foresee that you yourself will be able to describe it to us upon your return to Italy. Further instructions will follow.

***

Augustus is becoming divine. It had to happen. Once Augustus had decided that his adopted father was a god, and started calling himself "Son of a god", where else could he go? Maybe a flaming star shooting across the heavens will be seen when Augustus dies, and true godhead will thus be achieved. The nerve of the Princeps is almost amusing. Altars to his Guiding Spirit indeed! But Lucius, initially rather depressed by this letter, is gradually cheering up as he realises where he will place those altars... He will write home tomorrow – with the utmost discretion of course – and tell them all about it.

From Lucius Sestius at the end of the world to his sister Albinia in Rome:

You're going to laugh, and you are allowed to laugh. I, your own dear brother, whom you know so well, have written a poem, and a rather fine one too. No, actually it isn't. But it is a poem, and I wrote it seriously and out of inspiration, so I thought you should be the first to know. You would not believe the place I have just visited, so the only way I can tell you about it, is in a poem.

Here is the beginning of the end.
The colours are muted, and lifeless.
Here is a desert of water
Surrounded by a dull white sky.
Here is the sadness of loss –
Gulls crying their grief over and over.
The world can do no more
Than wait for this dull end.

I'm not actually as despairing as this would imply: this particular place, a headland above the wild Atlantic, struck me as bleak but I am not. And anyway, there is a grandeur about standing here and just looking at this vast expanse of raging sea, and knowing that I am so insignificant at its side... I have returned now to Asturica to a rapturous greeting from Sergius and the household, less so from Celi who is going through a difficult phase. We both miss Publius dreadfully, but in different ways: she cries and gets all wilted, I just miss him but carry on. Helice is very good with her, endlessly patient. I miss you all and especially, I hope you won't mind me saying, Decius. I always think he would know what to do. So, I am looking to distract myself, and have been driven to taking a bit of interest in the work. I have made sure that the three altars have been set up – I told you about the Princeps' suggestion in my last letter, didn't I? Well, I am sure you can guess where they have been placed.

And I have made some changes in the way the roads are surveyed and repaired that should make it all a bit more efficient. I potter around making my suggestions, write the odd report to the Governor, and so on. Sergius is deep in negotiations on my behalf for a plot of land to grow olive trees and make oil. He says that Spanish olive oil is going to be big! He loves it here, and I am almost certain that he will ask if he can stay on and manage the olives. I shall let him of course though I did have hopes that he and Marcella would get together. Ah well. And no, I haven't met anyone here before you ask. And yes, everyone is very nice, it is just that few of them have brought their womenfolk. You must remember that parts of this province have only been fully Roman for a couple of years. Anyway, I am hoping that Celi and I will be returning to Cosa soon – I don't know when, the Governor is making positive sounds about my experience which I realise are the precursor to being given more work. I don't know – I see the benefits of being here but I'm looking forward to seeing you all.

I hope you and Horace enjoy the poem…

Author's note

Lucius Sestius Quirinalis was a real Roman and followed the assassins of Julius Caesar to their bitter end - the Battle of Philippi. You can even see coins today which were minted by Lucius as part of the war effort. Along with many others such as the poet Horace and Marcus Tullius Cicero, Lucius was pardoned and allowed back to Rome. He became consul in 23 BCE following Augustus' illness, and his name later crops up in Spain at around 19 BCE. We do not know when he died. There are discussions of a conspiracy at about this time in the historical sources, though who was involved and even when it happened are confused. I have hypothesised most of the details, I'm afraid, but that is the joy of writing fiction: you can research all you like, in the end you write a story which pleases you - and, hopefully, your readers. If anyone wants to discuss anything about the history then please get in contact through my website:

www.luciussestius.com

Printed in Great Britain
by Amazon

82830953R00161